Alexander

Alexander

A Novel of Utopia

Klaus Mann

Translated by David Carter

ET REMOTISSIMA PROPE

Modern Voices

Modern Voices
Published by Hesperus Press Limited
4 Rickett Street, London SW6 1RU
www.hesperuspress.com

Originally published in German under the title *Alexander, Roman der Utopie*
in 1929
Copyright © 1983 by Rowohlt Taschenbuch Verlag GmbH bei Hamburg
First published by Hesperus Press Limited, 2007

Introduction and English language translation © David Carter, 2007

Designed and typeset by Fraser Muggeridge studio
Printed in Jordan by the Jordan National Press

ISBN: 1-84391-441-7
ISBN13: 978-1-184391-441-9

Contents

Foreword

It is difficult to be something and to have the air of being something. I have always feared the beautiful which had the air of being beautiful, the noble which had the air of nobility, the grand which had the air of being grand, and so on. As with physical elegance, moral elegance consists in a way in making itself invisible. It may be imagined with what fear I approached an Alexander... an Alexander the Great. It is fair to say that this Alexander made a brave appearance; in our era of short books it was a large volume. Furthermore it came to me from Klaus Mann, a young man who is closely accompanied by charm, intelligence and the most moving kind of fame, that of Thomas Mann, his father, who knows that greatness does not always dwell in great things. A little boy swinging on a little gate can move us more than the procession in *Parsifal*.

This family and familiar greatness of Thomas Mann illuminates a very gentle halo around Klaus Mann (a luminous child's hoop, if you will) and saves him from the pitfalls of malice.

Alexander! In secondary school he was a model in the drawing class, a profile in plaster, an eye in plaster, curls in plaster, and that nostril, that lip, cold enigmas in which the schoolboy quickly discovers a rearing horse. This profile had been brought alive for me, had been given a three-quarter turn, thanks to what was imagined to be the manual by Princess Bibesco: *The Asian Alexander*. It seems to be a manual at least, to judge by the format of the book, its cover of supple leather, its ribbon page-marker and the name of the Larousse company. This oriental Alexander disorientated me, but orientated the legend for me like a pearl, and orientated my mind towards a more human superhuman being.

I become bored as soon as I cannot sense the presence of that truth which derives from neither justice nor a code, but from a secret system of weights and measures. With Princess Bibesco the large vague form became clearer to the extent of becoming a small, precise and disturbing thing, not with the precision of a medal but with that of a flower: an upright hero, with curly hair like a hyacinth, and spreading around him a strong perfume.

The Alexander of plaster is replaced by this figure of hideous beauty, a veritable rebus of the same quality as the masterpieces of the modern style, the ectoplasm of which seems to be flowing from the mouth of a sleeping woman.

This time, by the intervention of a young poet, nourished, I repeat, by lines, figures and reliefs and not by that monumental fog of German legends, there is the profile of the whole face. Drawing the model full-face is the draughtsman's way of being frank.

Well, this is how Klaus Mann shifts the shadows of the myth, brings it closer to us and embodies it: Alexander has two student friends. There is one friend who watches him and whom he dominates; and another whom he watches and who dominates him.

Certain poets preserve their childhood; others find it again. They all remain serious, hard, hidden and frightening, as childhood is. I pity the people who despise this school fairy world, those battles in which a snowball can leave its mark on us forever and can forever dry up the springs of the heart.

Briefly, Alexander wants to surprise this friend whom nothing amazes, to put to sleep a little those too open eyes which observe him; and that will be the true motive for his exhausting march towards conquest, towards that victory which forces the conqueror further into loneliness, a loneliness which the smallest amount of progress will encumber with tourists and strew with greasy papers.

Sitting, as he believes, at the end of the world, Alexander asks himself: What more can I possess? One would like to reply to him: a telephone, a wristwatch, and a wireless set. Without defeat there exists no sure fame. It is through defeat that Christ makes his presence felt. A traitor enables him to win the battle; a traitor brought Napoleon down.

With what sadness this Alexander would fill us, stuffed full with success as his corpse will be stuffed full of honey by the women embalmers, this Alexander who was served by all kinds of good luck (his urine had the scent of violets), if Klaus Mann did not reveal him as weak, trying to please, taking the wrong route, killing his friend, witness and dear obstacle, and losing from that moment his only excuse for pride.

We shall see him punished by everything which warps him, punished by his marriage with the Queen of the Amazons, punished by his raids and the hatred he arouses, punished by the revolt of the pages, punished by that journey to the void until the reappearance of his love in the surprising and magnificent form of a supernatural creature who watches for his last sigh, to reveal to him, better than the Sphinx, and laughing at his surprise, the word which expresses the mystery of human existence and the purpose of life; a word which is too simple for the ear of a prince to hear, a purpose too near to tempt his hand.

I am happy to place a token of that friendship, which works that are only worthy of admiration cannot obtain, at the front of the book of one of my compatriots – I mean of a young man who is ill at ease living in this world and speaks without inane words the dialect of the heart.

– Jean Cocteau, 1931

Introduction

Alexander the Great hardly needs an introduction, but Klaus Mann is scarcely known nowadays outside his native Germany, except among a few devotees. Nevertheless he should be, and not just because he was one of the multi-talented offspring of that giant of early twentieth century literature, Thomas Mann (Klaus' sister Erika became an actress and his brother Golo, a leading historian). He wrote in a different vein to his father and with different concerns, not least because of his more openly gay lifestyle; Thomas Mann had always sublimated that side of himself in his works. Many of Klaus's writings imply critiques of the societies in which they are set without being explicitly political (unlike the works of his uncle Heinrich Mann, most famous internationally through the film version of one of his novels, *The Blue Angel*). Klaus was to explore issues of sexual identity, corruption, hypocrisy, and the self-destructive nature of genius more frankly than any other member of his family, with what might nowadays be described as a post-modern sensitivity.

He was born in 1906 as the oldest son of Thomas and Katia Mann and was already writing poems and novellas as a school-boy. In 1925 he founded a theatre group in Berlin with his sister Erika, Pamela Wedekind, the daughter of the famous dramatist Frank Wedekind, and the actor Gustav Gründgens, who was to become the leading interpreter of the great classic roles in German drama, including, for example, Mephistopheles in Goethe's *Faust* and was also to feature under an alias in Klaus' famous novel about Nazi Germany, *Mephisto* (1936). Klaus also managed to gain for himself some notoriety with his own early plays. Then in 1929 he set off with his sister on a trip round the world, financing everything through lectures and performances on the way.

Klaus Mann's first novel was *The Pious Dance* (*Der Fromme Tanz*, 1925). It was one of the first novels in Germany to deal openly with homosexuality; and its appearance inspired his father to write an essay *On Marriage*, in which he condemned homoeroticism. In his second novel he explored the complexity of human sexuality more thoroughly in relation to political idealism, and more especially to the imperial dream. Its focus on analysis of the close relationship between failure in human relationships and failure to realise impossible ideals (total knowledge and total control of a world, in which nevertheless freedom and love are able to flourish) is indicated by its subtitle: *Alexander, A Novel of Utopia* (*Alexander, Roman der Utopie*, 1929).

On its first publication the novel did not meet with much critical acclaim. The world was not ready for a revaluation of the greatest of the Macedonian conquerors which included descriptions of his private life in such intimate detail. Re-reading the novel in later years Klaus himself commented that he found it 'naive and cheeky'. He was doing himself an injustice however, for in the work he had respected the known historical facts, and his imaginative elaborations on the personal relations together with discussions on strategy are compatible with them. He had studied several of the sources thoroughly, including Aristotle and Plutarch, and the classic nineteenth century German history of Alexander, the *History of Alexander the Great* (1833), by Johann Gustav Droysen, which idealised power in accordance with a Hegelian concept of history.

The first part of the novel develops the image of Alexander as the glorious liberator, the beautiful young man, whom all adore and who can do no wrong, but progressively Alexander becomes a hollow man, estranged from those who would love him. A series of rejections, starting with that by his boyhood companion Clitus, who later becomes one of his generals, leads

Alexander to attempt to compensate, overcompensate in fact, for his perceived inadequacies in a headlong, lifelong pursuit of empire. If individuals cannot and will not love him, then whole peoples shall. His initial success is very much due to the fact that he is liberating many countries from the cruel yoke of the Persian empire under Darius Codomannus, and after every victory he is welcomed with the love and adoration he craves, but by the time he has dragged his armies through Bactria, Sogdiana and over the Hindu Kush into India, he is hated by all the races he conquers: he is no longer a panacea but a plague. It might be argued that Mann is simplifying the motivation of a great man, reducing it to a matter of unsatisfied love, but, as his friend Jean Cocteau writes in his preface to the first French edition, the conflicts of childhood can influence one's personality for the rest of one's life: one should not despise 'those battles in which a snowball can leave its mark on us forever and forever dry up the springs of the heart'.

The ending of the novel can be understood from a Christian perspective. In his final hallucinatory state Alexander communes with an archangel, who at one point seems to resemble the young blond soldier who had never wavered in his devotion to Alexander. It becomes clear that Alexander has misconceived the nature of love. He had actually killed Clitus, when the latter, acting as a kind of court jester, had revealed to the king the inadequacy of his capacity for love, through a retelling of the epic love of Gilgamesh for the youth Enkidu. Finally too Alexander fails, from a false sense of priorities, to come in time to the deathbed of the one man, Hephaestion, who truly loved and understood him. The archangel, out of concern more than anger, points out to Alexander his basic error: 'You have sacrificed another, not yourself.' He promises Alexander however that he will be able to return in another form. The implication is clearly that it will be in the form of one who knows that he must sacrifice himself. It cannot be incidental that at his first encounter with the archangel, Alexander wounded him in both hands. Another was to come later who would himself finally be wounded in both hands.

An intriguing part of the novel is the penultimate section, entitled 'Temptation' (the German word 'Verführung' can also suggest the act of seduction, but I felt the latter rendering to be too sexually specific in its connotations). In his unquenchable thirst for knowledge about all things Alexander becomes fascinated by Indian mysticism and seeks wisdom through three old wise men who chant to him mysteriously and hypnotically about the nature of Brahman, the ultimate reality underlying all phenomena according to Hindu scriptures. He is tempted and succumbs, almost losing his self in the process, but finally manages to tear himself away from them, with an unfeeling disregard for nature in his flight. Shortly after this the Indian queen Kandake tempts him into loss of self by other means, through a narcotically induced state but also through sexual seduction until he loses all will power. His life is threatened and he has to be saved by another. When he recovers from these experiences his self-reliance and determination have only been strengthened the more. As ever Alexander recovers from weakness and defeat through exertion of will.

It is timely to reconsider Klaus Mann's account of Alexander's life, which has been the subject in recent years of a television documentary and a Hollywood film. There have of course been other literary treatments, notably Mary Renault's trilogy: *Fire From Heaven* (1969), tracing his life from the age of four till his father's death; *The Persian Boy* (1972), about Alexander's campaigns after the conquest of Persia from the perspective of his boy companion Bagoas; and *Funeral Games* (1981), which focuses on the struggle for succession after Alexander's death. In general however it must be said that Renault's account is uncritical and romanticised. More recently there has been another trilogy by the Italian professor of classical archaeology and journalist Valerio Massimo Manfredi. These three volumes were published together in 1998, appearing in English in 2001: *Alexander: Child of a Dream*, *Alexander: The Sands of Ammon*, and *Alexander: The Ends of the Earth*. While being historically sound the works do not explore Alexander's emotional life deeply, downplaying the gay element; emotions are described but not analysed. The film *Alexander the Great* (1956), directed by Robert Rossen, suffers from the rather wooden respectful style with which epic subjects were treated in the period. There is much careful grouping of figures and big set speeches in theatrical style. There is not a hint of anything untoward in Alexander's sexual proclivities in Richard Burton's portrayal of the king, and he failed to hide approaching middle age convincingly under his blond wig. A more recent version of the story, Oliver Stone's *Alexander* (2004), with Colin Farrell as the king, explores the close relationship between Alexander and Hephaestion more frankly, but is still a little coy in handling it. In an interview with *The Guardian* (10th August 2007), concerning the director's final cut of the film, Stone stressed that the Warner Bros studio wanted him to 'cut out all the homosexuality and everything that reeks of anything incestuous'. He did try to keep them happy by including scenes with Alexander and his wife Roxana making love (which the king never manages to achieve in Mann's version). In Stone's words: 'He had to father some kind of heir, but he didn't work too hard at it did he?'

A stimulating account of Alexander's life and an evocation of just how strenuous his campaigns were are provided by the historian Michael Wood's three-part documentary *In the Footsteps of Alexander* (1998). Wood constantly cross-checks legend with the major historical sources in the earliest biographies, especially those of Plutarch, Arrian, and Curtius (Quintus Curtius Rufus), whose *History of Alexander* proves to be stimulating and evocative. In an interview included on the DVD of the documentary Wood also points out that Alexander's hatred of his father and close relationship to his mother clearly invite a psychoanalytic interpretation of his obsession with conquest: 'There's clearly something heavily Freudian going on in all this.' But later he adds: 'The Freudian thing... no one has got to the bottom of it.' Except perhaps Klaus Mann? Mann's Alexander clearly fits closely Wood's description of him as 'broken in the end by the loneliness and insecurity of absolute power'.

There are countless Greek personal names and Greek versions of place names in Mann's novel. Fortunately the author generally identifies the characters by their military role, or relation to Alexander, so that it is not necessary to burden this edition with copious notes. Listing modern geographical equivalents to the names of places, rivers, and cities etc. would also unduly increase the weight and price of the present volume. The notes therefore only include a few clarifications which aid easy reading. Readers who are keen to track down references in more detail are referred to the excellent glossaries, indexes and maps in some editions of Curtius' history. For the transliteration of the Greek names I have followed the English conventions rather than rely on the German renderings. Klaus Mann occasionally switches tenses abruptly and I have incorporated this in my translation when this does not lead to confusion in English. His style is also a blend of formal, poetic and at times even flowery elements with occasional colloquialisms; I have endeavoured to reflect this as faithfully as possible in English.

Finally I owe a great debt of gratitude to those friends who have helped me to resolve ambiguities and obscurities in the

German text. They are, in alphabetical order, Benjamin Barthold, Philippe Blanvillain, Alan Miles and Philip Morris. I am also very grateful to Katherine Venn and Rebecca Morris for all their practical advice.

– David Carter, 2007

Alexander

Awakening

I

There were the sun, enchanted animals and swiftly flowing waters. Concerning the animals Alexander knew that the souls of the deceased dwelt in them, and that it was better to handle this little dog and that little donkey gently, for perhaps they might be your grandfather transformed. And in the ripples of the brooks and the mountain rivers there also dwelt beings, which were mysterious, but so loveable as well, that you could listen to them for hours, when they joked around, danced and burbled away. Similar beings lived in the trees and bushes, and especially charming little ones in the flowers, which one was not allowed to pick for that reason.

Life was completely beautiful, as long as the father stayed in the background. This he did for the most part, and he only talked with the child on festive occasions, during which he liked to tease it in a rough way. The child did not cry, but looked at the bearded man, who was roaring with laughter, in a piercing way. But the man did not notice how full of hate and angry the child's look was.

Everything seemed good, even the mother's snakes, and it was only the father whom he rejected. Why did the father laugh in such an unpleasant way, and if you did not laugh with him, he became sullen. It smelt of sweat and alcohol when you were close to him, but of herbs and her beautiful hair close to the mother.

Leonidas, who called himself a pedagogue, although he was at best an attendant, was a good person, even if he did hawk and let wind as well; and Landike, the stout and asthmatic wet nurse, was also a good person. The way she staggered around, with her kind-hearted face! It was comfortable being with her, and her bosom, which rose and fell in a friendly way, was a refuge, which you could rely on. Her stories were not so marvellous as those of the mother, but they touched your heart. Landike told of the vine made of gold with emerald grapes, of the golden river and the Sun Well,[1] and of all kinds of adventures, pranks and foolish behaviour of the lesser and the medium level gods, but she did not dare to touch on the great gods, for she had a reverent attitude.

But when the mother told a story, the rest of the world sunk out of sight, and there remained only her deep, evenly rumbling voice.

It was rare indeed that Olympias spoke, for she mostly remained silent, and looked in an unfathomable way from beneath her stubbornly lowered brow. Characteristic of this look, which, under the long pointed eyelashes, was profoundly mocking, was an uncanny force drawing you in, and it was both impassioned and ice cold. Also very disturbing was her mouth, a large mouth, with thin, strongly curved lips, reminding you of the mouth of a lion at rest. Her hair, which she wore short, was shaggy and curly, and her neglected, slender hands had something wild and predatory about them. Many considered the queen to be very stupid, but then others thought she was mentally disturbed. She was completely inaccessible to logical consideration and was stubbornly dogmatic to the point of blindness. As she was known to be hot-tempered and even brutal, nobody dared to contradict her; many, who had nevertheless risked it, had felt her hand on their face, making it burn. Even Philip was familiar with these well-aimed boxes round the ears.

Most of the time she was silent, sitting there and brooding, and at most she mumbled gloomily that she was tired. The whole court discussed what forces she kept company with at midnight. Why was she so exhausted during the daytime?

Because at night she conjured up the most evil spirits. That was more indecent than if she had deceived Philip with a mortal. Egyptian priests and Babylonian magicians had initiated her into the most dubious secret cults, and she definitely knew more about Orpheus and Dionysus than was proper. What did she get up to with all those snakes, which lived in baskets near her bed? There was no end of gossip about that.

Whenever she was in a good mood as evening approached, she let the young prince Alexander come to her. She kissed and pressed him passionately, and he became dizzy when he breathed the smell of her hair, which had a bitter overpowering quality. She looked up at him in an impassioned and mocking way, and then began suddenly to tell a story, interrupting herself as she did so with little bursts of timid laughter and also putting her bony hand to her forehead in a pointless way.

Again and again she felt impelled to tell the story of Orpheus, who was torn apart by the maenads. They tore him into tiny pieces, because they loved him and were drunk, but he, since the loss of his Eurydice, did not like any women any more. It was the nine Muses, who, wailing, gathered together his bloody parts and buried them on a beautiful mountain. Olympias sang with her booming voice the songs, which were by Orpheus, and then her child felt more solemn than when at prayer. She hummed and droned and shook her head with its unruly hair, and even if Alexander was already crying, she went on humming and droning. 'It's the harmony which makes you cry,' she said, teaching him in a dreamy way. 'In the same way I, as a child, cried about the circling figures in the stars…'

Somehow related to the story of Orpheus, but even more mysterious in its way, was the Egyptian fairy tale of the divine King Osiris, killed by his brother Typhon, who was as cunning as he was evil. How he set about it was horrifying and complicated. For he had a chest specially made, which had exactly the same noble proportions as Osiris. After doing this he pretended, with his friends, among whom was his guileless brother, that he wanted to try out a game, the senselessness of which should have been obvious: for each of the companions was to lay himself in the box, until the one was found who fitted in most exactly. Of course nobody fitted in, except Osiris, and then they closed the lid on him. Those horrible men threw him into the river, so that his corpse would flow into the ocean. Washed up on a wooded bank, he was found by Isis, who was lover, sister and mother to him, and who was searching for him most devotedly. She nursed, adorned and caressed the poor body of her sweet spouse, but hardly had she left him alone, to see her little son Horus, than Typhon seized the royal corpse and cut it into fourteen pieces.

Mysteriously intertwined with the story of the royal god Osiris was that of Tammuz, who had lorded it in Babylon, and of the handsomely built Adonis, known in Asia Minor. All of these spilled their blood, and all of them were lamented by their mothers-cum-lovers, who were called Isis, Ashtar, Astarte or Cybele.

'*God has to be killed.*' With this the Queen finished her fairy tale with sensual cruelty, laughing in a horrible way and putting her hand to her forehead in a meaningless way.

Alexander listened to her with fearful interest; he was already dreaming of the bodies cut up into pieces. With profound cunning and scheming Olympias awoke horror in him and made his teeth chatter with fear. So much more wonderful did the effect, which followed, seem.

For cutting up the god into pieces was the condition for the miracle of his resurrection; the misery had to have been great, so that the rejoicing might be endless.

Though the women had wept for a long time over their Tammuz, or Adonis, and beaten their breasts, he came again, and revealed himself to them in his second and truly alive state. Olympias grasped the wrist of her son who was trembling with fear, and thus they stared together at the bloody parts of the body, which had been torn to shreds, and still seemed to twitch a little. Now they also began to weep, with the mourning women who were rocking themselves to and fro, with a noiseless but urgent chant of misery. They stared with eyes already blinded by tears at the place where the dead man was lying in his blessed blood, and sang, sobbed and rocked to and fro in the dance. Not until they had wept for a long time and beaten themselves, did they partake of happiness; at last the Lost One came again; in great glory the Decimated One stood there, and his was the splendour, the power and utter magnificence.

So Demeter was happy every year when the lost daughter returned in health. Olympias also told her story to her enchanted son. 'I am her priestess,' she whispered, with her hand covering her mouth, 'I served her on Samothrace and experienced it all – '

She revealed to her child and only to him, what she knew: the mystery of the bloody sacrifice and the resurrection in the light.

From when did it become clear that the grey Landike, swinging to and fro, disappeared in a twilight of gentle shadows? When did it suddenly become clear that that tottering gentleman Leonidas was not to be taken seriously, and that one was permitted to laugh when he gave a little cough and put on airs? The awakening came, without his being aware of it, gradually.

A decisive outward change came when he moved into the men's quarters. The child was removed from the provocative influence of Olympias, and only on festive occasions was the mother allowed to see him and caress him. Admittedly Philip also kept in the background temporarily, being occupied with political affairs. What is more children did not interest him, and he decided not to concern himself personally with Alexander, until the boy was fifteen years old. At this time he was not yet thirteen.

Philip trusted his Greek teachers. They were sophisticated and skilful men who always had a proper smile at their disposal. As he paid them well, the king thought that they must also be able. They promised to introduce the prince to the basic principles of mathematics, and to provide him with some knowledge of rhetoric and history; he should even learn to play the lyre.

His Highness was so gifted, the well-paid men asserted flatteringly to the king, that he should naturally lack nothing. Among themselves they mocked the barbarian Philip, who worshipped their culture like a parvenu, but the latter, it could not be denied, had been blessed by the gods with a fatal talent for political intrigue. There was not yet any trace of that in the crown prince, and the Greek teachers doubted very much if it would ever manifest itself in him.

For this boy was decidedly backward for his years. So much reserve was not possible: he must be lacking in talent. Admittedly he was not completely without grace, but it was an awkward grace, that of a disabled person, which had something not manly, not energetic about it. Only his eyes puzzled even the teachers. Beneath the high-vaulted black curves of his brows, which gave the effect of being constantly raised, with even his forehead seeming to wrinkle easily, those eyes had a strangely dilated, bright and seductive look. It was the magically urgent look of his mother, but not at all soft, like the night, and vague, and also actually not at all mocking. Rather, it was sharp, scrutinising and of a steely grey. Unfortunately this grey had the disturbing quality of turning into a blackish and even into a blackish-violet colour, indeed in such a way, that the colour of one eye became intensively darker than that of the other. Then the face of this happy and gentle boy, who still played for hours, kind and solitary, with flowers or small animals, acquired something that almost aroused fear; around the gentle mouth which had the sweetness of immaturity, muscles played, which led one to expect the most dangerous things later in life.

As friends and for close companionship for the prince some boys from the high levels of Macedonian aristocracy had been selected. Among these were Clitus and Hephaestion.

Alexander, Clitus and Hephaestion were mostly kept separate from the others, and only at mealtimes, during lessons and the obligatory games did they meet up with them.

However matters were complicated between the three of them, or, more precisely, between Alexander and Clitus, and it was the gentle Hephaestion who had to suffer from this. While Alexander and Clitus seemed to be fencing with each other in silent conflicts, Hephaestion remained a neutral mediator, gentle, agreeable and with the same tenderness towards both. His beautiful dark face was a little too large and too serious for his age, with a wonderfully shaped mouth, a noble brow and a fine solemn way of looking. Only where his cheeks were did it seem a little too shallow, not completely filled out, not alive in every muscle. Hephaestion had a touching and loveably complicated way of bowing, and he did it extensively, not without a roguish grandeur and with the hint of a smile. When he parted his lips, his teeth glistened with bluish enamel.

Clitus on the other hand seemed to be alarmingly childlike. In his soft cheeks there was almost always a laugh. His small, straight nose, which was very narrow at the base, broadened like that of a baby at the tip. His hair fell down over a low and bright brow; below his evenly drawn out long black eyebrows his cheerful eyes had a lively and confusingly shimmering language of their own.

In the games of his imagination the most outrageous things happened. The immortals came to him, and Clitus celebrated marriage with all the goddesses of Olympus. In between jokes and tall stories he quoted philosophers. Although it did not seem to suit him, he knew quite a lot.

He hated being touched, and shunned and despised caresses. As though his skin were oversensitive, he shuddered if someone stroked his loose-hanging hair. He did not regard lust highly, and mocked Alexander and Hephaestion when they yielded to it. The air in which he lived was purer than that in which others thrive. He was vain about his beauty, and loved and admired his image passionately, wherever it presented itself to him in mirrors or in stretches of water. But he scoffed at and ill-treated those who loved him for the sake of his beauty.

His self-confidence seemed to be brilliant and hard like a jewel. He allowed himself to make little jokes about his genius and the prettiness he was blessed with, and boasted, lied, and made up stories. He laughed and made clumsy little movements with his hands. But he mocked those who had really achieved something: Antipatros, Parmenion, all the grey-haired dignitaries and generals were the object of his impudent and swift comments. Without having the need for recognition, he indulged himself deeply on his own in dreams of enterprise, which never amounted to anything, but he just planned things and had fun.

Alexander thought that, compared with Clitus, he himself was becoming problematic and clumsy. What was developing behind his own brow was dull, confused and questionable; but in Clitus everything seemed to be magically ordered. When Alexander imagined Clitus' thoughts, he had an incomparably lovely vision, which evoked his envy, of geometrically arranged dancing figures. Which criss-crossed each other in effortless clarity. But in him however, in Alexander, there was a dark struggle and conflict.

Although Clitus, as was necessary according to custom and a sense of tact, behaved very politely and even humbly towards the prince, the latter nevertheless always believed he could sense his half amused, half inexplicably serious aggression. To overcome this aggression, and to win the child over, who remained inaccessible in his isolation, became the sole and burning ambition of Alexander. It went so far, that he found himself being the wooer of this boy. For two years he had only one goal: to conquer him! He had decided irreversibly in his heart: if anyone can be my lifelong companion, it is he. I want only one friend: this one. *He is preordained for me*, Alexander thought with blind and impassioned stubbornness. I want him, I must have him. It shall be my first, my most important conquest. – But Clitus evaded him.

Standing wistfully to one side was Hephaestion. He could understand the situation with melancholy clarity, but was silently content with the fact that he was the third person who was able to mediate between them and reconcile them. Often, when Alexander was at his wit's end, he found consolation in the always ready intimacy of the faithful Hephaestion, who renounced without ever having possessed. He knew that there would never be any other human being in his life apart from Alexander. But with a sad, secret pride, he also knew that Alexander needed him, that he was necessary and irreplaceable to him.

Alexander was driven to provoke a decision, the necessary outcome of which was clear to him in his heart. Thus he stood one night in the room, narrow and bare like a cell, which was Clitus' bedroom. It was winter and icy cold. Alexander had only put a light cloth over himself quickly, and thus he stood in the doorway shivering. Clitus hardly gave a glance in his direction. He was lying calmly on his back, looking steadfastly at the ceiling.

That face was almost always seen to be laughing, so it was much more remarkable therefore to find it suddenly deadly serious. Above all the cheerful eyes had changed, and the pupils seemed to have become broader and blacker. Alexander, as though paralysed with shyness, sat down by him on the edge of his bed. Clitus remained motionless. 'I'm looking at one spot,' he said in a harsh tone. 'I'm waiting till it moves.' 'Do you *want* it to move then?' Alexander asked him softly, and it seemed to him that he was watching, very much without permission, a very secret and forbidden game. 'I don't want it to,' replied Clitus, just as softly but much more clearly. 'Someone else wants it to. Someone inside me. But I don't know him.' And he kept cruelly silent. Alexander crouched by his bed, his teeth chattering with the frost. Nevertheless he devoured with his eyes this stony, empty chamber with an incomparable tenderness: the poor bed and on the bed the child, the contours of whose body stood out under the thin blanket. As he could not bear any silence he finally asked again: 'Is it moving now?' He lay his face on Clitus' pillow, so that his hair came close to Clitus' cheek. '*You're disturbing me very much*,' said Clitus, without looking at him.

At this merciless reply Alexander started as at a judgement passed on him. He knew that at that moment a decision affecting his whole life had been uttered. He believed it was in order for him to weep, but he just trembled. Now he did not even dare any more to ask the other for a corner of his blanket.

Suddenly, with a voice full of jubilation, Clitus shouted: 'They're moving – Oh!' He told the other hastily, his eyes radiant with happiness: 'You see, I've been aiming at two of them. If they collide, there'll be a disaster! I'm so pleased! – Bang! Hey, that was some noise – ' He became silent and was shattered. As after a great effort he closed his eyes.

Alexander stayed, although the most natural sense of honour required that he should go. He did not dare to move any more, for fear of disturbing the other, inexorably silent, in his adventures. He felt himself further removed from this strict dreamer than from another star. Nevertheless he stayed: he could not find the strength to go. His last thought was that it was all the same to him. Indeed he did not even dare to meet Clitus' look any more. And so he buried his face in his hands.

From that night on, in which Clitus had spoken those decisive words which could no longer be made good, the difficult bond of friendship between the three was at an end. It was Clitus who withdrew.

Alexander changed quickly. It was as though he drew strength from his most painful defeat. He became more self-confident, more beautiful, harder and more elastic. Only Hephaestion saw the soft side of him. He understood everything, without Alexander having said anything. He was the only one in whose arms Prince Alexander was granted the chance of being able to cry. A few weeks later Alexander became all at once the celebrated favourite of the court and of Macedonia. He had achieved his first heroic deed, by mastering, at only thirteen years old, the young and dangerous stallion Bucephalas.

There was general gossip and talk about the terrible wildness of the Thessalian steed, which, afraid of its own shadow, had thrown off everyone and which even the bravest refused to break in. So the boy jumped onto its unsaddled back. The pressure of his thighs was so incomparably strong, and his fist gripped in such a loving way, certain of victory, that the young animal, after having reared up briefly, began to prance around happily and finally trotted calmly.

For the first time flowers and ribbons fluttered around Alexander's young face; for the first time the soldiers paid homage to him. They shouted 'Master of Steeds! Ruler of Men!' He laughed, blissfully confused as he rode by. The whole capital was uttering his name. Suddenly they also realised how beautiful he was. 'He's mastered Bucephalas, the wild horse, and the beautiful boy is only thirteen years old,' the women called to each other; and the men thought of Macedonia's future. It was said that King Philip was supposed to have cried with happiness.

Among those waving stood Hephaestion, with radiant eyes. But away from it all, in the background, Alexander noticed Clitus immediately in the surging crowd. He stood there casually, with his stomach protruding a little, and his arms hanging down. He seemed to be smiling, but you could not tell in what way.

On his horse Bucephalas, Alexander, whom the crowd cheered on account of his grace, suddenly felt himself to be ugly and clumsy in the midst of his triumph.

2

The great reputation of Aristotle,[2] who came to Pella as a teacher, preceded him from Greece. People were affected all the more pleasantly by him when he was discovered to be the perfect courtier, who always had a suitable smile and a civil word. It was known that he had already been active in various princely courts; his father Nicomachos of Stagiros, had even already been at the court in Pella, in fact as the personal physician of the Macedonian king Amyntas.

Philip made him acquainted with his son. He did it in a complicated, embarrassed fashion: 'Your new mentor, my child,' and he laughed in an inappropriate way as he did so. In front of Aristotle he immediately mentioned the frescoes of Zeuxis,[3] and a certain Euphraios of Orea, a deeply learned pupil of Plato's, about whom he had never spoken, but now suddenly asserted, that he had been his closest friend for years.

Aristotle overlooked the loud-voiced insecure behaviour of the king with refined facial expressions, and with several light bows he mentioned for his part something of the extremely famous culture of Macedonia. Only Alexander was suffering in the background. He held his head at an angle, chewed his lip and his eyes went dark. Now his father even clapped the foreign scholar on the shoulder, at which the latter smiled indulgently.

The lessons took place in a nymphs' grove near Myeza, about one hour from Pella. Aristotle had chosen the garden himself, finding it suitable and charming, remote from the hurly-burly of the city, but which could be reached comfortably. Philip, to whom he explained this in elegant speech, said afterwards that he was judicious and a master of the art of living. The lectures and discussions were sometimes attended by selected friends of the prince: Hephaestion and the brown-haired Philotas, the son of Parmenion, Craterus, Meleagrus, Coenus, but sometimes the teacher and his pupil would walk alone. The intimate talks turned out to be the most productive.

Whenever they met in the morning on the shady promenade, the prince would bow with the most superior politeness. Between him and the philosopher the most careful good manners were constantly maintained. Pupil and master vied with each other in refined correctness.

When Aristotle made a joke, Alexander laughed enchanted, with his head leaning slightly back and with a glance at the witty man, who shimmered damply with the heat. Alexander was very clever too at guessing, while they were strolling about, when the tutor wanted to stand still, for Aristotle had that habit, as many teachers do, of standing still while walking, with a raised forefinger and wrinkled brow, to expound on something especially important. The sensitive pupil already knew his master so well, that he could always sense his wish in advance, a few seconds earlier than the man himself and slowed his pace, so that Aristotle might believe that he was stopping to please the capricious prince, and not in any way because of his own eccentricity.

Less polite was the look with which the attentive young listener occasionally scrutinised the lecturer quite briefly but the more concentrated for that. He studied very precisely the wrinkles that played around the eyes of his educator in complex patterns, and which hollowed out channels and fine furrows down from the bags below the eyes in the thin brown cheeks of fleshless skin and played around the loose but agitated mouth with its bluish lips in amusingly unpredictable ways. Alexander knew that face, observed again and again in indecent detail by now, and was often himself ashamed how well he knew it: that dark, wrinkled face with the white beard, in which the worn out but still tense mouth moved with a bluish hue; the sharp grey eyes with their easily irritated lids, and pinched together out of short-sightedness or nervousness; and the significantly wrinkled, endlessly mobile forehead. On the grey robe lay the great lean hairy hands, wrinkled, brown and intelligent, like the old face, with their large round bright fingernails, which gave the impression that they were fixed only loosely and could easily fall out, like old men's teeth. – Alexander knew only too well that long wrinkled forefinger, which rose instructively, swayed wearily, seemed to freeze, shook forcibly, and suddenly sank down, as though it had died.

Alexander asked, wanted to know and never got enough. 'Your curiosity is insatiable,' said the educator, gently but affectionately scolding him; around the eyes and the lips the wrinkles played indulgently. Then once more, in a different tone, quite seriously, with a steely, concentrated icy-grey look, right in the middle of the waiting face of the boy at his side, he said, with fear and admiration in his subdued voice: 'Your curiosity is insatiable, may the gods help me: it's true!'

Without flinching, Alexander bore the look, which pierced through him. Uninhibited he enquired further about the things which interested him, demanded information, asked for instructions, flattered him, wooed him, flirted and enticed him. Aristotle was wary of looking at him again, which made the boy's voice become even more seductive, sweetly veiled, with a pale silvery quality; and suddenly bright and ringing clear, lighting up, as when light forces its way through beautiful twilight. If the master turned, distracted by the marvel of this voice, and looked at him again, then he was startled at the face, held out towards him, waiting for an answer, with its mocking expression. This face wanted to *know*, it wanted to know an enormous amount, an immeasurable amount. It insisted that this was no laughing matter.

So Aristotle held lectures, formulated and explained things. He talked of the art of rhetoric, its tasks, its possibilities, and dangers. Using examples he explained and criticised the styles and mannerisms of the great Greek orators, both the classical and the modern ones; some he found fault with, and others he singled out for praise with a raised forefinger. All rhetoric was bad, which became a playful end in itself, and he thought little of the Sophists.[4] In Athens an eloquent man had allowed himself, from his delight in paradox, to be tempted to give a talk devoted to the topic of 'In Praise of Mice'. Such light-hearted things the philosopher found contemptible. He considered the last classical rhetorician to be Isocrates, who was incidentally a special admirer of Philip.

He defined the concept of poetry, laid down its essential laws, by means of the use of quotations which often became declamations. When he recited from Homer or from the great tragedians, Alexander found that he could have been an actor. His cheeks became heated and his eyes excited, and he could make his voice both resound and murmur. Without the prince knowing why, his teacher fell in his estimation in such moments.

He attempted to explain the anatomy of the human body and the laws governing its inner life, which he called psychology. He went on to animals, which he divided into families. Finally he dealt with them in general, and later went into inexorable details, by describing the characteristics, living habits and needs of all living creatures. Alexander heard about the hermit crab and the desert lion, and finally Aristotle tried to provide information about the psychology of animals, but in this he failed somewhat.

He lectured on rocks, flowers and types of trees. Then he dwelt on the mystery of nature in general. He became enthusiastic and often stood still while they were walking, as he described the mysterious process of chemical compounds and solutions. 'One should never talk of "genesis" but always only of "coalescence",' he demanded also angrily. 'And also never of "passing away" but always only of "dissolving". There is no "passing away": only a change in state. – This was already taught by Anaxagoras by the way.'

He liked to come back to Anaxagoras. 'He is my forerunner,' he used to say gravely. 'He realised that the universe forms a unity and that the different forms of matter of which it consists are not separated from each other or cut off as though by an axe, neither hot from cold, nor cold from hot.'

There were parts at which he stopped in his walking and which Alexander sensitively anticipated. 'Do you hear, Prince? There is no possibility of something having a separate existence by itself, for *everything contains a part of everything else in it*.' And then with a pathos which was rare for him he added: 'Only the mind[5] – the mind, Alexander, is a simple thing, its own master and not mixed with any other thing.' That old lover of the mind, his head inclined to one side, explained, sensually, almost lasciviously: 'For, as you well understand, it is the finest, purest and hardest, the most irresistible, the noblest and most irreplaceable of all things.'

He paused before he started to walk around again and teach. He gossiped about his predecessors, whose illustrious line he began with Thales of Milet and finished with Plato. For every one of them, he had, apart from respectful recognition, an excellently formulated spiteful remark.

Alexander was interested most in Pythagoras, whose adventurous and important life-story he knew: this most restless of all seekers after the truth had travelled via Egypt, Babylon and Persia as far as India. His insatiability shocked and fascinated the prince deeply, and he attempted to express this.

But Aristotle closed his ears to this. 'That Pythagoras!' he groaned, with his elbows pointing up at an acute angle, like angry wings, having put his hands to his big ears, which had white hairs inside them. 'Oh, that old mystery-making swindler. His detestable lack of precision, which was unfortunately taken for profundity, has truly destroyed too many men. Beware, Prince Alexander! Don't you know that the master Plato, towards the end of his life, under the influence of number mysticism, went crazy?'

His excitement would not go down for a long time. Hurt, he nevertheless cruelly ridiculed his great teacher's attempt to combine the doctrine of the Ideas[6] with the mystically Orphic revelations of the hated Pythagoras. He called the latter the Anti-Greek and an immoral seducer of minds. He asserted that every intellectual conscience should be outraged at the doctrine of the transmigration of souls, metempsychosis, at the concept of pre-existence and of the Fall. He was so outraged that he stamped his feet and shouted.

Alexander smiled at this. He kept politely quiet, but he thought silently that even the little he knew of the secret doctrine of the ill-at-ease Pythagoras tempted and attracted him more than the whole clear and lucidly wise system of his grumbling mentor, Aristotle.

He protested, still resentful, as though he had been personally insulted, against the concept of personal immortality. 'All that's unverified drivel,' he concluded spitefully. 'What remains is nothing but that which is indivisible in us, the mind, which I call "nous".' This feels nothing any more, however, and is completely impersonal.

Finally he came to Speusippos, who led the Academy as Plato's successor and whom he called the 'little nephew of the exalted dead man'. 'He has given himself up finally and irrecoverably to that pseudo-Egyptian obscurantism,' he stated bitterly but triumphantly.

Whenever he came to speak about Speusippos and the present state of the Academy, he immediately became especially venomous; he liked to refer then to the incomparably more interesting school, which he himself wanted to found. On such occasions Alexander, suddenly bored, looked away. He had become again only the ambitious old man, who bowed in front of King Philip with his insipid courtier's smile.

They sat and they strolled around. On the beautiful garden paths there were patches of sunlight, which Alexander found amusing. They moved as the foliage moved in the wind.

Smiling at the patches of sunlight, the prince asked almost affectionately: 'Tell me about the Last Things!'

'The Last Thing is the mind,' asserted the philosopher stubbornly. And Alexander, with a mischievousness, which worried and scared his master, said: 'Then tell me, Master, about the mind.'

They sat down, for Aristotle easily became tired. The stone bank was cool, and in the tree above them birds were singing. Alexander heard what he had already often heard and what continued to interest him to the most extreme degree, and indeed never completely satisfied him: Aristotle's doctrine of the 'nous', of the unmoved principle, which was the ultimate and mysterious beginning and impetus of all movement. 'That complete Being, which consists of *only thought*, and indeed only about itself, as the only object worthy of itself.' He held forth with a certain dry effusiveness, carried away by the idea, which was developing, but still pedantic even in his enthusiasm.

Alexander, who listened with a concentration which gave him a dark look, never ceased to consider *what was missing for him here*. 'What is it that doesn't satisfy me here?' he thought constantly, as he listened.

Long mornings in the garden filled with complicated conversations. The old man's faculty of reason, which analysed, ordered and sorted things, wooed, with a perseverance which only comes of love, the not easily satisfied soul of the boy, which was nowhere at rest and had a boundless will.

There was no field which they left untouched. Everywhere there were problems, but they were all to be solved. In the words of the scholar everything became part of the scheme of things.

He explained the essence of matter, which was made up of four elements, with a fifth one which is ether. Out of this the stars were made. He became somewhat more imprecise, when it came to the position of the Earth in space. In contrast to Pythagoras, who conceived it differently, he regarded the Earth as fixed, and likewise the stars and planets, and also the Sun, which for their part were fixed onto a hollow sphere, which revolved. He asserted, with that irritability to which he was prone when he felt insecure, that space should be viewed as limited, and that empty space was inconceivable and therefore did not exist, whereas time on the other hand was without a beginning or an end. Thus he could not avoid the concept of eternity, but dwelt on it only fleetingly, as the gloomy look which came into the eyes of his pupil with this theme made him anxious.

The last morning which he spent with Alexander he devoted to the question about the goal of human life, but his answer did not satisfy. That virtue should be the final aim of human existence, sounded rather weak, and so much more painful was it to hear that finally virtue and happiness were identical. The son of Olympias was completely outraged at this crafty eudemonic[7] ethic.

Thus in their last hour together teacher and pupil were remoter from each other than in their first: the old friend of wisdom had wooed in vain. He had enriched the boy entrusted to him in particular respects but disappointed him on the whole.

Aristotle, who was only used to respect, felt, for the first time in his life, that he had been seen through, judged and rejected, and by the very person whom he had specifically tried to influence and to please. This failure paralysed him and sobered him up, digging even deeper wrinkles down from his eyes to his flaccid and excitable mouth. 'This period of instruction has been the strictest schooling for me,' he admitted to himself. He was sadder, as though he had lost his ability or even his knowledge. Only the man who has loved in vain is as sad as this.

When King Philip asked the philosopher at the reception for his leave-taking about the impression that the prince had made on him, he smiled in a fitting way. 'Prince Alexander,' he said cautiously, 'is without question the most gifted young person, whom I have ever had the pleasure of meeting. The question is only whether he will understand how to focus his genius and to turn it to good use. He loves the infinite, likes to digress, hints at something without carrying it through. – Admittedly he is very young,' he finished with a bow.

His Majesty nodded anxiously.

Incidentally, Aristotle was not, by chance, introduced to Queen Olympias until the day of his departure. She assessed him with a lowered brow and a long look full of mocking doubt. While he was uttering his elegant phrases, this look became darker, until it became hostile and even hateful. Alexander concluded his judgement on his teacher to Hephaestion: 'He is perhaps a genius. But there are pedants of genius.' In addition he made fun of the fact that Aristotle, out of fear of catching cold and gastroenteritis, constantly carried a little leather bag filled with hot oil on his stomach.

'That's how careful he is!' Thus judgement was passed on him.

The philosopher, who in spite of the little bag of oil departed with a slight stomach upset and badly depressed, left his pupil, in order to impress him for one last time, with a saying of Democritus, as a warning for his life:

'I would rather discover one single causal connection, than become King of Persia.' His stomach upset would have become worse, if he had seen the smile with which the boy had put aside this legacy.

3

King Philip could trace his lineage back to Heracles. This did not help in any way, and just as little did it help that Olympias named Achilles as the progenitor of her tribe. He was still not taken seriously in Athens, with all the respect in which he was held. It is true that in the court at Pella, Euripides had been a regular guest, in the time of the reign of Archelaos I, and one of the Macedonian kings, Alesandros I, had even been allowed to come to the Olympic Games.

Nevertheless Demosthenes had been allowed to say publicly that the Macedonians were Barbarians, not even good enough to serve as slaves for Hellas.[8] Philip did not forget it, even if he joked about it. What was the point then of all the expenditure on culture which he undertook. He told everyone who wanted to hear it, how much the frescoes of Zeuxis had cost: a whole four hundred talents. As teacher of his oldest son he had appointed Aristotle, who was so highly regarded. It was all to no avail: they feared him in Greece, but they did not regard him as one of their equals.

Sometimes he said to himself: the fact that they were afraid of him was the main thing. He was rich, since he had acquired Amphipolis and with it the gold mines. They could joke and call him a parvenu, but he could buy himself what he liked.

He provided himself with an army, whose cleanliness and discipline became proverbial, but there was also education. For the young officers, for the noble youths of his entourage, lectures became obligatory: the lads had to learn Greek tragedians and Homer by heart, and anyone who got stuck was mercilessly whipped. A lively appreciation of culture prevailed. – He provided Greek teachers for his child; cute Thessalian dancing girls; astrologers from the East; embalmers from Egypt, who had to wrap up and perfume his dead relatives; catamites from Athens, because pederasty was in fashion, though it did not appeal to him at all; and above all Greeks, Greeks of all kinds and professions. It was ridiculous how many one could buy: actors, men of literature and rhetoricians, ointment blenders, cooks, and a band of dancers. They arrived carefully prepared, intelligent and morally corrupt; they stayed as long as one wanted, or rather somewhat longer.

They stayed and had a good time; but what they reported back to Athens was not exactly flattering to the king, by whom they were kept. They mentioned the frescoes of Zeuxis only cursorily, but instead they described in detail the crude aspects of that powerful but uncivilised capital. How the families, who were influential there, looked like a boorish, uncouth rabble. It was certain that none of them could spell correctly, and it remained questionable whether they washed more often than once a month. In circles of their society customs had continued to flourish, the antiquated nature of which would strike every city dweller as grotesque. For instance, whoever had not yet killed an enemy had to stand at banquets, instead of sitting or lying down, and the same was so for anyone who had not yet succeeded in killing a boar as it leaped.

A special role was played in the amusing accounts of the gossips by the strange queen with the seductive eyes and lion-like mouth, whose barbarous piety caused offence. Such intimate contact with subterranean beings was scandalous: she went too far with her snakes and her secret sacrifices.

It was said that the son, whom she loved with such indecent affection – while she was quite indifferent towards the later born daughter, the pale little Cleopatra[9] – was probably not conceived in a natural way, and certainly not by her husband. A mysterious man was said to have been with her, but the question was only in what form. Had he shot into her lap as a bolt of lightning, or had he approached her as an animal in the forest? She had given herself to a deity, that was the essence of the rumour, admittedly it could hardly have been to one of the Olympian ones, the illustrious ones, but on the contrary one of the chthonic ones, who dwell in the depths. Or he had come to her from afar, for she had summoned him magically with much cunning, from Babylon, from Egypt. It was no chance that on the night of Alexander's birth the shrine of the mother of the gods of Ephesus had burnt down in very suspicious circumstances, and all this was mysteriously related.

So the parasites from Greece surrounded Olympias completely with mystery. Only the relationship with the king caused simply amusement. In Athens they used to cover up such things in more charming ways. That Philip had married her, the daughter of the monarch of Epiros, with the right of inheritance, only for political reasons, was known anyway; but it was hardly necessary to hate each other so much. From her eyes shot black flames of antipathy, when she had to greet her husband on official occasions. She bowed her head, scarcely lowering her eyelids out of disgust nor the corners of her mouth, with such obvious contempt, that it escaped no one. But the king for his part made a fool of her when he could. The very way he carried on with other women in public was disgraceful. That little Thessalian whore Philina he treated as though she were his real wife, and with the bastard Arrhidaeus he had from her he was more loving than with Alexander, although it seemed that poor Arrhidaeus would become an idiot.

Things became much worse, when he started to love Cleopatra, who was from a good family. Her uncle, Attalos, was a black-bearded schemer from the immediate entourage of the king. At the great drinking binges he was one of those who could hold his drink the best. He always sat there upright and level-headed near the king, whom he entertained with indecent jokes. In with the jokes he blended with evil skill pieces of advice to his own advantage. In this way he managed to bring the king round to deciding to have a public wedding with the curvaceous Cleopatra.

The little Greeks shook with malicious amusement: at last it would come to a proper juicy scandal.

And it did come to that, as noisy a one as the mob, lusting after sensation, could have wished for. The marriage of the king with his niece made Attalos imprudent: it was too much of a triumph, and for the first time he drank more plentifully than he could take it. He slurred and burped and his vulgar mouth stood out thick and red in the undergrowth of his beard. With a shaky hand he pointed to Prince Alexander, who sat opposite him motionless: 'Now his time is past' and he spat and laughed as he shouted. 'Now the prince who is the rightful heir is coming, the real Macedonian, the son of Cleopatra!' Then he got a heavy mug in his face, and was bleeding. He gave a dull roar and struck out. Alexander, who had hurled it, was standing upright, twitching with a dangerous blazing look.

On the other side Philip rose up from the embrace of the drunken Cleopatra, who lay across the table with the white abundance of her breasts. He shouted and stamped: his own uncle had been insulted. As Alexander's silence, trembling with hatred, stimulated him to raving and rage, he rushed up to him, staggering, with his stretched out fist shaking and his face swollen with anger. His faithful companions Parmenion and Antipatros held him back. But the impudent Greeks taunted him, giggled and stirred him up. 'I'll beat him!' shouted the king, but the crown prince waited for him motionless. Close in front of him his father stumbled, struck out, vomited, and lay stained with mess at his feet. Alexander turned away, without a further glance for the man lying down. Several of his friends followed him.

The next morning the prince left the capital with his deeply offended mother. He himself, induced by skilful intermediaries, returned after a few weeks. Olympias stayed away from Pella for more than a year at the court of Epiros with her relatives.

At that time Alexander was fifteen years old.

With an exactness, born of hate, Alexander observed, judged and scrutinised his father's politics. He came to the conclusion that he found it excellent but at the same time abominable.

Alexander, as a sixteen- and seventeen-year-old, did not yet know himself what he wanted, or knew it only in that vague marvellous way you know the wonderful dream of the previous night. But it became daily clearer that Philip's goal was not his, although it might outwardly seem to be similar. Philip planned to start the campaign against Asia, after he had first gained hegemony over Greece. The pan-Hellenic campaign of revenge was the pretext, by which he could strive for this hegemony.

'I'm hard on you,' he said to the Greeks, whom he impudently suppressed, 'but only, so that one day you will be unified under my rule. I want what's best for you, I want your nation to rise up, and it is *me* you should thank, when the Great King[10] has atoned for the ignominy done to you at one time.'

All that he wanted was to become a Greek national hero, and the Asiatic campaign was intended to make him one. This coarse but cunning man proceeded step by step, and was never impetuous, but always crafty and consistent. His son observed, in both disgust and admiration, these cruelly shrewd and calculated steps.

Naturally Demosthenes made mistakes with every word he uttered: this ruthless lawyer did not seem to have much grasp of psychology. What a narrow-minded misunderstanding, to suspect that Philip's enterprises were directed against Athens, for nothing mattered to him so much as recognition of his heroism, especially in Athens. To have a memorial there, and be a hero there, that was the sole ardent goal of his vanity.

So what did this excited lawyer want? He even went so far as to get involved with the Persian king out of hysterical hatred of Philip. As an honest nationalist he should have encouraged an alliance between Macedonia and Athens, instead of pouring scorn on it and preventing it. Or was he obsessed with the idea of the absolute supremacy of Athens? He knew his fellow countrymen, to whom he told harsh truths in his pedagogic zeal, too well, not to know that such a thing was impossible.

Although he found them obsessive and short-sighted, the crown prince of Macedonia read with a certain pleasure the rhetorical chants full of hatred of the old nationalistic democrat, which accompanied all his father's enterprises and subverted them in a sufficiently crude way for the street mob. This schemer with a rather dark past even achieved a number of things on a big political scale. Had not his career begun with a trial against his own guardian, during which he was said to have made use of some really bad tricks? After all he did all the same bring about the alliance between Athens and Thebes, admittedly when it was not of much use any more.

For Philip had in the meantime gone too far. Alexander despised the hot-tempered old Demosthenes the more thoroughly, because in the end he did not achieve anything after all. Anyone who operated using such unscrupulous means must be successful. The other man, Philip, that jovial and uncultured ruffian, was not even the rightful king of Macedonia, for he was only standing in for his sickly nephew, old Perdiccas' son. But he was successful with all his tricks and intrigues. Alexander surveyed the sequence of these fatal triumphs during the nights when he could not sleep.

He had become tenacious, tenacious and disgraceful. Inexorably and cunningly he had conquered one power after the other, and bound one regent after another to him. Finally it had gone so far that Macedonia, the day before yesterday still an overlooked country of shepherds, stood forth as the prevailing power. Philip proclaimed before a large gathering: 'Under our leadership United Greece will proceed against the Asiatic arch-enemy.'

But the emotional demagogue in Athens, Demosthenes, wanted things to be different. The Hellenic alliance was established against Philip and even one between Athens and Thebes.

Lying on his bed full of spite Alexander considered things: 'Certainly, when it came to an argument, even I wanted our victory, although actually only my father will enjoy it. After all it was *my* intervention, which decided the battle of Chaironea – '

That was then the second time that Philip wept with joy over his son. His insensitivity filled Alexander with nausea. '*He doesn't notice anything,*' he thought, completely disgusted, and he turned away curtly, almost impolitely, when his emotional father wanted to embrace him. The latter hesitates, does not understand, and stands there clumsily with his eyes open. Alexander, having turned away to the side, assesses the vigorous and yet already ageing man with a quick glance of such merciless cruelty, as only sons have for their fathers: the tough, grey-speckled pointed beard, the sensuous and brutal mouth, which was constantly moist, the sturdy nose, and the clever, sneaky little eyes. The only thing that the son does not see is that those eyes are now wet. Nor does he see the movingly awkward pleading and helpless quality of Philip's gesture. He only hears how his father murmurs, with a solemnity which does not suit him, and which has a comical effect: 'My son, I conquer for you, everything is for you – you shall be a greater king than I.'

Then with a remnant of pity, Alexander finally turns his face completely away, so that Philip does not see his angry and contemptuous smile.

After the battle of Chaironea it was proved just how naive the policies of Demosthenes had always been: while the King of Macedonia punished Thebes all the same by placing a garrison there, he handled conquered Athens with kid gloves. It was promised freedom and autonomy, and to regain their prisoners they did not even have to pay any ransom.

Instead Philip had the satisfaction of becoming an honorary citizen of the city, which had fought against him so passionately, and along with him his General Parmenion and his son Alexander.

4

Alexander and the idiot Arrhidaeus were almost friends, although many at court played off the poor son of a whore against the rightful crown prince for political ends. His slovenly mother, the grossly made-up Philina, had long been up and away, and no one knew in which capital city she was hanging around. But many found it pleasanter to have a missing courtesan as the queen and mother, than this aggressive but inscrutable Olympias. Yet others, above all the party of the cunning Attalos, pinned their hopes on the son, with whom the new queen, Cleopatra, was pregnant.

Arrhidaeus had matted hair falling down over a low-hanging square forehead darkened with melancholy. His wide mouth, always distorted as though he were about to cry, could only slur, and in addition his shaky bad-smelling hands moved helplessly; and his big Adam's apple, which was pointed and stuck out, danced sadly to the same rhythm. Admittedly you could tell by his eyes that he was Alexander's brother. They had a deep absent-minded look, and their colour was goldish-brown, but other shades blended with this. However idiotic the movements of his whining mouth, and the gestures of his unsavoury old man's hands, more than these those forgetful eyes had their own profound language.

In a corner of a cellar, where it was warm and dirty, Arrhidaeus used to crouch, with his hands wrapped round his bony knees. Why did he laugh softly? Because the small mice and fat rats teased him. Here Alexander visited him and stayed many hours. They sat in silence. Sometimes they talked, but nobody ever found out what about. Sometimes they held each other by both hands, and leaned their faces close together. Finally their foreheads touched. Now it was obvious that they in fact resembled each other.

Alexander never talked with his half-brother about the monkey business which a few plotters got up to with Arrhidaeus' name, and it also remained questionable, whether he would have understood him. Even when the scandal about the daughter of the monarch, Pixodaros, of Caria, divided the whole court society into two camps, the two did not mention anything about it in their quiet dialogues; they had other things to tell each other.

Outwardly the crown prince certainly made great use of this new and coarsest lack of tact by his father. It concerned the fact that the Carian monarch had had the proposal presented via a solemn legation, that his eldest daughter should marry the crown prince who was the legal heir. Philip had received the envoys very politely, provided them with one of his amusing evenings – which Alexander was prudently by no means called upon to attend – and finally announced that the princess should have the prince, that his name was Arrhidaeus, and that he was good-looking, clever and energetic. Old Pixodaros, who had not been initiated into the intimate affairs of the Macedonian court, said yes, and expressed his thanks too. Alexander learned all about this. The group around him presented it as a great scandal: now Philip was serving up the fruits of his vulgar passions, which had turned out badly, as heir to the throne, and, what was more, to a foreign country. He should not have been allowed to go so far; the supporters of Olympias and her son were furious. On his own initiative Alexander sent messengers to the confused Pixodaros, telling him that Philip had played a trick on him, that Arrhidaeus was no more than a crazy whore's child, and that they had wanted to put a poor bastard into the marriage bed of his princess. There was a great outburst of anger by the ambitious old man, and the legation, which he now for his part sent off, had a tough message to deliver. The affair threatened to have the worst consequences for foreign relations. To partially save the situation Philip had to summon up all his diplomatic skills. His most distinguished general, Parmenion, with a face like a faithful tomcat, set out to take the greetings, gifts and apologies of his lord to Caria.

The brothers did not talk about all these insignificant superficial occurrences, when they crouched down together in their mysterious dialogue, brow to brow, in the hole of a cellar.

The little Greeks could never have hoped for so much amusement at this barbarian court. It was more lively even than in Athens. Hardly did the affair with the Carian princess begin to be forgotten about, than the pricelessly funny story of Philip and the page boy Pausanias occurred. What happened was that the king let himself go again thoroughly, and in fact, for a change, not with a woman but by raping this lad, the sweet and sentimental Pausanias, in public at the dining table. He did it in a complicated and formal way; although he seemed to be very drunk, he was concerned even in this act to keep his royal bearing. In a solemn but admittedly wavering voice he ordered the boy to undress, and place himself in a comfortable position. The whole hall yelled; only those sitting closest to him saw that the abused child was trembling all over his body with rage and shame. His face was white, and his poor eyes were swimming with tears.

Pausanias had the best figure of all the noble pages, a magnificent creature, with a slow, completely womanly beauty. His mouth, which pouted and seemed to blossom when he smiled, drove men and women crazy, as did the coy or sentimentally sorrowful look in his grey eyes, which he was able to shade with his long carefully pointed eyelashes. Above the completely clear, beautifully curved brow, as delicate as ivory, the chestnut-brown hair rose up in a gleaming silky mound. His gait was that of a great hetaera, and he swung his shoulders and hips in a pleasing way.

He was completely without vivacity but extremely hysterical. The fixed obsession in his heart was that he was in love with Clitus. While half the capital city desired him, acknowledged as the most attractive boy of the high aristocracy, he clung to Clitus, who was generally considered to be unprepossessing, with a faithfulness which was painful to watch. His masochism yearned for humiliation: Clitus had not even stroked his hand.

After the scandal at the royal table, poor Pausanias, just like an insulted lady, dashed into the room of the one he loved in vain. His indignation made him even more beautiful than he usually was, and with tangled hair across his distraught face, he ran up and down in front of Clitus' bed.

'If he had asked me to go into his bedroom, good, I wouldn't have said no, although, as the gods know, he's not my taste! But like that! Such degrading lack of consideration!' He swept to and fro like a princess, whom it is intended to send into exile, stopped, gathered up the train of the dress that he was not wearing, and swept on.

Clitus, in his bed, smiled more and more mysteriously. There was a malicious gleam in his eyes, as he said in a voice cooing with gentleness: 'What is more he boasted about it already beforehand. He's a frisky old man, you have to admit it all the same. Your reputation at court is lost. Now you are a little catamite, like those that come from Greece, and who will willingly do it for an evening meal.' He stayed slyly quiet, hummed something, and behaved as if the matter did not interest him any more.

Pausanias stamped, became flushed and finally wept. He sank down, shaken by sobs, onto his knees in front of Clitus' bed. 'Such meanness,' he whispered through his tears, with his moist face in his friend's pillows. 'Now you don't respect me any more.' This thought was more than he could bear, and his sobbing became a spasm; he threw himself to and fro as though he were being struck with a whip.

Suddenly he held his breath and even forgot to let his tears flow. Had a miracle occurred? Clitus had his hands in his hair. Now he even felt his mouth, that inaccessible object. First in his hair, and then on his neck, which no longer trembled but was still with happiness. At the same time he heard the gentle and dear voice, which hypnotised him.

'Now pay close attention, my dear Pausanias! There is still just one way out for you, but if you don't take it, you will remain forever humiliated. But you are a man, my little Pausanias. Just listen – '

Pausanias listened.

In the half-light of dawn Clitus was alone. He crouched on his bed with his knees drawn up and his hands wrapped around them, silent for a long time, and just smiling and rocking his head as though in time with jolly melodies.

When the birds began to sing outside, he turned his head towards the window. Speaking into the grey morning light, which was becoming surrounded with pink clouds, he said in a fresh cheerful voice: 'I'll see him on the throne – quite soon – That'll be fun – '

He whistled something, as a breeze blew coolly against him, and he drew the blanket closer around him. He lay back, and closed his eyes, still smiling.

The same morning came the answer from the oracle which Philip had questioned, concerning the Asiatic campaign:

'Behold, the bull is garlanded, the sacrifice is waiting.'

Philip found the pronouncement ambiguous and confusing: the question remained: *who* was the bull. He summoned some scholars, who politely interpreted the riddle in the following way: Persia was the bull, already garlanded, already prepared for its fall. But still there remained a certain unrest in Philip.

But he believed he should not wait any longer, and all of a sudden it became urgent for him. He was overpowered by a nervousness, which he had hitherto never known. Prematurely in fact, he sent a part of his army, under the leadership of Parmenion and Attalos, across the Hellespont.

Before he followed them with the remaining troops, the wedding of the little princess Cleopatra to a young prince from

Epiros was to be celebrated, and indeed in a very dignified way in Aegeae. On such occasions Philip showed himself to be conservative, almost sentimental. Aegeae, Macedonia's former capital, lay abandoned and desolate. It was traditionally considered to be the city for coronations, weddings and funeral festivities. The entire court left Pella, together with the inquisitive part of the population: in Aegeae there was to be Greek theatre, a masquerade and a procession. It was embarrassing that Olympia refused to accompany them, but stayed stubbornly at home.

Generally the mood in the leading family was not a happy one. Philip, surrounded by his officers, showed a rather forced cheerfulness, as though he were planning a specially great joke for that day. He roared out hints about it and slapped his men on the shoulders in a noisy way, which caused pain; and also he had been smelling of alcohol since early morning. It struck many as very tactless, that even on this highly official occasion he had his second spouse, the woman Cleopatra, at his side. What is more she was full of hopes and far too splendidly dressed up for her condition. So much more unprepossessing was the effect made by the young Cleopatra, Alexander's dull little sister, with the sadly empty face. Her small face was pale like a little bit of snow, and her sad eyes looked around in search of help. She did not know her young prince at all, and did not seem to look forward to seeing him especially. Moreover on the evening before the departure to Aegeae she argued again with her irritable mother, and the immediate circle around the ladies knew that the queen had even hit her daughter and they told of blue marks on her back and one of her delicate breasts. To go along with the coarse jokes of her half-drunken father was impossible for her, for the very reason that she did not understand them.

Neither did Alexander laugh during the journey. He stayed apart with some of his friends; among these moreover Clitus was missing, and, which was less noticeable, the disgraced Pausanias. No one knew where they had both disappeared to.

The friendly Hephaestion tried to cheer up his gloomy prince, by telling him in a gentle voice stories of scandals in court society. The others also tried to be cheerful, Philotas, the son of Parmenion, Nearchos, Craterus, Perdiccas, Ptolemy, and Coenus. They indulged in little indecent thoughts: 'You can imagine why pretty Pausanias hasn't come today. He can't walk or sit on a horse any more; King Philip injured him.' They roared with laughter. But Alexander did not turn a hair. The joke which King Philip had thought up for the wedding celebration was even more inappropriate than anyone could have feared.

The procession of the gods went off to general satisfaction: the wagons had been magnificently equipped, the actors dressed up very much like the gods, and the people looked at all the holy luxury with reverence and eagerness. But the cries of rejoicing died on their lips, when, in the midst of the blessed ones of Olympus, the grotesque mask appeared. This red-speckled monster swelled up like a turkey, and had a ridiculous bird's beak as its nose and abominable donkey's ears. Horrified whispering ran through the crowd that the disguised figure was none other than King Philip. That was going too far, they grumbled: it was blasphemy. The Greek legations did not conceal the fact that they were extremely shocked, and the Asiatic ones looked on calmly but disgusted. There was perplexity and stunned whispering in the court society: His Majesty had indubitably lost all sense of embarrassment and shame, to insult every religious feeling in people so audaciously. Did he want to imply in this disgusting manner, that he himself was a god? Things had not gone that far yet, and even the old soldiers grumbled.

They looked around inquisitively but nervously for the crown prince: what did he think, what sort of expression did he have on his face at his father's gaffe? Alexander looked gloomily to one side. His friends stirred him on, but he waved them aside. They advised: 'Speak to the people, Alexander! At this moment they all hate him! He makes himself into a god and what a god! Just look at how he swells himself up and rocks to and fro! Nobody claps, nobody cheers.'

Philip, in his blasphemous outfit, passed by in the icy silence. If one person had laughed at least! But in inexorable silence they looked at his megalomaniac excess. As no one found it comical, his funny gestures became more and more repulsive. He seemed to be extremely drunk; otherwise he would not have moved in such an indecent way.

At that moment, as the painfulness had increased to the point of being unbearable, an elegant figure veiled in black, that seemed to have shot up out of the ground, leaped onto the step of the wagon, and barely had anyone noticed the glint of a knife, when the king was already falling down and gave a dull roar; dark blood smeared the golden wood of his vehicle. The wagon did not stop immediately, but went on a few paces. Philip, who hung down towards the ground, with the knife in his throat, spitting, uttering a death rattle and bleeding, was dragged along, with his hair sweeping along in the dust, and his comical mask was pushed aside. Beneath could be seen suddenly his chalky white face with its mouth gaping with fear.

The cry which rose from the crowd sounded as much like one of relief as one of horror. Everyone had felt that this deed had *had* to happen at that moment, for how else should the next seconds have passed. Nevertheless curses and stones were already flying at the murderer, who had been seized by soldiers. They tore the cloth from his face, and it was Pausanias whom they were holding. With big completely empty eyes, brown like a deer's, he stared at those who were gripping him. He moved like a sleepwalker. They wanted to hit him in the face, but were moved by his young countenance, which was as white as a sheet, and by his helpless, stupid and desperate beauty.

There was general confusion, and out of the yelling and cursing of the men there rose sharply the hysterical cries of the women. It was indecent how happy the Greeks were. They rejoiced and threw up their arms: 'He's dead, Philip is dead!' They would have most liked to run immediately back to Athens with their happy news. In the midst of the chaos no one noticed that poor little Cleopatra, the forgotten bride, collapsed in a faint with tiny weak cries. The more audibly did the older Cleopatra, Philip's actual widow, lament. Voluptuously, as in her rapturous pleasures, she indulged herself in her pain: it was magnificent to see, how she pulled out her hair, tugged at her dress, and shook her fat white breasts in despair. She howled with her widely open mouth, and sank down, only to raise herself up again the more imposingly and tragically, every inch the lamenting queen in the carefully disordered arrangement of the pleats in her garments.

Even the old generals had lost control of themselves, stamped around and cursed and swore amongst themselves. Only Alexander stood motionless, surrounded by his friends. With a faraway but mysteriously radiant look he watched Pausanias being dragged away. Then he let his gaze, still radiant, rest on his father, from whom the mask had been removed and the blood and dirt had been washed off. He had been previously laid out on the golden wagon, which had had to serve him for his final offensive amusing game. His wife Cleopatra threw herself over the corpse, spreading out her white arms in a fine sweep. Alexander's gaze, which scrutinised everything, became colder and colder and more and more inscrutable.

Very gradually a smile developed on his calm face. His friends shouted more and more enthusiastically around him: 'Long live Alexander, our young king! Our young king – Long let him live! – Long let him live!' Alexander smiled at these shouts, not yet for the sake of the people, but to himself, feeling quite enchanted.

As they raised him up on their shoulders, he greeted the crowd around him for the first time, with a broad, radiant gesture. Many were still lamenting, gathered around Philip's corpse, but the others were already greeting the youth, who was now their leader. Above all the twenty-year-olds turned away from the dead man. These greeted Alexander who gave them that wave of his expressing certain victory, with that smile, which seemed divine to them.

When he came to stand somewhere on firm ground again, someone touched his shoulder gently but firmly. He turned and looked into grey shimmering, cheerful and deep eyes. 'Come!' said Clitus to him. 'It's your mother. She's waiting for you urgently!'

5

Olympias received her son alone and solemnly in the vaulted central hall of the palace, which was decorated with frescoes of Zeuxis, Philip's pride. She sat in the middle of the room on the throne, but by no means in garments of state, nor specially prepared or dressed up, but rather unkempt as ever, with hair that looked unruly with anger. With her broad brow lowered, she looked at the prince with her seductively deep gaze. As he approached her with elastic movements, bowed to kiss her forehead and hand, she smiled, but not only in a motherly way.

Alexander stood before her and waited respectfully to hear what she would say. She scrutinised his figure at first not with a tender look but rather as though she were examining him. Only gradually did her look become tender. Alexander, with his head held to one side, remained patiently silent, until she had looked him up and down thoroughly.

Finally she turned her eyes away from him, stretched herself, and raised her arms. 'We've done it!' she shouted to the vaulted ceiling, her voice resounding with jubilation, and again, more quietly but more blissfully: 'We've done it, Alexander!'

At which she drew him to her, with a violence which charmed and startled him. 'Listen!' she whispered, close to his face – he could smell her shaggy hair, her excited breath, the irresistible scent of herbs and all kinds of dried plants – 'Listen: *now I'm going to give you your mission.*' – What was coming next? Alexander held his breath, and with all the ardour in his heart he waited for her decisive utterance.

But she began dreamily and vaguely. 'There were times,' she said, as in former times when she had told him about Orpheus, torn apart, 'beautiful times of peaceful happiness, when the world was better organised, than we poor souls are familiar with, and human life passed gently and contentedly, until the solemn hour of death. At that time, my son, it was Woman who ruled and Man who was subordinate to her. We women are milder, cleverer and more diligent than you, and we also know more about the gods. Under our rule the earth was almost a paradise.'

Alexander's eyes were imploring: the mission! But Olympias did not hurry. She told her story at a leisurely pace: 'The rule of Man soon destroyed everything that was good, what we had built up over centuries. Philip combined in himself all the bad attributes of men. He was *the* Man, and that is why I hated him. It's fortunate that you are not really his son.' She smiled in an underhand way.

Alexander leaped at her, and forgetting all ceremony, grabbed her by the shoulder and shouted roughly in her face: 'Not his son, Olympias? I don't believe a word of it.' He was really afraid that she might be mad, for she shook her head, smiling in an odd way: 'Not his son,' with a quiet stubbornness. 'The gods be thanked that he is dead. I heartily desired it,' she said simply, almost tenderly. With a firm, joyfully sober voice she added, with her bright face turned towards Alexander: '*For now you are here, my son.*'

She grasped both his hands, and now all the dreaminess had gone from her, and she spoke clearly and cheerfully: 'Already this year Philip would have undertaken a campaign to Asia, but for what purpose? To make, if it were in some way possible for him, Macedonian colonies of Asia; to force on those peoples, who are the wisest and most mature people, his impious crudely masculine belief in gods; to make the whole world more unhappy than it already is today under the rule of Man.' She shuddered at the thought. 'It is really good, that he is dead!' she said once more and finally. She turned towards her son emotionally again.

'To you however your mother gives the mission. Go to Asia, and it will submit itself to you *lovingly*, for you are beautiful, the grandson of Achilles. Maternal Asia will obey you, for you have been given the mission by your mother. The aim of the mission is not to conquer, for men have already conquered so much. A wedding will have to be arranged – '

As she jumped up, he saw that her face was streaming with tears. Then he too wept, and she enclosed him in her arms as though he were still the child who wanted to hear fairy tales. Mother and son sealed their alliance amidst tears in the solemnly bare banqueting hall. 'I'll come to Babylon and will become Empress when you have made your conquest!' she said, her wet face lying against his, which was just as wet. 'When you are dead, I will take power alone. That must be fixed explicitly in your will. For you will not live very long.' From her half-closed eyes she scrutinised once more his young face, this time in an oddly flirtatious way, and almost maliciously: 'You will not live very long.' Then she wept again, pulling him to her more intimately.

Again the dazed Alexander heard her enchanting whispering words at his ear. 'You yourself will not live very long, my sweet son, and I don't know if you will ever be happy. But you are chosen to bring happiness to mankind, my Alexander! You will achieve it by the power of your beauty and your youth. For you are young, Alexander, you see, and that is the marvellous thing about it.' Her words died in her mouth. She kissed him, and into the kiss she whispered, almost inaudibly: 'I was naturally not innocent of the death of Philip – I had made an arrangement with Clitus – little Pausanias had been asked to – '

At this Alexander let go of her; she should not have said so much. She too noticed at once that she had gone too far, and she sat there on the throne again in all her royal dignity, with her eyelids lowered which made her inapproachable. To the prince, who bowed deeply, she held out her hand to receive his kiss. 'You know the will of your mother,' she said above him icily. He stood up, and they looked each other severely in the eyes. The most important matter had remained unspoken: he did not ask her about Clitus, who was secretly controlling his fate. He only added, with emphatic politeness: 'Your will has always been mine.'

They parted solemnly from each other.

Philip is dead, and with dazzling exuberance the actions of the new king begin. Had they already been rejoicing in Athens? And made the poor little regicide into an honorary citizen in absentia? And heaved a sigh of relief because they believed themselves already freed from the new tiresome hegemony? Athens armed itself, and with it the Aetolians and the Ambachiotans, the Eleans and the Arcadians.

On the throne the much-hated youth was surrounded with nothing but danger; everywhere conspiracies were being prepared against him: Greece, among the barbarians of the north, in Asia and even in his own court. The disagreeable Attalos with the coarsely sensual mouth in the undergrowth of his luxuriant pointed beard, and who has come back from Asia Minor, spins his threads probably as far as Susa and Babylon. King Philip's long-standing generals can be seen standing together and whispering: above all Parmenion, so capable that he has turned grey with it, displays an expression prophesying doom. The name of a certain Prince Amuntas, old King Perdiccas' son, is mentioned again and again: they say that it is he to whom the throne is rightfully due, for Philip for his part had taken over power only as his guardian.

Cleopatra, widow of the murdered monarch, strides around with a mere display of grief. She meets her young stepson with a show of offended dignity. In intimate circles she hints cautiously, that she may consider Olympias and her son by no means innocent of the murder of the great Philip. Also Arrhidaeus, the melancholy whore's son, has his supporters.

In this chaos a real frenzy of activity takes hold of Alexander. Friends advise him to be cautious, warn him, and ask him to consider all sorts of things. Hephaestion reproaches him, with loving concern, in long evening conversations about how absurdly dangerous his situation is. 'They're all against you; the Orient and the Occident, Greece and Macedonia are in alliance against you.' Alexander laughs radiantly.

Before starting his campaigns, he seeks advice from Amphyctyonan about the Thermopyleans; he renews the union with Corinth, and allows himself to be paid homage to as the absolute 'commander of the Hellenes'. Thus, to the amazement of the various nations, this barely twenty-year-old man takes on the succession to his father.

In his heart, by the hour and by the minute, the great plan of his life matures: it fills and torments him and causes him to wake up at night and smile with happiness; it lends brightness to his voice and a gleam to his eyes. Admittedly there are many affairs which must be put in order beforehand: the peoples around Macedonia who have become rebellious must be pacified. With Thessaly he quickly establishes reconciliation: the other remaining ones are: the Thracians, the Getae, the Triballians and the Illyrians. He conquers the Triballians who once imprudently attacked Philip, beats their prince Symos, without losing any of his own men; and he conquers the Illyrians at the Pass of Pelion.

As he has been wounded, it is believed in Athens that he is already dead. They rejoice again and take up arms, and evil old Demosthenes, because it does not matter, accepts three hundred talents from the Great King. Suddenly Alexander is standing in front of Thebes. As the city remains stubborn, it must atone horribly and in Athens tales are told of conflagrations, bodies cut into pieces and soiled shrines. People look at this youth with the wide uncanny eyes and the brilliant voice in awe and fear. Even Demosthenes begins to suspect what storm-like force is at work here. So Athens concludes peace.

The most urgent things have been done; and with incomparable impatience Alexander plunges himself into the preparations for the fantastic enterprise, that his mind is set on. He plans, decides, organises. A pretext for having Attalos executed for high treason has been easily found; also Amyntas has already been removed, and the young king only protects Arrhidaeus, but nobody understands why. Olympias, indulging herself in her power, gives the order to strangle Cleopatra, who was her worst enemy and rival; she has the embryo taken out of the belly of the corpse, and burns it uttering horrific curses.

With a brutality, which no one would have suspected him of having, Alexander orders everything according to his wishes.

He is not seen by anyone to be cheerful or broody any more, and even towards Hephaestion he is matter of fact and brief. His eyes have the almost black, concentrated and harshly shining look, which those around him fear. Around the mouth are steel-hard muscles.

Outwardly the justification for his Asiatic campaign is the concept of pan-Hellenic revenge: what Xerxes did to the Greeks, Macedonia wants to take revenge for on Darius Codomannus.[11] He claims to be executing Philip's will, and only to be carrying out what the latter had planned. But in doing this he distances himself further and further from Philip's ideas. His father wanted only what was reasonable and limited, but he is attracted only by what is boundless. Philip had at first only concerned himself with the geography of Asia Minor; Alexander is already studying the climatic conditions of Iran, and obtaining reports about Bactria and Sogdiana.

Ships are armed. Greece, Thessaly and Thrace send troops. In the meantime he, in drunken, blind generosity, gives away almost everything which is his, all his private possessions, as though he wants to free himself forcibly from every tie.

Parmenion, with his face like a tomcat and the look in his eye of the faithful soldier looking up in deep respect, asked most respectfully for the fact to be considered that to leave the country without a successor to the throne was irresponsible, especially in such dangerous times. He suggested various ladies of the high aristocracy, and also foreign princesses, who might be suitable as a spouse, never forgetting in the process, with the benign but indecent smile of an old man, to praise the physical merits of the girl in question. The young king laughed briefly and contemptuously; Hephaestion, who was with him, laughed with him.

As the winter drew to a close, King Alexander set off with an army of thirty thousand foot-soldiers and five hundred cavalrymen towards the Hellespont. He took leave of his mother only ceremonially, in the presence of several officers. Since their decisive discussion, he had not talked with her alone again.

Antipatros was installed as Regent of the Empire.

They moved along the coast via Amphipolis, and then Abdera, Maroneia and Cardia, and on the twentieth day were in Sestos. The fleet was already waiting at the Hellespont. On the other side lay Troy.

Alexander, at the bow of the ship, was dreaming with wide open eyes. His dreams became too great, and he had to talk about them. So he tried, his voice trembling with fear that he could not make himself clear, and only give hints, which no one understood.

'If this is successful, Hephaestion, then the goal of mankind will be reached. Blood will flow, but the goal will be reached – Oh, Hephaestion – ' He went silent, for he noticed already, that the other man did not understand anything. He noticed that he, as ever, was alone. Loneliness made him humble and no longer proud; he tried to come closer to the man who was standing next to him like a stranger.

Hephaestion saw how in the restless darkness Alexander's head sank down towards him. Both felt on their lips the taste of the salty water. Behind the clouds drifting in shreds, through which a spring gale was blowing, the stars came out rarely and palely.

'But you must help me,' begged Alexander, who was suddenly fighting back the tears, his brow against Hephaestion's cool one.

The latter replied gently and firmly, as though reminding him of his duty: 'It is the hour which mellows you. You know that you do not need my help. For you are strongest when alone,

Alexander! I only disturb you – ' He became silent, moved by his own renunciation, having, in his gentleness, no idea how it affected the other man.

Alexander's heated face, around which his locks hung tangled like snakes, drew back. In the morning light it seemed to grow palely rigid. The mouth became harsh, and wrinkles appeared on the beautiful brow.

This was the second time that he had been turned away. 'Now I will never offer myself again,' he thought, calmly after his exuberance.

As Hephaestion felt for his hand, he let him hold it, but without returning the other's pressure. He turned his gaze, which had become severe, towards the water, which was becoming pale and rippled in the freezing cold.

Victory

I

They sacrificed to Zeus, who protects landings, to Heracles, and finally to the Ilian Athene. To the latter Alexander dedicated all his weapons, for which admittedly, in a pious but advantageous deal, he took the holy weapons from her temple treasure. Amongst these there was a shield, of which it was said that it had belonged to Achilles, whom the king called his ancestor.

On that morning Alexander was united in enthusiastic comradeship with his soldiers, who were as young as he. They all loved each other: all of them were no older than twenty-five. The year was also just beginning – and the campaign would be a big one.

They fought with each other like boys: whoever was the strongest was decorated with flowers. They felt the sun blissfully on their bodies and with a cheerful shiver the wind that came from the sea.

They rejoiced loudest when the young king came out of his tent with his friends. They had left their clothes inside and were naked: Alexander, Clitus, Hephaestion, Coenus, Philotas, Craterus and Perdiccas. The army went wild: their leaders were beautiful and strong like demigods.

Their bodies had been exercised in the gymnasium and become brown. They moved around more freely naked and more naturally than in their leather tunics; they stretched themselves, laughed and suddenly threw themselves at each other and wrestled. Two pairs were having a contest, and the others watched, applauded and encouraged or scolded, if one infringed the rules.

Not for nothing were they young Greeks, and they soon took the contest seriously. The slender Clitus, who was improbably dexterous, defeated the hot-tempered Philotas, covered with black hair and as strong as a bear. At this the latter ground his teeth, and his father Parmenion ground his teeth too under his grey beard. Craterus, who kept to the permitted holds too closely, was, after defending himself bravely by the way, defeated by Perdiccas, who did not take it so seriously.

After the wrestling they went on to throwing the discus, and the running.

Alexander and Clitus were the fastest, so they had to compete against each other again as a pair. Half the army took a passionate interest in it.

It seemed as though Alexander would be the winner. You could see that he ran straining with all his energy, panting, with a grim expression and his jaws biting together. Clitus, quite effortlessly, kept a few metres behind the king. He did not overtake him until shortly before the finish. Alexander noticed this, panted even harder and summoned up his remaining energy. It was unquestionably too late, as Clitus had as good as won. Then, two metres before the finish, he slowed down his pace; at the last moment, with the crowd shouting with excitement, he let the other man pass the line in first place after all.

Those standing nearby had hardly noticed that Clitus had *let* Alexander win, out of sympathy, courtesy or mockery; and that he could have won himself, and indeed without panting. He stood sly and happy to one side, while the king was greeted with solemn cries.

Alexander, who knew, gave only cursory thanks, not daring to look at Clitus again.

Everywhere men were wrestling, jumping and running. Many had run to the sea, and they could be heard rejoicing and yelling, whenever they sprayed each other with water. They embraced each other, in such an effusive mood were they due to their own self-confidence, youth and the fine weather.

This motley gang, thrown together by politics and chance, had never felt so much that they were Greeks and never so enthusiastically as a community. The one who led them, however, the youth, he was more than human.

They saw him, their Alexander, strolling around in an embrace with his friend Hephaestion, and they felt truly that it was Achilles with Patroclus. Alexander's body was brighter, more muscular, and more elastic than that of Hephaestion, who appeared brownish, somewhat softer and with a tendency to a charming ponderousness. Both turned round in surprise, when they were suddenly cheered at. Hephaestion smiled thankfully, for he heard them call him Patroclus, at which he blushed and looked down modestly at the ground. Alexander, whom they greeted with an enthusiastic shout as Achilles, thanked them by raising his arm in a formal way, greeting them and laughing.

Of course no one had noticed the hastily taken and secret sidelong glance, with which he wanted to try and establish whether Clitus was watching the scene. But he was sitting somewhere in hiding, playing with flowers and spinning stories full of lies.

At night most of the men slept in the open air, many entwined together in pairs. They breathed calmly after the day which had been marvellous.

Just as calmly breathed the young leaders in their tents. They dreamed of the fabulous wars, on the sites of which they had wrestled together that day in their play; many of them hid Homer, together with their daggers, under their pillows. But they also dreamed of those even greater wars, the even more fabulous heroes of which *they* would be.

The only restless one was Alexander, who sat up and stared embittered into the darkness.

'*Why did he let me go ahead?* That he can defeat me is bad enough, but that he does not even do it – Oh, Clitus – Clitus –'

In the lifetime of his cousin, Artaxerxes Ochos, as cruel as he was clever, Darius Codomannus had been first head of the postal services and then Satrap of Armenia. After the demonic hermaphrodite Bagoas from Egypt had first murdered Great King Ochus, whose creature and favourite he was, and then his successor Arses, Darius, who came from a branch of the Achaemenids, acquired the tiara. The only vigorous act of his life was to demand, with gentle but inexorable politeness, of the fat horrible Bagoas, when the latter served him with a poisoned goblet soon after he started his rule, that he drink it himself; which he, for good or evil, had to do. Thoughtful but with indifference Codomannus watched, as the fat monster died in convulsions before his eyes.

Darius had a melancholy idyllic disposition, but however, when it mattered, was not squeamish or sentimental, but rather of a cruelty which was as silent as it was resolute. It is true he did not take any pleasure in it however, as did for instance his cousin Artaxerxes. Rather it disgusted him, if he had to go as far as torturing and executions: it caused him nausea rather than delight, albeit quite temporarily.

He consoled himself with flowers and educated conversations. In addition he was attached to and very much in awe of his mother Sisygambis, an energetic old woman, who for her part somewhat despised him; and he was also attached with chivalrous tenderness to his pretty and melancholy young wife, who had given him two daughters.

The Great King was not a majestic figure, somewhat stocky and almost small, with too huge a head, which he held at an angle when thinking; also he had thoughtful yet empty eyes of a beautiful brown.

As a young man he had not had a pleasant life. The postal services caused him a lot of bother, and as Satrap of Armenia the mountain people called the Cadusians had become a nuisance to him. As his power of resistance was not very great, the forty-year-old already felt tired; the affairs of his enormous empire, which stretched from the Indus to the Hellenic Sea, from Jaxartes to the Libyan Desert, which he barely knew, were not of too burning an interest to him. He let the satraps do as they pleased, which they did impudently enough and to the bitter dismay of the populace. For the rest he relied on his Greek mercenaries with whose help Artaxerxes had already put down the Egyptian rebellion, and on the cavalry provided for him by rougher countries.

The sudden incursion of Philip's troops into his area of Asia Minor had really unnerved and frightened him. He transferred the protection of the empire to Greek mercenaries and gave supreme command over them to the Rhodian Memnon, whose tough skill he valued. After a short time he could heave a sigh of relief and give thanks to Ahura-Mazda. Philip was murdered and the Macedonian troops went away.

What did this Alexander want, of whom it was said, that he was young and had very uncanny eyes? The Great King had a restless night, and the next morning he summoned his leading men to a meeting.

He received them in his ceremonial outfit, though he was very pale. The heavily padded tunic, a foot deep and drawn in at the waist, made him clumsy and hindered him; in addition there was the cylindrical cap, the carefully frizzled beard, heavy earrings, in his left hand the prescribed long staff, and in his right the flower, with which he played nervously.

Apart from Memnon, various influential lords had been announced, some of whom belonged to the court, and others who were staying in Babylon temporarily on account of some business matters or for their amusement: Arsites, the Satrap of Phrygia on the Hellespont, Spithridates, Satrap of Lydia and Ionia, Atizyes of Greater Phrygia, Mithrobuzanes of Cappadocia, Omares, who, coming from an old family, was regarded as especially distinguished. They came clattering in, in their black beards and covered in gold. The obligatory falling at the feet of Darius was more hinted at than carried out; only Memnon, the Greek, touched the floor before the feet of his lord with his brow in a demonstratively detailed manner, at which the latter cleared his throat nervously.

The Great King had an oddly cursory and absent-minded manner of communicating to his advisers what the matter was about, which the latter, who knew of course exactly what the matter concerned, confirmed amongst themselves, with partly anxious and partly scornful side glances; only Memnon, with his deeply furrowed brow lowered, remained haughty and completely indifferent.

'In short, this young Macedonian is a threat to my empire,' the monarch finished his exposition suddenly with surprising impatience.

At this the advisers ventured to contradict. They were of the strong opinion that one could in no way speak of a 'threat'. It was more a question of a young intruder of, it was true, remarkable impudence, but without all other supplies to help him. One would have to, as indeed a matter of honour, show him quickly and vigorously, what it means to raid Persian territory in such an insolent way.

The smug talk of his noblemen seemed to quickly tire and bore the king. He nodded and remained silent, sometimes looking anxiously at Memnon, who chewed his lip but otherwise did not move his yellow, beardless face, and looked down at the ground, remaining unapproachable.

After endless meaningless words, the subject of which was Persia's greatness in general, they finally came to the practical part of the debate: to the battle which they were to undertake against Alexander, what troops were to be employed, and which terrain they considered to be the most favourable. Here at last Memnon intervened, and provided precise and exact proposals, and soon he alone was controlling and leading the discussion. As a result Darius also became more lively. Only when the problem arose, to whom the supreme command was to be assigned, did the Greek general become quiet again. After an excruciatingly painful pause, it was the Great King, who, in an uncertain voice, suggested Memnon; but the others immediately contradicted him.

They irritatedly let it be understood that to entrust to a foreigner the command over an army, which was to defend the national honour, was really going too far. Memnon, who knew that he was hated, again looked icily indifferent, chewed at his lower lip and remained silent.

Finally the result was that various generals should take over together the supreme command: apart from Memnon also Arsites, Spithridates and several others.

Memnon indicated his acceptance with a small movement of his hand, but the king seemed to be cross: he had trust in no one but the taciturn, elegant and cunning Greek.

On the same day, to show people that the court was in good spirits, an especially marvellous excursion was undertaken: he appeared in broad crimson breeches with the tiara wound round with a diadem of precious stones. Ahead of his decorated coach trotted a hundred single horses, and it was followed by a hundred more. Alongside ran slaves.

At the River Granicus Alexander finds himself opposite the Persian force. He decides on a quick attack.

Old Parmenion approaches him; he warns him: the superior force of the enemy is considerable, and there are said to be twenty thousand cavalrymen, as many Greek mercenaries, and infantry; the terrain, with the steeply sloping river banks, would conceivably be unfavourable to an attacker.

'Follow my advice!' concluded the vigorous and cautious old man. 'Delay this first decisive battle!'

Alexander, full of tense impatience, and eager for his first decision, rejects this haughtily and impatiently. 'I conquered the Hellespont, so am I to fear this little stream?' The old man, grey and venerable, who finds this response lacking in objectivity and takes it personally, withdraws feeling insulted.

On the other side it is Memnon who advises against the engagement. His instinct senses that Alexander, full of energy, as he is today will win victory by sheer defiance, against any terrain. In a few weeks, the Greek calculates, this daredevil will be weaker.

But the Persian officers scoff at his cautiousness. That was all they needed: wait and withdraw! It was high time the Macedonian got to know them. – Memnon lowered his eyes haughtily at such empty phrases. What is more, against his explicit advice, and only for reasons of national vanity and out of ostentation, the Persian cavalry were placed at the front, right on the bank, while the Greek mercenaries were placed further back.

Alexander himself led the Macedonian attack. He could be recognised on the other side by the white plume on his helmet which was fluttering. He and his young soldiers came through the torrents of water with a battle song, and behind the trumpets sounded, sure of victory.

He and his young soldiers shouted for joy in doing battle. They were still as cheerful as they were a few days before while playing, but with a wilder cheerfulness, which was ready for death.

From the steep banks arrows and missiles came towards them, and twenty-five Macedonian horsemen fell during the attack. But with such enthusiastic impetuosity did the others take the steep bank, that the superior Persian force shrank back in horror. On the slippery damp ground of the bank the hand-to-hand fighting became more and more horrible. Many plunged into the water, the narrow course of which became filled with corpses.

Where Alexander's white feather was, the fight was most furiously intense. The curved swords of the Persians and the light spears of the Macedonians clashed against each other, and crossed each other, making a moving roof and grille which cast shadows over the heated heads of those wrestling below. Alexander laughed with heroic exuberance, for his weapon split right down the middle. An officer threw his to him, as though they were playing ball.

With this the king pushed from the steed the little Persian cavalry general, who, snorting with anger more loudly than his steaming animal, came leaping towards him. A jangling comrade was already preparing to revenge him. Alexander received him with his whirring blows.

He had the borrowed sword still in the wound of the second man, when a third was already brandishing his sabre behind him. He noticed directly above him something curved glinting; before he could become alarmed he was already falling. With the weapon fell also the man who had brandished it. Alexander saw him sink down sideways from his steed, roaring coarsely. It was the one who had almost killed him, and now blackish blood gushed out of the embroidery on his garment.

But Alexander, the man who had escaped death, felt a hand on his shoulder, which he recognised by its pressure: it was gentle and firm. He obeyed, and let himself be led from the throng without exercising his will. He thought dreamily as he was riding: this hand is brownish and muscular, quite thin, with noble, firm joints, and light nails which come to a point. So now it has saved my life.

When he looked into Clitus' face, it was full of a seriousness which was so intense, so impenetrable, as Alexander had only found once before in him: in that night, when the fateful phrase 'You're disturbing me very much' had been uttered. 'What's happening behind that brow?' thought the rescued man in his suffering.

At the same time he said, when they were already away from the fighting but with arrows still whizzing around them, 'You have saved my life. How would you like me to show my thanks to you?'

Clitus, lowering his brow, was suddenly quite the old joker again, courteous, and with that smile that was, incredibly, interpretable in a hundred ways.

'You show me thanks, Alexander, by being alive.'

For the twenty-five horsemen fallen in the attack bronze statues were cast by Lysippos. Three hundred complete sets of armour went to Athens as gifts dedicated to Pallas Athene. Alexander thanked his army with rapture, weeping with happiness. 'With this victory the power of the Great King is destroyed as far as the Taurus Mountains. This is the beginning, my friends. Now no one can resist us.'

His dazzling words were answered by rejoicing, joyful singing and a shower of flowers.

2

Memnon, as a Greek and an aristocrat, hated Alexander with a personally bitter and grievous hatred. For him he was nothing but a half-barbarian, the revolutionary upstart, whose appearance brings disorder. Also he could not forgive him or his father that day at Chaironea, least of all for the mercy that had been shown to Athens at that time and that he felt to be humiliating, while the democratic city, which had become vulgar, still thanked the lenient conquerors nicely.

To Syrphax, the head of the Persian garrison in Ephesos, he said contemptuously: 'Passionate individuals like these have always brought misfortune, when they ventured into the world of facts. After their dictatorship comes chaos – I prefer small tyrants.' And he looked at Syrphax in an insulting way. 'They keep things in order.'

It was clear that he despised his new friends, but they did not notice it. They clung to Memnon as to a saviour, for their power was beginning to become shaky everywhere. With Alexander a storm of a new feeling for freedom was spreading over the land, which had been oppressed for so long. Ionia was awakening, and the Persian-oriented rule by oligarchy seemed, thanks to this terrible Macedonian boy, to have gone downhill.

In Ephesos the lords amused themselves as much as possible; Memnon, with a bitter cheerfulness, joined in. The holy treasure of Artemis was plundered, and Philip's statue was knocked down.

Disturbingly, the most unpleasant news reports were arriving every day: Sardes, the residence of the Lydian satrapy, had opened its gates to the conqueror, who appeared as a sign of freedom, and Mithrines himself, the Persian commanding officer of the garrison, came together with the dignitaries of the city, to receive the intruder solemnly.

'The people rejoiced,' Memnon related among the circle of Syrphax and his friends. They grinned scornfully. Here they only heard the people whispering and complaining.

There was one stroke of bad luck after the other for the lords in Ephesos: Tralles and Magnesia had surrendered voluntarily and everywhere the rule by aristocrats was being abolished, in Chios and Lesbos.

'We are sitting in the middle of an earthquake,' said Memnon, whose face became more and more yellow. He chewed at his lower lip, staring embittered straight ahead of him. 'What is more all this is superfluous,' he asserted with a painful stubbornness. 'The Battle of Granicus River could have been won. Persian vanity spoilt everything.'

What use were his remarks to the petty tyrants, who were sitting in the middle of the earthquake? It really made their skin creep. Memnon still had the energy to mock, but his friends were not laughing any more. Things were becoming restless in the streets of Ephesos. The storm was approaching –

'Alexander is said to be so beautiful,' asserted the yellow-faced Memnon with a sarcasm that his companions found to be uncalled for in this situation, 'that even his fleeing enemies have to turn round towards him, when he is after them. So it will be delightful for you to get to know him.'

He himself went away, to Halicarnassus, so it is said.

Syrphax hardly dares to go onto the street any more, for now the mob in Ephesos is already rejoicing, as the one in Sardes has done: they know that the Macedonian army is already advancing.

'The liberator's coming!' rejoices the mob. Syrphax trembles and sobs in his palace, which is surrounded. 'It's blatant revolution,' whimpers the little lord, who had held up his head so inexorably: 'Won't Persia help me now? I have always acted in the Great King's interest.'

As Persia does not help, he flees by night into the Temple of Artemis, which he has plundered only a few days ago. The people are not in the mood for piety, and he is torn from the altar. And aren't those stones which are flying? They are well-aimed and the petty tyrant collapses. They laugh at his last comical twitching movement; and in with this laughter is mixed a greater noise, a rejoicing.

'The liberator has arrived!'

At the head of the cavalry column the youth on the white horse is so covered with flowers that he is almost unrecognisable. He rides without a helmet, shaking his curly soft strawberry-blond hair from his brow occasionally with a defiant gesture. The women who throw the flowers are mad about his hair. 'It has a crimson shimmer,' they whisper blissfully. 'And how young he looks. He's got a mouth like a child. And such soft cheeks.'

'But I'm sure that mouth can be very strict,' others whisper in great awe. 'I'm sure it can be terrible. You can tell by his eyes.'

He paid homage to the Mother of the Gods with a great sacrifice, which was his first action in Ephesos, and his whole army had to be present in Gala. It is true however that beforehand he had been alone with her for many hours.

He knew more about her than most who had worshipped her. The history of her holiness was lost in the venerable obscurity of Egypt. Olympias had taken him to the point where the virgin, whom the Greeks call Artemis, becomes identical with the Asiatic mother, who loses her lover and son, weeps for them and sees them resurrected. The son of Olympias felt himself doubly and mysteriously related to the Ephesian deity, as she had spoken to him in the night of his birth with such terrible signs. The fire, with which she had herself adorned and decorated, united her for ever with Alexander.

He stood for a long time eye to eye with her. Between them a silent dialogue of great import seemed to be taking place. Was a mission being renewed here, solemnly repeated, being set again?

The portrait, which Alexander had made by Apelles, he dedicated to the goddess' temple. It represented the young conqueror with a brilliant gesture, brandishing a lightning bolt in his hand. The gesture however with which he handed it over and set it up was humble.

He stayed in Ephesos for a few days, putting things in order and governing affairs. To everyone who came to him with requests, he gave a hearing; everything down to the smallest detail, gripped his attention and interested him.

A few days after the great sacrificial festival the king set off with his army for Milet.

He reported to his mother:

'Since my stay in Ephesos and the visit to the Great Mother I feel I'm stronger than ever.

'Asia Minor is cheering me; they were sick of Persian rule. It's being fulfilled, Olympias, it's being fulfilled.'

After the conquest of Milet, Alexander disbanded the fleet; thus he gave up the idea of a conflict with the Persians at sea. 'At sea they could be superior to us,' he explained to his confidants, when he informed them of his decision. 'Our triumphal procession must not be disturbed by the disgrace of a single defeat. I want to conquer land and free land, not water.'

So much more important did Halicarnassus in Caria become for him, which controlled the entrance to the Aegean Sea. The remains of Persian power in Asia Minor had gathered together in this famous and strong city.

At the entrance to the Carian empire a vivacious woman of an effusive disposition was waiting for him, Princess Ada, who claimed that she was the legal mistress of the Carian land, and had been shamefully deceived by her treacherous relative Othontopates, who was at that time arming himself against Alexander in Halicarnassus.

Princess Ada was so incomparably talkative, that she took the breath away from everyone who heard her. She wore expensive but rather slovenly clothes, had an aristocratic face like a male sheep, with a long nose, eyes of a watery brightness and a chattering mouth. She immediately took it for granted that Alexander was her liberator and knight, for which she already thanked him beforehand in her talkative way.

'You are too kind,' she immediately enthused, when she was introduced to him. 'These fellows have been harassing me.' And she told him as coherently as she could, her family story, which was as sad as it was complicated.

'I could have made it!' she exclaimed at the end of her intricate novel, which dealt with the fates of her forefathers, cousins and aunts. 'I did make it for a few months, but then my brother Pixodaros deposed me. Oh you eternal gods, what a rogue he was! Your clever father wanted to really fool him with his half-witted Arrhidaeus. Well, finally Pixodaros also died, and do you think I gained what was rightfully mine? Othontopates took what was due to me. And what do you think he gave to me? The mountain fortress of Alinda! The mountain fortress! Oh, you eternal gods!'

Ada could not console herself about the mountain fortress. Again and again she cried out 'Alinda!' and raised her eyes wretchedly towards the sky. Naively and cordially she confided in the young hero, who, she believed, had set off from Pella, with the sole purpose of helping her and to procure her rights.

Alexander found her droll and kind, and the absolute trust that she put in him flattered him a little; so he treated her with gently ironical courtesy. She for her part insisted on heaping presents and tasty morsels on him, and daily she sent dishes, little baskets and bowls full of sugary things, roasted things, preserved and fresh things; rosy and prickly fruit, sweet, perfumed and many-coloured things; oily and greasy things, and delicate, nourishing and surprising things. Alexander enjoyed it and had flirtatious expressions of thanks delivered to her.

'I think she wants to marry me,' he said to Hephaestion, grinning as he gnawed at an almond pastry. She intended something more exceptional: she wanted to adopt him. This notion he found so crazy that he said yes to it. 'You can never have enough mothers', was his opinion, and he let himself be kissed by her on his brow and cheeks.

In addition he also made use of his relationship with her in a political way: now he could claim to be fighting for her rights, when he attacked Halicarnassus.

Behind the walls of the city Memnon did as he pleased more energetically and cleverly than Othontopates, who was the official commanding officer.

'We must hold this city to the last, to the very last,' he demanded again and again, when he discussed the defence possibilities with the leaders, elders and engineers. 'With its three forts it is almost impregnable. Never forget, that it signifies our last base in Asia Minor; *the last base of order,*' he warned them. 'If it falls, the flood cannot be stopped any more.'

It was unstoppable, and all the trenches and fortifications, which Memnon laid out were of no use. 'Then he will conquer nothing but rubble,' said the irreconcilable man. He had the town set on fire, and withdrew with Othontopates and the troops to the island where the royal castle was.

'That's the second Greek city that's burning for him,' he remarked with a cruel satisfaction. 'First Thebes, and now Halicarnassus. This is what the liberation of Greece proves to be like. Here is his freedom.' And with these words he indicated scornfully the sea of flames. 'That's how he wanted it. It's chaos.'

'Is that the freedom, which I wanted to bring?' thought Alexander, making his entry between buildings that were crashing down. 'The second city of the Greeks, which is burning for me.'

All the same he conquered Caria, and Ada got her satrapy back. She wept with happiness and embraced, repeatedly and closely, her saviour and son, whom she had not been wrong about. He even allowed her to keep the revenues from the province, which were large.

'You are good!' she sobbed again and again. 'You are so good, Alexander.' He nodded thoughtfully, and almost sadly.

Nevertheless it seemed to do him good, that she chattered in such a lively way and believed in him so unconditionally.

He could even allow himself to send those of his soldiers, who were newly married and had young wives at home, to their loved ones in Macedonia and Greece, which gave rise to some jokes and some coarse teasing.

Parmenion was instructed to move with a part of the troops to Sardis, where he was to stay for the winter. Thus, first of all, the old man was left out of things. Alexander himself set off into Inner Asia Minor, to take Lycia, which had been Persian since Cyrus' time.

In how many towns does he ride on white Bucephalas through the gate decorated with flowers? How often is he received with a shower of flowers, the cheering of the men and the young boys, and the infatuated murmuring of the women: 'How young he looks – He's got a mouth like a child and such soft cheeks – Look, he's not wearing a helmet; what a lot of curls in his strawberry-blond hair. Look, he shakes it from his brow with such a beautiful defiant movement – You almost can't see his face, he's so covered with flowers – Have you heard? His face is said to be so beautiful that fleeing enemies have to turn round towards him, when he's after them. But you can see his eyes though between the flowers – '

Were there any dangers for him? The attack was discovered, which was carried out against him by a gloomy young man, Alexandros of the Lyncestae, the son-in-law of Antipatros, and who was paid a large bribe by Persia. The soldiers rejoiced. 'No daggers can strike the favourite of the gods!'

In the small towns which surrendered to him they celebrated with joyful festivities. They boozed and had women, and at night Alexander went into the market place singing with his friends, to decorate the picture of a Greek poet, Theodectes, with flowers.

The warm night sent them warm rain from her beautiful darkness, which made their hair and faces wet. They embraced each other, and lay wet faces against each other.

3

Memnon reported to the Great King in Susa.

'Alexander's conquests on the mainland are indisputable. I hope that Your Majesty has been informed truthfully in this respect. Sagalossos has really fallen, and Celaenae, the residence of the Phrygian satrap, has surrendered voluntarily.

'In all these cases it has been a matter of the chance successes of a bold adventurer, for whom the game has been made only too easy by our own mistakes. As matters stand, his downfall will be most certain, if we let him win and conquer a little bit more in Inner Asia Minor, while we retrieve along the coast road what he has already acquired. In this way we'll cut off his link with Macedonia.

'At the same time it would be advisable to strengthen the number of our agents in Greece. In the long run Alexander's situation is untenable, if the spitefulness against him in his motherland increases. Sparta seems to be on the point of rebellion. In Athens they are sullen, for Alexander treats the illustrious city with less consideration than his father did. First he just downright refuses, without giving any reasons, the Athenian request, to set free the prisoners from Granicus.'

His report was concise and detailed, and also honest, in contrast to that which the courtiers wrote. His suggestions were clear. Darius, who wanted an end to the affair soon in order to be able to devote himself to his idyllic inclinations again, decided to give full authority to Memnon, to the bitter annoyance of the Persian aristocracy.

Memnon became supreme commander of the fleet.

The great occasion of his life had arrived, and he made use of it with passionate energy. His face, which had been wrinkled and worn out, became tighter; it was still yellowish, but had become ten years younger. Ambition and hatred made his gait elastic.

He knew that he was isolated, alone with his plans and his considerations. The Persians who surrounded him were malevolent towards him. The only man who enjoyed a sort of position of trust with him, was Pharnabazus, his fairly insignificant nephew.

His extensively laid out intrigues and wheelings and dealings and the threatening majesty of his fleet succeeded in winning back Chios, Lesbos and many other cities for Persia. Only Mytilene still resisted.

He decided to lay siege to this city.

On the third day he felt himself becoming feverish. Something in him was becoming weaker, and he did not understand where this weakness and paralysis were coming from. They must herald serious illness. Had someone in his circle poisoned him, someone bribed by Alexander or an adversary at court? Had higher powers sent this bad nausea? Then the higher powers were favourably disposed towards Alexander. This thought disturbed Memnon most.

The next morning he was unable to stand up. He was tormented by shivering, and every movement, even clear thought hurt. He asked his nephew Pharnabazus to come to his bed. The good lad was completely taken aback to find his uncle so changed; finally he even began to weep, which made the sick man impatient. 'Don't weep!' he said gruffly, 'I'll be dead in a few hours.'

Behind his brow, where so much had been thought and which was deeply lined with wrinkles, his mind was still at work. 'If

I had conquered Mytilene as well, then this Macedonian youth would have been lost. It would have been the end of him, his ruin. I'm dying just at the right time for him.'

After a sorrowful pause he added: 'If one of these Persians has poisoned me, it is a sign from the gods, that they are ready for their downfall. Ready, ready, ready!' He shouted and thrust forward the upper part of his body in pain. 'Now nobody else can resist the breakthrough of this barbarian. No Asian can hate him the way I do, only a Greek. He is the enemy of Greece more than of Persia. He mixes everything up and confuses everything. But we were the pure ones.'

He sank back down again, and his quince-yellow, distinguished and worn-out face rested in pain. The chin stuck up in a point and his mouth seemed to sink in like that of an old man. Only in the passionate dark eyes could one see that he was still thinking, as inexorably and passionately as ever.

In conclusion to this last great flow of thought he said softly: 'He's lucky, that Alexander. The gods have given him good luck.' With his brow sinking sadly forward, without hope, but proudly, he said: 'I was the last man he had to fear.'

With a tired and resigned solemnity he turned to his nephew again, who was listening anxiously. 'I name you my successor,' he said weakly. 'Assure the Great King of my loyalty and devotion – '

The news of the death of his important adversary reached Alexander in Gordium. It did not put him in a happy mood, rather in a solemn one. Every new proof of the favour of the gods moved him deeply almost to tears. He informed his mother of the new favour in refined language:

'The mysterious gods, to whom you pray for me, have destroyed my worst enemy. They bless me with their great favour, for the sake of the mission, in accordance with the meaning of which I strive to act.'

On this day they showed him in the Phrygian royal castle the holy cart, in which Midas had driven among the people, so that, according to the oracle, his divinity could be recognised. They showed him also, on the shaft of the cart, the knot which seemed to be woven together from the fibre of a cornel-cherry tree in a way which could not be unravelled, and neither the beginning nor the end was visible. This knot, said the prophecy, must be unravelled by whoever wanted to rule over Asia.

Alexander bent over it, and examined it with his eyes narrowed; he felt around it with his fingers, and finally even sniffed at it, to see what it smelled like. It smelled rather rotten; an old knot, toughly matted together. It felt sticky with age, and if you grasped it firmly it would surely fall apart like a little bit of ash. To unravel it would indeed have involved a nasty effort. With a gesture showing him to be thoughtful and absent-minded Alexander drew his short sword from its sheath; he poked around and played in the rather unsavoury mass with the point of his sword, and suddenly, with no one prepared for it, he cut at it. The knot crumbled and fell apart.

The city fathers who were conducting the tour, tried to show horror in their eyes. But Alexander bowed gently as after a successful trick, and he showed his most radiant smile.

'Thus the prophecy has been fulfilled – ' The old men ran or toddled off, to inform their people about the miracle.

In Gordium the various units of the Macedonian army united together: Parmenion came from his winter rest in Sardes with his unit, the newlyweds came back from their recreational leave, and with them a large number of newly enlisted men, three thousand on foot, and six hundred and fifty on horse.

While the large camp prepared itself for departure, Alexander was having weighty meetings. It proved to be necessary to create a new fleet, to maintain contact with the motherland, for Mytilene had after all surrendered to Pharnabazus, and Memnon's intrigues were having an after effect.

'Athens will refuse to supply us with ships.' Parmenion put forward this idea for consideration. Someone interjected: 'They are bound to it by treaty.' The old man shook his head. 'Nevertheless.'

It was Alexander who cut the discussion short: 'I will give the order to stop all merchant ships coming from Pontos, to take possession of them and fit them out as warships.'

In no way did he contemplate handling the illustrious city with kid gloves. Brutal and certain of victory he looked around him.

It was spring and Alexander was burning with desire to force some new decisions which would be definite. And with him waited his troops, who were burning with desire as much as he.

He led them through Cappadocia, beyond the Halys River, towards Tarsus and Anchiale; and on the way they occupied the land side of Cilicia.

The achievements demanded by him in his impatience were often enormous. Every morning he awoke with the same obsession: 'We did not get far enough yesterday. Today we must go further, further, much further.' The newly enlisted men still had to get used to these forced marches. They covered the greatest stretches at night, for by day the heat was terrible, and they preferred to be in the water, when they were not sleeping.

They always shouted with joy, when they splashed about in the ice-cold rivers. The campaign had not yet lasted too long, the great adventures were still ahead of them, and Babylon lay there in her fat splendour waiting for them.

When Alexander saw their brown bodies, he could not stay there alone in his clothes; he threw them off, for he belonged among those who were splashing each other and rejoicing.

He belonged among them, he was one of them, nothing but their enthusiastic comrade. He was twenty years old, like them, brown like them, muscular like them, and his hair grew like theirs. Intoxicated by a sense of community spirit, he forgot everything, which separated him from them, his experiences, ambition, even his suffering. His yearning to be nothing but a young man among young men and take part in the bond between them, which seemed to him to be more splendid and fresher than the bond between Man and Woman, and was stronger than everything else. – Thus he jumped into the water with them.

This time he had to pay for it, for he had become heated up, but the water was icy cold. He became very ill. His fever became so alarmingly high, that it was doubtful whether he would recover, and panic threatened to break out in the army. He had bathed with them, and now he was dying –

His doctor was a young Indian, who was called Philippos and whom the king loved very much. Whenever he brought him medicine, Alexander smiled thankfully and in a friendly way, even on the day when he was half dazed. Whenever this brownish gentle young person sat at his bedside, he slept more easily and better. Above all his dreams were more pleasant then. For Alexander was afraid of his dreams.

'When I'm asleep I often experience such disgusting things,' he told, in his exhausted condition, the young healer, who visited him in the mornings. 'Last night I was standing by a river, beneath a blazing sun. Out of the river there rose some youths – how old could they have been? No older than sixteen or seventeen years old, some perhaps only fifteen; I envied them, for they seemed to be freezing. They were lean and brown, and on their chests, arms, backs, and thighs they had faint goose pimples, because they had been so long in the water. Do you know that? When boys have been in the water too long their lips acquire a moving bluish colour, and tremble. And also they get great frozen eyes, which are also moving. Yes, that is how the children were standing, quite slender and shivering.

'But I was wearing a thick purple robe, and was completely buttoned up in nothing but hot, blazing purple. That's why I was so hot. Also my head had been wrapped up in a solemn way. The sweat ran down over the nape of my neck and my brow, and I was swelling up with the heat, and becoming fatter and fatter under the robe of state. I stood there, a swollen purple figure dripping with sweat, opposite the slender brown youths. Finally it seems that I exploded. It was dreadful.'

He kept silent in disgust. The Indian had to sit with him for a long time, until he had calmed down.

Alexander also smiled on the morning, when a letter had warned him about the learned scholar: he had been bribed and was trying to murder him with his potion. The letter was from no less a man than Parmenion himself, who claimed to be informed most accurately about the evil intentions of the doctor and to be afraid for the life of his king. Alexander handed the letter over to the man under suspicion for him to read, while he himself slurped the concoction which tasted pleasantly of herbs. Philippos wanted to defend himself, making furious gestures, but the king laughed between his blankets and clothes and waved him aside.

'As Parmenion warns me about you,' he said with amusement, 'you'll certainly make me well.'

He slept well, and the next day was almost recovered.

They took Tarsus, then Anchiale, which had been built by Sardanapalus. On the statue of the King of the Assyrians they found this inscription:

'Anchiale and Tarsus were founded by Sardanapal in one day. But you, stranger, eat, drink and make love. Anything else that Man has is not worth talking about.'

This inscription seemed to occupy Alexander's thoughts a great deal. He went around thoughtfully for the rest of the day.

The news of the death of General Memnon put the Great King in a state of the most profound confusion; now he could think of no other way out at all. He just continued to sit there and shook his head, with tears running down his big cheeks.

This is how he was found by his mother, the vigorous Sisygambis, who mocked him coarsely: 'A fine king!' And as she said this she even pointed at him with her finger. She reminded him firmly of the fact, that he was an Achaemenid. 'The blood of Cyrus runs in your veins,' she cried threateningly. He shook his heavy head, sorrowful and in disbelief. 'Oh yes,' he said, full of worries.

Still he summoned a council of his leaders. He admitted to them, that he did not know any more what to do. The black-bearded, clanking gentlemen showed themselves to be more decisive: What was to be done? A huge battle was to be undertaken, which would finally bring destruction upon the stranger, and what is more with one blow, as he deserved. The army was standing ready, and it could be counted in hundreds of thousands: the Persian cavalry, and the Greek mercenaries were waiting. The king of kings only needed to put himself at their head. His presence, cried the black-bearded ones, as they clanked around, would inspire them and make them brave. Things could not turn out as they had at Granicus.

The king, gentle, distinguished and resigned, listened and nodded. That his personality could inspire an army and lead it to victory seemed inconceivable and strange to him; but he liked to hear them say it.

What Darius had really dreamed in the night before setting off to join the army, nobody discovered. He woke up distraught. Officially it was announced that he had seen the Macedonian camp in flames, a rather ridiculous fiction, which could only be taken seriously out of politeness.

Apparently haughty but in reality depressed to the point of a nervous breakdown, he set off, accompanied by his great harem, his eunuchs, his mutes, cooks, and soothsayers as well as the royal ladies.

He greeted the army with a rather dull speech. 'We must be victorious, for right is on our side,' he said sadly. After this he climbed back into his carriage, over which the baldachin swayed in all its sumptuousness. Next to him sat his mother, who scolded him about his speech which had been a disaster, his wife, and his two daughters, the elder of whom was called Statira.

The ponderous and very mixed mass of people, which regarded itself as the Great King's army, dragged itself slowly from the Euphrates towards Syria.

After the defeat Darius Codomannus fled unarmed, with his robe torn to pieces, on a mare towards the east: fled, fled, fled away from Alexander through Onchai and Thapsacus, until he was beyond the Euphrates. He wailed and babbled, and in his overexerted head, which wobbled as he galloped along, the confused painful thoughts hurt him.

'This horrible Alexander has supernatural powers, I could see it in his eyes. If those eyes had not looked at me in that way, oh, then this battle would not have been lost; then I would not have fled.

'Because those eyes looked at me, my kingdom is perishing,' he said in a confused way. 'That *I* turned back was the beginning of the catastrophe. The centre broke apart – '

The falling evening, windy night and the grey morning were audience to his despairing prattle. Sympathetic people handed him a jug of water and some bread. They did not recognise him. On his mare he was just a babbling, disturbed old man with a large head, who was riding towards the east in a pathological hurry.

In the meantime Alexander was looking at the royal treasures, tents and supplies, as well as the harem, everything that had been left behind in Damascus. The queen mother as well as the queen and the princesses were also his prisoners.

The suspicious old lady imagined that the worst was in store for her, and with icy calm she was prepared to be raped by at least ten Macedonian officers. Instead of this they hardly bothered about the high-class women. Alexander had given concise orders, to allow them all comforts, and to treat them with special courtesy. He himself did not even pay them a visit.

He and his friends had fun with the treasures, which they had found in the royal tents. They tried on the splendid robes decorated with precious stones, sniffed at the ointments and had food served to them in the golden dishes.

Alexander presented himself to his friends in the formal clothes of the Great King, and they rejoiced, clapped and laughed. As a joke he had them fall down before him. When they touched the ground in front of him with their foreheads, he suddenly became serious.

His riders and generals caught up with Darius, almost capturing him in fact. They brought him to his senses, and more brusquely than respectfully they reminded him what he was, what he owed to himself and the nation. Under their influence he drew up a note which began with the words: 'From the King of Kings, the Achaemenid, Son of Ahura-Mazda the Sun God, Darius Codomannus – To Alexander, the Macedonian.'

In the course of this letter he set forth in bitter words driven by pain, what the intruder had done to him; how he had, without being provoked by anything, destroyed the calm, peace and welfare of his great and beautiful empire. As the gods however, in their unfathomable wisdom, which was often so difficult to understand, had decided the great battle in his, Alexander's, favour, he was prepared, as one king to another, among equals, to make a deal with him. He should first return to him his ladies, of whom he was so fond, and then it could be agreed under what conditions the Macedonian army should vacate the territory, which did not belong to it.

To this peaceably unsuspecting offer the Great King received an answer, which was headed: 'King Alexander of Macedonia, Son of Philip, the Heraclide – to Darius,' and which began with the glorious sentence:

'As I am in fact Master of Asia...'

It stated, concisely, that a deal 'among equals' was inconceivable. Should Darius wish to approach Alexander, then only on condition that he recognise him unconditionally as his lord. Were he not to do that, then the decision would have to be left again for a battle to decide. – Concerning the ladies, he should himself come and fetch them and at the same time kneel at the feet of his lord.

Darius, on reading this reply, sat motionless for a long time, just shaking his head.

4

Alexander had adopted the habit, at decisive discussions, but also when alone, of hurrying up and down in the room, thinking things over, his hands behind his back and with his head bent down. He would stand still only with his closing words and, with his brow lowered, formulate his brief sentences.

Hurrying up and down in his tent he reflected on things and made decisions.

'If I wanted to act in accordance with the wishes of my officers and my army, I would immediately make good use of this great victory by setting off to Babylon.

'I can't allow myself to. I need the Phoenician merchant cities. I need, above all, Egypt.'

'I need Egypt,' he said aloud, stopping in the middle of the room. '*It belongs to my empire.*'

The presentiment which rose up before him was so great that he had to close his eyes. He saw 'The Empire', the eastern border of which was lost in uncertainty. Was Greece together with Macedonia anything more than an appendage to its magnificence? However his heart lay in Egypt: they were moving through a desert and deep within it they found the shrine. From there came the blessing, the confirmation.

'From there comes the confirmation.'

Alexander ordered his generals to come to an audience. He explained to them briefly what was to happen; they listened in amazement.

The most important merchant cities had already surrendered: Sidon, Aradus and Byblos. They were used to changing their masters and had been under Assyrian, Babylonian and Persian rule, one after the other. It had always been made possible for them to conduct their business, live in a lavish way and in real luxury.

Only Tyre remained refractory, considering itself, as an island city, to be impregnable.

The siege lasted several months.

After the conquest of Tyre and the fortress of Gaza, Alexander, accompanied only by small bands of men, visited the Jewish and Samaritan lands, where something strange happened to him. For here a priest greeted him, who was called Jaddua and seemed to be graver than all the magicians and conjurers, who came and went in Olympias' house. He raised the palms of his hands, shook his head, and his speech consisted of a nasal litany.

What he said went along the lines that Alexander was the one whose coming the Holy Scripture had so often foretold and proclaimed, who was sent by Jehova to free the chosen people from the Persian yoke. Alexander, who listened with courtly seriousness, was exceptionally pleased by this speech. Being used to guessing the identity of the deity, whose being was a secret, in every form and mask, he was also willing to believe in this one, which remained invisible but must be terribly severe and jealous.

Following the exact instructions of the priest, he made offerings to the secret one in his temple. It was in a town called Jerusalem.

Since the battle of Issus a year had passed. Finally they were ready to set off for Egypt.

It turned out that no battle was necessary there. The country surrendered to anyone who offered to free it from the Persian tyranny. It lay there majestically inflexible, thinking daily those ancient, pious and fixed thoughts. Thus it waited for the hero, who would come with his curved sword. When he came the Satrap Mazakos hurried towards him in a solemn manner and with a great escort. He handed over Memphis to the young stranger with the radiant eyes without any hindrance.

When Alexander sacrificed to the Apis Bull in the Temple of Ptah, the people wept and rejoiced on the streets with joy, for they believed that their saviour had come: their previous lord, Artaxerxes Ochus, had stabbed the blessed animal through with his sword instead of sacrificing to it.

'He has returned!' they shouted out on the streets. 'Our saviour has returned!'

He stepped onto the terrace, where all could see him. 'I have returned!' he cried and raised his arms.

Jaddua, the priest of the Invisible One, had recognised him, and now the people of the holy city also recognised him.

'I have returned!' he called out over the people, and then he proclaimed to it the happy news of his presence.

His presence, his entry into Memphis should remain in the memory as a festive event; great games were arranged, Greek artists and combatants were already on their way. 'There shall be a Greek-Egyptian contest,' he had it proclaimed. 'Enormous games to inaugurate the empire that I am founding.'

The people replied to him: 'He has returned!'

Incidentally Alexander stayed in the royal, holy cities for only a few days. It was a more remote and mysterious place which attracted him.

Concerning her relations with the very much hidden god Amun-Ré, whom the Greeks called Ammon-Zeus, Olympias had often made cursory but unforgettable hints. 'Greet the deity Amun from me!' had been one of her parting phrases, which she accompanied, as Alexander remembered with love and faint horror, with her enigmatically mocking smile and that way of looking up at you which drew you down – '*He knows everything*,' she had added.

This excursion, to which he was mysteriously and irresistibly drawn, Alexander justified to the others and to himself with reasons of political cunning.

'Our empire,' he explained to the generals on leaving, 'which grows beyond the boundaries of a Greek polis, needs more than just a national protector. That's why I am looking for the Greek-Egyptian deity.'

For Amun, who dwelt in an oasis, had also been worshipped in all periods by the Greeks. According to trustworthy reports both Perseus and Heracles had been guests at his shrine, and from the Delphic oracle the instruction had come, to obey

Amun before all other gods, to consult him, and to serve his will.

'This expedition is very much in our interest,' Alexander wrote to his mother, before he set off.

The journey through the Libyan Desert was long and exhausting. Loose sand flew into their thirsty faces, and there was no grassy place to rest on, no well from which to drink, and no palm tree under which they could have a good sleep.

The clever Egyptian boys who were guiding them, entertained the king with all kinds of pious fairy tales and anecdotes, which he knew in part from Olympias. He heard again, how Osiris had been taken in by his deformed brother; the knowledgeable youngsters recited to him the whole of Isis' extensive song of lament; finally they described in a very vivid way her bliss when she had him back again.

They also knew stories which were funny; for example, how the exceedingly eloquent Isis outwitted the sun god Ré, who had become old. They told of all kinds of holy animals, their influence and their power; and then, with a reverence filled with horror, of the realm of the dead, of its strange but strict customs and practices; and also of the aids, amulets and magic spells, with which one could protect oneself against evils.

Alexander inquired, investigated and asked; he had an insatiable curiosity. What was that about the sky over their heads? It could be regarded as an enormous venerable cow, on which the divine beings had set up home, but on the other hand it was a giant woman, which gave birth daily with joy and pain to the sun, moon and stars.

Everything merged together, and much was mysteriously confused. The great gods also could often not be distinguished from each other.

When evening came the clever youths talked in a melancholy way of the times when the pharaohs had still ruled over the land along the Nile in god-given splendour, and worshipped the High Being in the holy of holies. How long, said the well-informed boys sorrowfully, how very long ago those times were now and how much cruel power had dominated the empire of Osiris since then. Now it had become too late, and no one rebelled any more. 'Our land is old,' said the young boys in a melancholy way.

To distract them from their worries, Alexander asked again about Amun, whose shrine they were travelling to. They told of how he had come on a consecrated barge from the land of the Ethiopians to Thebes, with its hundred gates, and how long ago it was; how in Thebes his power and magnificence had grown greatly, especially, as in the course of time he had undergone a certain rejuvenation through marriage with Ré; how he had set off from Thebes to the hot desert, to rest at the oasis, and to reveal himself in a mysterious form to the seeking stranger, if he was worthy of it.

What could the boy guides, even if they were so clever and melancholy, say about the actual nature of the god with many names? It was unfathomable. They thought that he was also related to the god of procreation, Min of Coptos. It turned out however, that they thought he was related to everything and everyone, and above all to Osiris. His spouse was Mut, good and most highly versed in magic, who lived in the pond shaped like the crescent moon. The son of them both was none other than the Moon God.

With so many pious, though not always lucid conversations and inquiries they lost their direction and way. As there was no path, and only the hot hateful sand was blowing, they believed themselves to be almost lost. But the Mysterious One sent them great white birds, which came fluttering in front of them, croaking, and showing them the way. Thus they no longer feared going around in a circle. Good water also fell from the sky, which remained blue and cloudless; they received it with thankfully opened mouths, for they had been near to dying of thirst.

On the same day they reached the oasis, where olive trees and date palms thrived in peacefulness. The shrine lay in a beautiful peaceful spot, and nearby there flowed springs, which were full of health-giving salt. To the brick wall, which surrounded the building complex, there led the God's Path, which was wide and lit brightly by the sun, and which was set with figures of animals and sphinxes. Alexander forbad anyone to accompany him; he went alone down the road with his head lowered devoutly, and stood alone in front of the gate, which was flanked by two wide towers.

The person who opened it was a servant wearing a veil, who bowed deeply before him. In the broad forecourt surrounded by columns the high priest, the great visionary and completely initiated one, Psammon, was waiting for him.

The young king bowed over the frail hand, to kiss it. The ancient voice of experience above him, uttered through the white beard which impeded it: 'The God greets you my son.'

The rear hall, intended for more intimate functions, was painted with coloured signs and symbols and also full of figures. Alexander did not understand any of them.

Psammon, who set some fruit and drinks before him, said with the pensive look, which old relatives have, when they confirm family likenesses: 'You have the eyes of your mother, my son.'

Genuinely startled, Alexander asked: 'Did you know my mother then?' At which the old man nodded.

Alexander remained silent in astonishment. Then he enquired if he might put some questions, to which the old man made no objection. The first thing that the king wanted to know, with somewhat hypocritical interest, was whether 'all the murderers of his father were punished'.

Then what happened was that the high priest threatened him with his finger. A thousand wrinkles played on his wise face. Who would have thought that it could have become so tenderly coy. 'Now, now, my son,' he threatened with venerable coquettishness, 'you know full well, that no mortal can do any harm to *your father.* – But the murderer of Philip has been punished,' he added in a cooler tone.

At this unmistakable hint Alexander had blushed, and then he laughed, filled with delight, and a little embarrassed at it.

His next question was more open and impudent. It was: '*Will I know everything?*' – and his eyes were glowing as he spoke. 'Oh, you are inquisitive,' said the great visionary in a fatherly joking way. Alexander stretched himself sensually. He said only, 'Infinitely.'

The old man, whose sunken mouth was still smiling, inquired with a deep and scrutinising thoughtfulness in his gaze: '*Why do you want to know, my child?*' And Alexander said enthusiastically, with his arms spread, and a bright tone in his voice: 'To save people, father.' At this the initiate said, quite quietly, as though to himself:

'You're lying.'

Alexander seemed not to hear it, for his gaze shining with eagerness was still demanding an answer. Psammon hesitated, and said, jokingly again: 'Aristotle has taught you a lot.' At this the youth made a movement with his shoulder, and said like a defiant schoolboy: 'He himself did not know anything.'

The aged man looked into the distance, which seemed to be overcast. After a very reflective pause he said finally with a fleeting smile – for he now already knew what was coming: 'Let's leave that till later. Continue with your questions, my child.'

Alexander did not ask any more, he demanded, and what is more so loudly, that the temple resounded: 'Make me ruler of the world, father! Make me ruler of the world!'

An echo of his words reverberated, as though he had called into an abyss. It rang out and roared. At the same time it seemed to get darker.

Standing there, his body still stretched and trembling, he could feel the gaze of the high priest, which became filled with compassion. But when Psammon answered, he was already no longer close to Alexander, but further back, by the decorated wall, where the double bronze door in front of the most secret temple was locked. It was no longer the old man with the cheerful wrinkles any more, whose metallic voice now filled the vaulted room with an incomparable music. Alexander, who was already collapsing, heard the words: 'To you, son of a mortal, and offspring of my loins, I render the kingly honour of Ra and Horus. I give you courage and power over all countries and religions, insight into every mystery and strength to your arm, to fight all peoples. I promise you,' cried the voice, which was not that of Psammon, for it knew no compassion, 'all the suffering and the magnificence of the world.'

Did the bronze wings of the door fly open, or did the wall open? Nothing could be seen because of the brightness however. A light burst in which robbed the man lying down of his senses. It scorched his brow and his eyes. It made him happy and tortured him, until he sank down.

Thus he was consecrated for his magnificence and suffering.

Alexander left Egypt after he had founded near the sea, seven stades[12] distant from the island which Homer calls the Seal Island, a city which he named Alexandria.

5

He had come back changed from the Libyan trip. The older men complained, above all Parmenion, that he was more unapproachable and haughtier than ever, and the way he talked about his father, the great King Philip, they called unpardonable. The younger ones were of the opinion that these days a radiance emanated from him, as it had not even done that time in Troy. 'The god has blessed him with all his favour,' they told each other, subdued out of reverence for him. 'So he is truly his son.'

Before the battle of Gaugamela on the River Bumodos he slept better and more thoroughly than he had done since his childhood. As he was woken up he had the soft and ready face of a boy who has slept thoroughly and who is determined on the greatest adventure, for he knows he is accompanied by his angel. He sent a message to his mother: 'I feel that you are thinking of me at this moment, Olympias. I'm fighting the great battle!'

As lithe as ever, he stepped in front of his troops. The address which he shouted out to them was inspiring. 'This battle,' he proclaimed, his arm clanking as he raised it, 'is the last one in our struggle for and attempt to win Asia. It is no longer a matter of possessing Syria or Egypt, it's about ruling the boundless Orient!'

He was so beautiful, that they whispered to each other: that no mortal had fathered this youth, and the rumour must be true, that their king was the son of Zeus-Helios.

The belted upper garment, which he wore, was a piece of Sicilian work, and on top of it was the linen double armour, plundered at Issus. The iron helmet gleamed like the purest silver, as did the iron collar, set with precious stones. The short sword, hard, lightweight and dangerous was a present from the King of Cyprus. Everything about him sparkled. His troops gave thanks for his beauty, by rejoicing, as they were to die for him.

On the other side Darius had mobilised the last of his forces; it was known that from the remote satrapies of his empire more than one million men had gathered, forty thousand horses, and several hundred chariots, which, with their glinting scythes, were horribly effective. Companies of Bactrians, Sogdians, Turkestanis, Medians, Cedrosians and Persians, together with their lords, had arrived.

What was opposing Alexander's troops was no longer a hired army but a people's army; admittedly the man who was leading it seemed tired, even before the fight began. While the Macedonian king was receiving the cheers of his soldiers, whom he called his friends, Darius rode along the endless line, accompanied by the royal personages. They did not dare to cheer, for they were dazzled by his magnificent robe. Silent and submissive to their fate, they filled the flat landscape as far as the horizon, as though they had no other purpose.

The Great King spoke words which were intended to be encouraging; but only very few knew his language and they hardly understood him. They stuck out their foreign faces, submissive to their fate and stupid like cattle going to the slaughter: long rows of yellow faces, long rows of blackish, coffee-brown faces of animals to the slaughter with strong cheekbones, slant-eyed, and shaggy little beards; others with thick lips and a look which gleamed with a sad quality.

Darius lost the courage to speak any further; he turned and looked at his generals in search of help. Bessus, Satrap of Bactria, an evil little fellow with penetrating eyes, started to speak on his behalf: he bellowed out words expressive of bravery over the sea of people, which remained unmoved. Darius looked on sadly; when his officer hurled out statements which were especially expressive of certain victory, he nodded melancholy confirmation with his heavy head.

The Macedonians attacked as though possessed; they were in a state of raving and ecstasy. They never loved their Alexander so ardently. They had no other wish in this world, but to die near him. With the triumphant cry of 'Alala!' and bristling with spears, they overran the Persian centre, and then the left flank; on the right one Parmenion, who was sluggish and apathetic, would have spoilt almost everything. In the decisive moment, when Alexander with his elite was already after the Great King himself, who was fleeing aimlessly, there came breathless envoys from the dozy old general: saying that Parmenion needed help, or all was lost! Alexander replied abruptly and nervously, was the old man mad, believing that the centre could do without some forces in the middle of the battle?

Nevertheless he sent them, and in the meantime the Great King was miles away.

The city of Babylon, navel of the Orient, ruler of the Aramaic lowlands, and winter residence of the Great King, was handed over, after the unprecedented victory of Gaugamela, by the satrap Mazaeus to the Macedonian king without a single sword blow. Both the oldest and the richest citizens of the city waited for him in front of the wall with wreaths of flowers; among them were, on their little coloured asses, the Chaldeans from Borsippa, who know the future.

They went in through the Ishtar Gate, and along the processional route decorated with images of animals to the palace, which awaited them solemnly with its black statues. Around them there was nothing but flowers and the irresponsible howls of pleasure from the crowd, which greeted the new lord. The women stretched up on the tips of their toes and waved amorously: they saw that many of those soldiers were very handsome, almost all of them very young, and especially hand-some above all was the youth at the head of them, with the wide, radiant eyes, who did not laugh, when flowers fell onto his face, but just looked around in a marvellous way. Next to him the softer, darker one, with the friendly look, appeared equally desirable to many; he must be the favourite of the young king, for he kept so close to his side.

The Babylonian men with their prettily frizzled beards swung, to their heart's content, their tall coloured felt hats and their long, smooth walking sticks, the handles of which were decorated with lily buds and finely carved birds' heads. They were as pleased as children, because a new adventure was happening to them: a new lord, and, as he was young, he could not be bad.

Two hundred years ago Cyrus had conquered their city; how many princes she had obeyed before then!

During the first days after their entrance Alexander stayed only in the castle or in the gardens belonging to it, the white terraces of which, completely overloaded with flowers, ran down to the Euphrates. He sat as though magically fixed in the palace, to which all roads of this land ran, and which was the magnetic centre of a giant and complicated system of post-stations, relay runners and express carriages. He dictated orders and received legations. A gesture which aroused the delight of the populace but astonishment and even horror among those closest to him was that he allowed the satrap Mazaeus to retain his position: 'I have not come to hurt or destroy,' he explained. He added domineeringly: 'I have come, to set people free and make them happy.' As he said this he hurried to and fro with his head lowered.

He asked the greatest architects of the city to come to him and commissioned them to rebuild the shrines of Babylonian deities, the temples of Anu, Enlil, Ea, of Shamash, Ishtar and Sin, which

Xerxes had had destroyed; and also the seven-levelled building of the Bel-Marduk-Temple, which was, because it was inhabited by the god of the city, the holiest of all.

He received the various priesthoods, greeted them effusively and entertained them with pomp. 'Tell our people,' he concluded the speech which he directed at them, 'that serving its gods should be freely and splendidly revived, as in the times of Nebuchadnezzar.'

He wanted to be loved, and nothing was more important to him.

While they were shouting his name and praising him in all the streets and in the squares, he still did not dare to leave the palace. He was prevented, he did not understand why, by a nervousness which often increased to a state of fear.

In the meantime his soldiers, divided up into small groups, swarmed through the streets, the system of which was at the same time straight and primitive and also complicated. Again and again new prospects opened up and other perspectives appeared greyish-red or ochre-brown; in the evening they were drawn into the golden-violet semi-darkness.

During the first days the men from the mountains of Macedonia, and from the small Greek towns just stood in front of the sights with open mouths: the cube-shaped monumental buildings of granite, porphyry, basalt, from the reflective depth of which their own faces confronted them mysteriously darkened; the Assyrian stone statues, the winged bulls with men's heads, whose eternal smiling, staring, malicious, and inscrutable, frightened and confused them more than earlier the curved sabres and the chariots with scythes at Gaugamela, Issus and Granicus.

Many things already looked a little dilapidated, such as the great wall, to which they had devoutly wandered; and also the Temple of Marduk-Bel. 'Well,' they said good-naturedly, 'it'll be

good if our king can bring some life into this sleepy operation.'
All the same, the hanging gardens of Semiramis, which they had
already heard about at home, won their approval.

Finally they had enough of sights: only then did they notice,
that a sweetish-putrid smell hung about the city in all its corners
and alleys. It poured out of the temples and stores, out of the
clothes of the women and the styled hair of the men; in many
little alleys and backyards it intensified into an offensive but
fascinating stench. – The soldiers began to nudge each other in
the ribs and laugh in embarrassment, for suddenly they noticed
that women stood leaning against all the gateways and walls.

There was no question about it, you did not find them made-
up so splendidly in Athens, or in Pella. These ones wore broad
glittering necklaces, which jangled lightly and encouragingly
between their breasts, and coloured jewellery on their knuckles,
wrists and fat upper arms. In their broad, still thickly made-up
faces they had beautiful calm and enticing eyes, with rings
painted round them, and large dark-coloured mouths, from
which a pleasant scent came.

The soldiers, who had followed such heavily limbed ladies to
their remote little abodes, came back exhausted but blissful.
Such exceptional and fantastic delights they had never experienced anywhere. Even just hinting at them drove their friends
crazy.

In addition to this was the fact that in this country the most
pleasing girls seemed to be also the most pious; they called
themselves maid-servants of Ishtar and of Mylitta. In the most
complicated games and movements of their lust, thought out
with the profoundest cunning, they remained serious, even
solemn, as in the temple. 'They don't close their eyes,' reported
the lads, on returning from their embraces. 'They look at you
the whole time while doing it, so sleepily and holy, you become
quite dazed.'

When Alexander rode out for the first time, it was a holiday in the whole city. The men wore their most grandiose clothes, narrow, fringed, as white as blossom or as colourful as parrots; and in addition coloured hats below which their blue-black hair hung down carefully coiffured on the napes of their necks; the women had put on their most dazzling jewellery, and swung to and fro, full of promise, with their broad earrings, and huge necklaces. You almost could not see where the river was any more, so overcrowded was the water with decorated barques; and in between little boats drove around, many of them only hollowed-out tree-trunks, decked out with hides.

On his decorated steed Alexander, interested but suspicious, sniffed the enticingly insipid smell, which came from the opened dwellings, from the gutters and from the bodies of the women. He followed it, already almost seduced by it, into the narrowest alleys, where it became penetrating and took your breath away.

'It is a mixture of Arabian spices and decay,' the man riding next to him observed knowledgeably and dreamily. It was none other than Arrhidaeus, his very absent-minded half-brother, who had arrived with messages from Olympias and Antipatros in Pella, to congratulate Alexander on the great occasion.

It seemed somewhat strange that he appeared to know his way about in this rotten maze of alleys, as though he felt at home there. 'Here it smells strongest!' he promised in an indecent way and enticed the procession into more and more remote corners, which lay in a dirty haze.

The goods that were offered for sale here, looked mouldy, already in the process of decomposition, especially the confectionery; also the lustre of the spread-out silk fabrics had something suspicious about them.

Most disconcerting for Alexander was the appearance of the children. Eight- or twelve-year-old girls should not look like that; they already had the veiled eyes, both lecherous and pious, of their obliging mothers, and their broad dark-coloured mouths and sluggishly provocative attitude. Unfortunately many of the boys were also made-up, and Alexander hastily decided to forbid that kind of thing. While this was happening Arrhidaeus at his side said, with a dreamily tender look at the children: 'The dear little mice.' At which he salivated like an old man and laughed.

It went so far that the two brothers lost sight of their escort and would have almost got lost. A humble and beautiful little girl, whose trust Arrhidaeus seemed to have won, showed them finally the way back.

After this first time Alexander rode out daily; seldom with a large escort, often only with the dreamy Arrhidaeus, and often also, so it was told, disguised, alone, just to get to know about everything really thoroughly.

He tried out the materials and implements in the vaulted market halls, tasted the strongly spiced and the sweet foods in the eating places, and sniffed at the bottles full of oily sweet-smelling scents at the ointment dealers and hairdressers.

He visited the maidservants of Ishtar and had them show him their tricks and arts; but also the men, who occupied themselves with the courses of the stars, sitting with their mysterious diagrams and tables, and who predicted many things about his future.

Most often and most thoroughly he paid visits to certain ancient scholars of the scriptures, who lived in huts outside the city and who were well-informed about many things if not about everything.

Their clay-coloured, crumbling and narrow houses were filled by the gleam of the young king's armour, and the robe thrown splendidly around him. They were not humble towards him however; rather they were strict. For they knew that he was only young and had only been a man of action.

He had them recite to him the chronicle and history of Babylon again and again, explain and embellish them; the story of its ups and downs, its times of suffering, the epochs of its triumphs, and above all the history of its gods.

He listened engrossed, like a child listening to Homer, whenever he learned about how the long-dead people, the Sumerians, had come from the furthest east, invented the cuneiform script and founded in this country a civilised lifestyle; and how after them the Accadians had created their empire at the time when in Uruk, the Sky God was worshipped, in Ur the Moon, in Nippur Enlil, the Lord of the All Lands, in Erida the Water God Ea, but in Adab the Mother of the Gods, who has a great variety of names. Splendour was followed by decline, and this in its turn by another rise, and then new chieftains (who knows where they came from!) finally founded the empire the capital city of which was called Bâbili.

The old men in the clay-yellow huts recited the times of rise and fall, of foreign rule and being set free; from Hammurapi, who had given them wise laws, to Cyrus, the Achaemenid.

'And now you are here.' Thus they concluded their report with serious courtesy.

It seemed to be impossible to satisfy the enormous desire for knowledge of this young king. If you had told him things all night long, then in the morning he wanted to hear still more.

The whole great song of creation they had to sing and recite for him; and then the heroic battle of Marduk against Tiâmat, the Original Mother of All Things who had become malicious, and Kingu, her husband who made such an awful blaze; finally the creation of human beings from the blood of the sacrificed Kingu, during which he had the chance again to remember very similar stories, into which Olympias had initiated him. 'You are to destroy a god,' his mother had said.

Then there was the story of Afapas, who did not take the water of life as a false precaution; and the extremely horrific and unforgettable story of Ishtar, who travelled to the underworld, where the mighty Queen Ereshkigal tortured her with sixty illnesses and held her fast until Tammuz freed her.

Alexander's curiosity made him want to trace the history of the gods back to the time when Marduk was still called Tammuk, the true Son of the Abyss; for he knew, concerning Tammuz, that the mystery of his death and his resurrection must be related to that of Adonis; and further, to the still more mysterious point, where Tammuz and Osiris were still one person, as were Isis and Ishtar.

But the wise men were reluctant to let him go back so far: 'The nature of the gods is obscure,' they concluded without relenting.

The young Macedonian generals could be seen standing around in annoyed groups. They complained about their king, who was not doing things to their taste.

Philotas, the imposing and conceited son of Parmenion, asked spitefully, 'Can't you see it? His eyes are like those of someone intoxicated. He gives himself up to these Arabian fairy tales and stories of devils like a vice. While he is becoming a depraved Oriental, my father has to work for him, occupying Susa, and fighting the thieving Uxian people.'

Outraged Craterus, Perdiccas, Coenus and Nearchus nodded amongst themselves. They all felt insulted, because Alexander surrounded himself more and more with Egyptian and Persian leaders but clearly neglected them. Out of hurt vanity they played the role of the morally outraged. 'The Orient has cast a spell over him and is unmanning him,' they said sternly.

After a stay of many weeks came the long yearned for order to leave Babylon. Admittedly the great departure was put off once again for a few days, for which an embarrassing and rather ridiculous incident was responsible: Arrhidaeus had got lost. As might have been expected, the disadvantaged man, who spent his youth sitting babbling in a hole of a cellar, had got the idea of trying to go out for a walk on his own, probably in those little alleys, the smell of which he loved so much.

He did not come back, and searching did not help. Had he hidden himself or had he been murdered? The maze of little alleys had swallowed him up, and they would have to give him up, hush the matter up, as far as possible, and leave without him.

The march went out of the lowlands up into the highlands of Iran, where the old royal cities of Persepolis and Pasargadai were to be taken.

Up here the air blew more purely than in Babylon, where the smells and depravities of so many civilisations were mixed up together. They were in the real home of the Persian monarchy; the palace with the forty columns, which rose up in enormous terraces, and belonged to Xerxes, who died at the Acropolis in Athens. In front of the portal there lay the colossal statues in the Assyrian style, malicious-looking chimera at rest, of a man and a steed or a bull.

With a feeling of triumph, which was mixed with awe, Alexander entered, passing the threatening statues.

Inside the throne was awaiting them. It had been that of Xerxes. Animal figures rested on the side, and the rich baldachin was decorated with symbols. Alexander received the representatives of the city sitting on the throne.

Finally he also received his own friends; they wanted to smile, when they saw him in the midst of all the strange splendour, but he remained unapproachable. This made them mock him somewhat. They greeted him bowing deeply, but there was irony in their bow. Only Hephaestion kissed his hand with chivalrous seriousness. 'You are the King of Asia,' he said, as though confirming it, and at the same time with a secret undertone of compassion.

Alexander, above him, repeated with a remarkably inhuman voice, which made a metallic sound high up in the wide room:

'*I am the King of Asia.*'

He was especially majestic and strict with old Parmenion, who had requested an important discussion. The general approached respectfully but self-confidently. He had served King Philip faithfully for decades, he asserted with an oversensitive look from below that had turned somewhat bloody; his lean, wrinkled cheeks and sideburns trembled. The old man said he thought he might be allowed the right to warn the young king.

The look, with which Alexander assessed him from beneath his high-arched brows, was more threatening than questioning: 'I have often *not* followed your warnings; never to my disadvantage,' he said in a cutting tone. The general did not let himself be confused by this in any way. Rather he even became emotional. 'We have reached our goal!' he cried imploringly, and added 'Philip would never have gone further.' 'Not even as far as here,' said the man on the throne grimly.

To go on further from here, the general explained with pedagogic sternness, would be a crime against the nation. Now it could only be a question of organising the conquered territories in a new way. 'Our goal is realised,' cried the grey-bearded man in a begging tone. 'The Hellenic disgrace of the past has been amply revenged. If we now go further, we'll lose our connection with the homeland. We must make the new territories into Greek colonies!'

The inhuman voice from the throne replied: 'I don't want colonies. I want a world empire.'

Parmenion warned: 'Then the world empire will devour Greece. It will be more than we can cope with. Stop, Alexander!' He raised his arms defensively, as though floods of water were already pressing on him.

At this Alexander said, with an iciness, which made the blood in the veins of the old soldier congeal:

'*What concern is Greece to me?*'

'Then of course…' In his horror Parmenion could not even find the strength to be indignant.

He stared at the earth, and wasn't he even weeping? He was hurt bitterly. And meanwhile where did his young king let his gaze wander?

'We're going to the east,' he said calmly and peacefully; while the old man was weeping, the gaze of the young man lost itself in infinite distance.

In that night a conflagration broke out in the king's palace in Persepolis, which reduced large parts of the castle as well as the adjoining buildings to ashes; nobody knew how it had originated. The rumour arose that the king himself had had the fire started, but nobody dared to say this aloud. What could his purpose have been in doing it? That would have been almost the act of a madman. His triumph was clear enough, and he did not need to underline it in this way, which made enemies and destroyed without bringing any advantage.

It struck people as alarming, that Alexander had been seen, as long as the blaze lasted, walking in the courtyards of the palace, staring into the blaze with a weird avid gaze. Whenever a column crashed down, he listened to the noise with his eyes closed, as though it were a kind of music, which soothed his heart.

Thus Clitus found him. They both stood alone opposite each other, for the first time again since how long? Hadn't it been at Granicus?

On the face of Clitus were playing the reflections of the fire. They danced across his brow, down his cheeks, ignited sparks in his eyes and toyed around his mouth. His face was blessed and flattered by the light, but the king's face was in the dark.

'But it was *I* who lit this fire,' felt Alexander in painful spite.

The Test

I

Darius fled. It seemed to him that the danger became less, the further eastward he came. So he left Ekbatana and sent his caravans, harem, the rest of his gems ahead of him to Ragai, to the entrance to the Caspian passes. He followed, and with him were the rest of the chiliarchs led by Narbazanes. Close behind him was Alexander, who was not a monarch any more for him, but fate.

His wife had died in childbirth, but the vigorously inexorable Sisygambis was still alive, and also his two brown-haired daughters. He had to keep himself alive for their sakes, for them above all; and after them for the empire, the capital of which had been taken from him provisionally by fate in the form of a catastrophic young man, but which was only waiting to be set free by him, Darius Codomannus, the Achaemenid and hereditary ruler.

His weak and damaged soul escaped into piety. In the long meditations he consulted the deity, to find out why it had arranged everything in such an incomprehensible way. There was no question about it, it was a case of the primal conflict between Good and Evil, which was taught by Zarathustra Spitama. This rabble-rouser from Macedonia was the brilliant envoy of the impure power, and it had never revealed itself in such a fateful and blinding way. Who else could be competent to fight against it, if not the grandson of the great Cyrus, to whom the crown belonged. 'One day the dispute will end – and evil will pass away,' proclaimed Zarathustra.

Admittedly there were also the bad times of conflict. The prophet himself asked us to consider 'Whether there was not a possibility at all that the Good could have an effect, or whether

99

only cleverness counted in this world?' But behind the doubts came the confidence, and he had never been so confident, not even in Babylon on his decorated throne. For the prophet had left us these words:

'But what is conquest, what defeat! The die is already cast. Only he who is within you lives.'

For him the die was already cast, but it was necessary to threaten the adversary: 'But woe to you, if you were faithless!'

His immediate circle, who had known him to be modestly idyllic and often disheartened, were astonished to see him erect in the hour of most extreme danger. Now they understood for the first time, that despite his head being too large and his dreamy eyes, he was a nobleman, and almost a hero.

He summoned his leaders to disclose to them that he wanted to try once more to do battle with Alexander. 'The gods are with me,' he said profoundly and proudly. He had to endure being contradicted. At first they hesitated, and then they admitted openly: to risk their lives for something which was at that moment hopeless, seemed pointless. They should move further to the east, to Bactria, Sogdiana, and gather new masses of people.

The Great King revealed himself to be more disappointed than angry. He became quiet and thoughtful: So, didn't God want the decisive battle yet? He only became angry, when Narbazanes came out with his impudent suggestion.

This hardened old courtier behaved, as though there was nothing unusual about that which, with a calm expression, he put forward for consideration. Whether it would not be generally more beneficial to the interest of the great cause, he put forward cautiously for consideration, if Darius were to abdicate, to renounce the tiara, in order to hand it over perhaps to the satrap Bessus? The latter enjoyed great respect in all the eastern lands, Narbazanes explained with tenacious politeness, as the Great King was seen to turn pale; the Scythians and the Indians were his allies. In addition he was considered to be related to the royal house.

He did not get any further, for Darius was already reaching for his dagger. With a wry smile Narbazanes drew back; he was followed by Bessus, a small, muscular fellow and typical Mongolian, with a hanging black moustache in his yellow, strongly boned face.

The mood in which they continued their journey, was dull and at the same time agitated. Bessus and his group kept themselves apart in wily silence. The heroic courage and power of the Great King appeared, after such a short boost, to have thoroughly disappeared, and he rested almost apathetically in his carriage. When, in the village of Thara, three men in disguise, who were Bessus, Narbazanes and Baisaentes, broke into his tent, he was scarcely startled. He hardly defended himself, when he was tied up.

The very same night Bessus had himself declared supreme commander of the army and monarchic deputy. Darius Codomannus, who contented himself with shaking his head sadly, was taken on with them as a prisoner.

Alexander received news of these events immediately, and he decided, that he still had to have the deposed and captured Codomannus, and he set out after the treacherous caravan in a forced march. The hunt lasted four days and four nights, horses were ridden to death, soldiers were left exhausted on the road, and finally Alexander was alone with a few officers.

In a wilderness they found the royal carriage. It had been deserted by all the troops and scouts, and even the horses had been unharnessed. Darius Codomannus leaned against the cushions with his head, which was finally just tired, sunk forward. From the imaginatively complicated embroidery on the breast of his fine robe there seeped blood, in several places. He could not have been dead long, as his hand, which Alexander took hold of cautiously, was not yet cold.

Alexander also touched his forehead, his nose and the lightly bloated mouth. In order to identify it more clearly in the semi-darkness of the carriage he felt the large dead face, which he had never seen alive; he examined it thoroughly, with gloomy curiosity.

'So that was my enemy,' he said finally, with melancholy as well as in contempt. He beckoned to one of the officers to spread the cloth over the corpse. 'What is the new man called?' he suddenly asked absent-mindedly, as though it concerned a trivial matter. 'Bessus – Bessus – ' He repeated the name, as though he were trying out its taste on his tongue. Then he turned, and quickly left the carriage.

The murderers of the king were miles away; Bessus on the way to Bactria, and Narbazanes to Hyrcania.

The body of Darius Codomannus was transferred on Alexander's orders to Persepolis. The funeral of the last Achaemenid was attended by the Queen Mother Sisygambis.

The satrap of Hyrcania was to be taken, because of the importance of its coasts which had many harbours. Its capital surrendered. They should not rest there for long. The next goal was Bactria, the residence of the Bactrian satrapy.

They had not yet known such wild areas, and the army often grumbled; for they went through dreadful forests, where they had to make a way for themselves with axes. The campaign had been fun even if it was often bloody. In these lands it revealed its hard and sobering face. There was not even fame to be won, only the awful little raids to be warded off, with which the wily inhabitants tormented the army. In Susia, the first city, which they came upon in the satrapy of Areia, the regent of the country, Satibarzanes, came to meet them, to offer his submission. He appeared to be polite and gentle, though admittedly he had malicious eyes.

He kissed the ground in front of Alexander frequently, and added flattering remarks in elegant Persian. The king found him quite unsympathetic, and it disturbed him also, that he smelt so strongly of inferior perfumes; on the other hand his submissive manner pleased him.

The news that he brought was sensational and shocking: Bessus had had himself proclaimed Great King, and wore the tiara, which he had stolen from the poor Darius, and he called himself in his terrible audacity Artaxerxes, Lord of Asia. Satibarzanes, skilled in matters of propriety, related this story with suitable indignation, though at the same time a small malicious grin was unfortunately noticeable around his agile mouth.

For Alexander there was only one thing to do: inexorable pursuit of Bessus, who laid claim to be that which he, the Macedonian, since the conquest of Babylon and Persepolis, actually was. In great haste he gave gifts to and praised the bent figure of Satibarzanes and turned towards the east again.

Suddenly: there was insurrection at his rear. It was not for nothing that Satibarzanes had grinned so underhandedly: hardly were the Macedonian forces out of sight, than the scheming friend of Bessus was already breaking his word, which he had only given, to keep Alexander in a false sense of security. Artacoama, the capital of Areia, was the centre of the uprising. The Macedonian legation was attacked and mown down, and their leader was murdered.

Alexander saw himself cut off, and so he had to give up the pursuit of the usurper – *provisionally*, as he decided in fury. When he reached the faithless capital again, he found it in complete disarray and panic. Satibarzanes was already up and away and had fled to Bessus.

Although Alexander knew, that the rebellious troops had only been seduced, he had a bloodbath instigated among them: thirteen thousand of them were partly slaughtered, partly sold as slaves.

The Regent of the Empire, Antipater, made reports back home about the seriousness of the situation.

King Agis of Sparta had an agreement with the Persian naval power, and now he had had Crete occupied by his brother Agesilaos. He went as far as open rebellion, and the indefatigable old Demosthenes offered him his moral support, still stirring things up from the speaker's rostrum and demanding the 'restoration of freedom for the states'.

The situation was dangerous; nevertheless the letters of his mother the queen were still quarrelsome, obstinate and filled with her own affairs. The policies that she pursued were perverse and often confused. With a stubbornness which no one could understand or approve of, she insisted on being the lawful mistress of the land of Molossos. In her letters she was always complaining again and again about Cleopatra, her anaemic daughter, whom she had never liked, but now hated; for she made claims on the same area.

The poor young girl had become a widow, and, there was no question about it, her son belonged on the throne of Molossos, but as he was underage, she herself belonged there, however anaemic she might be. Only the gods knew from where Olympias derived her rights. In any case her obsession with this throne, which was not fitting for her, seemed crazy at a moment when the whole of Greece was threatening insurrection against Macedonia.

The judicious and sensible, always somewhat long-winded and pedantically written reports of his highest official Alexander read with concern, but the overwrought and quarrelsome ones of his mother on the other hand he read in sorrow.

The tension was finally released: Antipater's messengers proclaimed the victory of the Macedonian arms over the Spartan rebels at Megalopolis. They could heave a sigh of relief: Agis himself was dead, and the rebellion dealt with, but only after the brave resistance of the Lacedaemonians.

Alexander congratulated his regent; at the same time he wrote to his mother, more sternly than ever before:

'Your behaviour, which does not always seem to be reasonable, makes it difficult for me to bring to completion the mission which you yourself have given me. I have come far, but am still a long way from my goal. The worst lies ahead of me. It's becoming harder and harder.

'Never forget, that I am suffering for the sake of your mission. It is your dream that I am fulfilling while suffering a thousand agonies.

'Oh, Mother: I write to you with blood on my hands.'

2

From the high mountain valley of Kabul seven passes lead over the Hindu Kush to the area of the Oxus River.

When Alexander's order went out to the army, that they were to cross over the mountains, the soldiers thought that he was now really out of his mind. They knew of no example from the history of all periods and peoples, of an army having been capable of mastering such a mountain range. On top of that it was winter and they knew that Bessus, who was escaping further and further east, had plundered and laid waste the land. They grumbled, but Alexander stepped before them. He was dazzling and stretched himself up as he did before the great decisive battles.

'If nothing else does it, the crossing of these mountains will make you immortal. Nothing *can* be impossible for you, because I am your king.'

It became even more horrible than they had feared. In order not to starve, they had to slaughter the horses; the water that they took with them in skins, ran out. They ate snow and raw meat. The villages which they passed through could offer them nothing, no bread nor a bed. Many froze to death, fell down or stayed by the roadside.

On the fifteenth day they reached the first Bactrian settlement, Drapsaca, and a little later the capital. Everywhere Bessus had just set off, and escaped eastward. It seemed that he wanted to entice the Macedonians, fool them, to lead them ever further astray into the innermost part of Asia, which must be endless.

Now they were certainly at its heart, and it was said that this was the homeland of Zarathustra. So, from here the doctrine of Good and Evil had spread out over the whole of Iran.

With a gloomy and respectful gaze Alexander looked out over the majestic and barren landscape. Compared with its inexorability, how harmless was the self-indulgent sumptuousness of Asia Minor and of opulent Babylon. Here primevally fissured mountains raised their blackish craters in a boundless arid plain of scree. In the face of this cruel landscape the king realised with clenched teeth: now things were becoming serious. For just *one* step further, and it would be the final wilderness. An absolute wasteland opened up, where no lands were marked off from each other, where neither Persian nor Greek, neither Zarathustra nor Dionysus were known. There the Scythians, who eat human flesh, eked out their lives.

'*We've reached the limit,*' thought Alexander with horror as he viewed this landscape.

They had set off for Bactria; for Bessus was already in Sogdiana and with him an army of cavalry and quite a lot of leaders, among whom were the hypocritical Satibarzanes and a very dangerous man called Spitamenes, Satrap of Sogdiana.

Bessus, as tenacious and muscular as he was, appeared to be under a lot of strain. Since he had gained power, he was no longer as consistent and clever as the time when he was still treacherously striving for it. The dark-eyed Mongol had had a certain barbarian élan. Since he styled himself Artaxerxes, his only thought was taking flight.

So his friends became fed up with him, especially the wily Spitamenes. One day he sent to Alexander some messengers, who betrayed the place where Bessus was staying. Alexander thanked them and sent off his bodyguard Ptolemaeus with six thousand men. Finally they had got this most unpleasant of all his enemies.

He had to atone for it in a horrific way. The irritated and exhausted Alexander wanted to hear him whine. So he gave the order to place him, naked, and clad only in iron fetters, on the way which he rode along with his officers. The Greeks laughed, because the feared regicide was small and malformed. On his yellow, muscular dwarf's body his hair grew in irregular black tufts. On the scarred chest especially it thrived in the form of ugly little pointed beards.

Alexander, looking down haughtily from his horse, asked him why, as satrap and a favourite, he had murdered his Great King and stolen the tiara from him. The slant-eyed fellow said, with a last wretched attempt at diplomacy, bowing naked: 'To please you, my king.'

Then he was whipped more than ever.

He was transported already half-dead to Ecbatana, where on the occasion of some festival or other he was to be executed.

The border, behind which the Scythian wilderness began, was protected by seven border forts, the most important of which were Cyrus and Gaza. Alexander left some Macedonian garrisons in them, and he himself camped a little further on by the River Tanais, which was called Iaxartes, the great river.

The king was not by nature inclined to mistrust people, in spite of everything which he had experienced. His self-confidence was too strong for that. He took the word of honour of this Spitamenes just as seriously as he had taken that of Satibarzanes. Oddly enough he did not think of saying to himself that this man, who had betrayed Bessus, his ally, would remain loyal even much less to a stranger.

On the contrary he was surprised, when there was a rebellion again behind him. He was speechless, for now he felt, that he was seriously and bitterly hated, but he was used to love. The situation was as bad as it had been years ago, when the youth succeeded to Philip and had to fight at the four points of the compass. It was worse, for at that time there was little which he had to lose; now however it seemed that his enormous daring was being revenged. A power was trying to engulf him, which he thought had been dealt with after the royal cities had been captured: Asia.

He hurried back and forth in his tent with lowered brow and a dark look in his eyes, and dictated orders. This behaviour, and that embittered play of muscles around his mouth, was well-known. He looked that way, whenever he was venturing his great operations, whenever he felt that everything was at stake.

Behind him was the Sogdian rebellion; in front of him the Scythians who were also becoming rebellious. In the border towns they had killed his garrisons. From beyond the borders, from the Steppes, new hordes broke through, who murdered and robbed.

In his tent Alexander dictated:

No man in Gaza and Cyropolis should remain alive; every house was to be set on fire.

His orders were carried out with inexorable exactness. The Macedonian army passed through the country meting out punishment everywhere, and after four days they were outside Samarkand. What they left behind them were burning cities and the howls of rage of the barbarians. If I am to be hated, thought the king in resolute defiance, then let it be completely.

He was used to getting to know every condition to the utmost limit of its possibility. Wherever he had been, there had been cheering, flowers and rejoicing; now he was greeted by horror and despair. He had brought peace and liberation to Asia Minor, and he had been their darling and saviour; in Sogdiana he left behind him oppression and misery.

Spitamenes had already fled, this time to the hordes of the Massagetae. After Samarkand had been chastised, the army, which seemed to this country to be nothing else but an affliction, withdrew to Zariaspa, situated in Bactria, for their winter rest.

Their lifestyle had become at the same time more luxurious and more joyless. The enthusiastic comradeship, which had bound them together at Granicus had long disappeared. Between the king and those who had been his friends, there now stood the Persian dignitaries, who honoured the monarch as divine, by kissing the floor in front of him. Alexander was becoming more and more intimate with them.

Also amongst the Macedonian generals there was tension and distrust, and each one had his group. Philotas, the brown-haired, self-satisfied son of Parmenion, showed off most prominently. Perdiccas and Craterus believed that militarily they had the greatest merit. And Hephaestion was still considered to be the favourite and confidant of the king. To one side was Clitus, and no one knew where they stood with him.

Among them were the men of letters, conducting their intrigues: those like the boastful Callisthenes, who were always talking of Hellenic freedom and criticised every attitude of the king, and the others, who licked his boots in glorification of him. The traders did their little bits of profiteering, as did the whores, who travelled with them for what they could get.

Since they had got to know oriental comfort, they lived at their ease and even luxuriously. Everybody had his crazy habit: one wore gold nails on his shoes, the other had the sand he used for his physical exercise sent on after him on camels. There was great expenditure on ointments and refined essences, and also on unusual and spicy foods. They got used to Persian costume more and more, and many attached importance like dandies to their long costumes with narrow waists. Finally Clitus was the last one to be wearing the short white-leather battle tunic.

Thus the winter passed quarrelsomely and pleasurably. A special role in the life of the camp began to be played by a creature who was as dubious as he was charming and called Bagoas, who had been sent to Alexander from Babylon as his personal page boy. In intimate conversations it was rumoured that the finely made-up being, who was a skilful dancer, and who wore his silky black hair done up around his artistically made-up face, was a hermaphrodite like his demonic namesake, who had formerly been an evil spirit at the Persian court. Alexander certainly knew why he was attracted to him.

The winter resting period did not last very long, for the fiendish Spitamenes made his presence felt again. He broke into Sogdiana with his Massagetae; as they attempted to oppose him, he withdrew in disgrace to the east.

Alexander and his soldiers had never hated anyone so much; it was as though the knocked-off head of Bessus had grown back again but was much uglier. He was the dreadful ghost of the steppes, Inner Asia's irritating goblin. He made fools of them, till they went out of their minds. Hardly had he appeared and you had grasped at him, than you had nothing in your hand but emptiness, and he escaped out into the wasteland, from where there came horrible laughter.

He carried on his impudent game for months. It was a period of torture for his opponents. He was unbeatable, and his skill seemed to be supernatural. He was the force of evil in person.

The generals were in despair ten times over, but for Alexander there was no giving up. If the other was more mobile, then they would be more tenacious. Finally it was the Massagetae who had had enough of it. They feared that one day they would be beaten by Alexander, but that it would be in a terrible way. They fell upon Spitamenes, cut his head off and sent it to the Macedonian king.

He stuck it on the point of his sword and went in front of his army with it. He held out the victory trophy, with blackish drops of blood falling onto his shoes.

Thus he stood in front of the silent rows, a herald stained with blood and with his head awkwardly bowed. 'We've got him!' he shouted out over them; not radiant with the joy of victory however, but, satisfied as he was, tired out and gloomy.

3

The grimmer, more violent and unpredictable the king was, the clearer it was becoming, that more and more Clitus was becoming the favourite of the army.

The young general, who kept himself as far as possible from all public consultations, and almost never gave orders, had always had a small band of supporters. This was becoming larger. As all the other officers and dignitaries were becoming crueller and more bad-tempered, his gentle and dreamy cheerfulness was felt gratefully as a relief.

He seemed to stand above the situations they were in. That is why he was admired. His pieces of advice, which he used to give casually and as though in jest, always hit the nail on the head with amazing precision. And so gradually they took them more seriously than those of anybody else.

However his talent for political strategy did not seem to interest him in the least. He despised reality, still now as he had done as a child. Today as then the men of action were the object of his swift and mocking remarks. He made fun of the real world, in which he could have actually achieved everything. He took no victory seriously, and no defeat could have grieved him.

For his spirit played in regions, where the air is thinner, and in which mortals cannot thrive. Where he was at home, all the problems, tragedy and grave matters of this world of ours seemed to have resolved themselves into amusing and complicated figures, which shifted together like the geometry of dances.

His enemies said that he was childish, and he could not take anything seriously. They were wrong: for it was not that he could not have endured the real world. For him it was not worth the effort, because it was so coarse. He allowed another to be great in it, whom he himself had, out of curiosity, addiction to gambling and secret affection, helped to attain this greatness.

For more than the struggles of Asia it was the adventures and decisions about those points conjured up in the air by his imagination, which gripped him. He was too pure to take part in material conflicts. As he kept his body remote from all contacts, so also his mind, which was bored by everything related to physical weight and the body.

As he was completely pure, he was also completely cruel. Pity was as foreign to his heart as ambition.

In the course of the years he had not come one single step closer to Alexander, on whose colossal fate he was the only one, together with Olympias, to have influence.

By contrast a subtle alliance of a kind which it was difficult to interpret seemed to be developing between him and Hephaestion. After so many long years of a steadfastly intimate, self-denying and hopeless wooing of Alexander, who was more and more unapproachable and incomprehensible in the midst of his solitude, something in Hephaestion began to yield; a readiness, which had already been tested for too long, and a loyalty which felt as though it was becoming pointless, because the one whom it applied to, did not recognise it, overlooked it, did not notice its presence.

Clitus never spoke about Alexander with Hephaestion; his highly sensitive feelings avoided touching on this theme. He would just tell fairy tales when they were strolling together. So much more gratefully did Hephaestion attach himself to him, and found with joy and astonishment, that the unapproachable Clitus had adopted more human and softer tones towards him, and only towards him. 'It's pity,' he said to himself; but it still made him proud.

In the evenings Clitus gathered some friends around him at a well or by a column, and among them Hephaestion was always to be found. Clitus crouched down and invented stories, sometimes laughing softly as he did so and making pointless little movements with his hand. His face was as childlike as ever, and on his white cheeks there was a mischievousness, and on his bright forehead a cheerful but stern seriousness. Whenever he interrupted himself while speaking, it was to gaze around the circle with a shimmering grey and enticing look.

'No one jumps quicker than my little dragon pig,' he continued with his invented fairy tale, which had been dreamed up in the complicated way of children. 'If you leave it in peace, it is really quite cute. But if you irritate it, oh, ho…'

Under the enchantment of his puzzling, bright and gentle words, everyone breathed in a more subdued way.

Meanwhile Alexander was bawling out loud with his mates at a messy dining table.

After a great banquet, that the king had given for his officers, Clitus was called upon to tell one of his enchanted stories; it was above all Hephaestion who entreated him to do it. 'We'd all like it!' he called out warmly; and then added suddenly, somewhat confused, to Alexander: 'He does tell them so nicely. He always knows those stories that nobody has heard of; and he weaves them together with other stories – ' Clitus smiled inexplicably.

At the top of the table, in his magnificent Persian robe, Alexander gave a brief wave, without looking at either of them. 'Let him tell a story. – But something nice,' he added with a threatening smile.

'You probably all know already the fairy tale about which I've been thinking so much recently,' said Clitus, without paying any attention to Alexander, and with a mocking dreaminess which was disturbing. 'But you'll like it anyway –

'Now pay attention: You are in Uruk, the great gleaming city, and your mighty prince is called Gilgamesh. He is two thirds god, but one third only human. That must be unpleasant – ' He laughed, cruelly amused at the thought of the sufferings of the demigod; it seemed to Alexander as though he were looking at him as he laughed.

'He was very ambitious, allegedly for Uruk, but in reality for himself. "Uruk's splendour shall shine in all cities," he proclaimed loudly. Actually however, he only wanted to shine himself.

'The people, whom he exploited too cruelly and made use of, so that his own fame would grow, turned, in their need and helplessness, to the God of the Skies, Anu. The latter got in touch with Aruru, who was an expert in making things. She decided to create a man, Enkidu by name, who should be as strong as the exuberant Gilgamesh, so that Uruk's king would have an opponent and his exuberance would decrease, which was becoming an annoyance to the gods and causing alarm to mankind.'

Clitus smiled and was silent. He looked at his brownish delicate but firm hands, which were restless. 'It continues in a marvellous way,' he said smiling. 'In order to paralyse Enkidu's strength and innocence – for he played, in a way which was marvellous to see, with the strong animals of the wilderness – Gilgamesh, with his enormous cunning, sent a woman to him, and indeed one of excellent experience, and dedicated to Ishtar. In a love game which lasted six times twenty-four hours, she broke his strength. Enkidu, lured, initiated and corrupted by her, followed her, having suddenly become restless and thirsty for knowledge, to Uruk, the capital city that glittered afar. Gilgamesh, who had only been waiting for this, easily beat the weakened man in a duel, but in doing so he pressed against him lovingly, as one presses against a woman.'

Clitus closed his eyes for a second, as did Alexander with him. Both listened for a second to their innermost being, perhaps also to that of the other. For they knew that now came the story of a great friendship, which could have been their own, but which had not been granted to them. – With a look in his re-opened eyes that was all the brighter, the teller of the fairy tale continued.

'The friendship between the two of them grew enormously. Gilgamesh raised the youth, whom he had wanted to kill, to the prime position in his empire. Enkidu tolerated it, like a magnificent animal which is feted and groomed. They loved each other with all the force of their divine souls.'

Clitus laughed, looking round the circle with his shimmering grey eyes, and finally stopping at Alexander: 'I find that charming, how the old goddess Aruru had miscalculated. She wanted to create an abominable opponent for Gilgamesh and created for him something which provided his life with meaning and delight.'

Hephaestion also laughed, softly and feeling moved. Clitus continued with his story.

'Unfortunately Enkidu sometimes had nasty dreams; he probably could not get used to city life, which was sumptuous. So that things might get better, they made offerings to the sun god Shamash, by filling a bowl made of reddish stone with honey and a dish of lapis lazuli with butter and left both of them for the sun to lick up. But the deity would not be fobbed off and demanded an adventure of them. It was required that they should kill the monster Chumbaba, who wreaked havoc on the mountain of the gods in the cedar forest.

'As the omens were good, the two friends set off; but the risk was horrible. Nothing could be so frightening to see as Chumbaba: his eyes were made of fire, his mouth spat poison, and his reproductive organ was a hissing flame. Using his fiery horn like a spear he caught them both up and hurled them, so that they flew a hundred metres through the air, and then tried to stamp around on them. But they were swifter. They drove their spears into his neck. With their closely combined efforts they finally succeeded in finishing him off.'

Through the circle there ran a sigh of relief combined with a feeling of satisfaction. Alexander listened leaning forward with enraptured eyes, and also breathed with relief. They had won, with their closely combined efforts! – Meanwhile Clitus was already continuing, now in a triumphant voice.

'Made more beautiful through the delights of friendship and the happiness of victory, Gilgamesh flourished so magnificently beyond measure, that Ishtar herself, who knew a thing or two, made proposals to him. She had chosen the right man.

'The hero, who loathed her crude lust, shouted the most horrible things to her face. He was bold enough, to call her a sheath which is a burden to its wearer; an elephant which shakes off its cover; a shoe that pinches its owner. He spoke his opinion to her so openly as no one had spoken to her before, and reproached her harshly for everything she had ever committed, her cases of spitefulness, curses and tricks; and finally for *all* the lovers she had ever had – and there were not a few of them – how abominably she had behaved with them and treated them.

'Ishtar shouted, stamped her foot, and flew off to the heavens contemplating revenge.'

They knew Ishtar, all of them knew, Alexander too, that she could be equally cruel and charming. So they listened with a vague excitement to hear what would come. What came was even sadder than any one could have thought.

'At first it is true Ishtar underestimated her opponent, and sent the Dragon Bull against Gilgamesh, to stamp on him and tear him to pieces. But, with Enkidu fighting at his side, he was unbeatable, and destroyed the monster. As the beast had given its death rattle, he also tore off a leg, in scorn and mockery, and threw it into Ishtar's face, at which, in an angry rage, she began to dance, sing and rejoice.

'But now she struck him in a sensitive spot,' said Clitus, and everyone knew where she struck him. 'She sent a fever to Enkidu, his beloved. The beautiful young man lay down exhausted, and, oh, in his fantasies he accused the prostitute, who had once enticed him out of the wilderness, out of his innocence and loneliness to Uruk. He wished, with his last breath, that drunkards and thirsty men would beat her on the buttocks.'

At this point Clitus had a smile, which was both mocking and sad and caused an anger to rise in Alexander, which grew darkly, and which he himself found incomprehensible at first. Both sadly and mockingly Clitus continued.

'These curses were of course especially painful for Gilgamesh, for without the prostitute that Enkidu was now cursing, they would never have come together. Enkidu died in the arms of his friend, without having recognised him again. Gilgamesh went rigid with pain.'

Clitus was also silent and just shook his head, worried. 'And such great deeds they had achieved together,' he pondered as he shook his head. 'Now the king uttered a lament: "You look grim and cannot hear my voice." He spread his cloak over him as if over his bride.'

Alexander was frightened at himself, for he had only a feeling of anger, not sorrow. His anger grew as Clitus continued his story.

'In Gilgamesh's great but impure soul there was mixed with the deep pain for his only beloved a fear for his own life, which was even deeper and fiercer. If he has died, who seemed to be life itself, how easily he, Gilgamesh, could be struck down. He was afraid therefore and his teeth chattered.

'Out of misery and helplessness he set out to visit the initiate Utnapishtim, who lived at the end of the world and could divulge to him the secret of Life. The journey to him lasted years, and at the end of it the Prince of Uruk, who was known to be covered completely with precious stones, was now wearing only rotten rags and furs.

'He went through all the cities of mankind, then through wilderness and desert, and finally through enchanted regions, past castles where dragons dwelt, through the realm of the scorpion people, which is difficult to reach, through confusing forests of precious stones, and finally to the great sea, which is the end of the world, and behind which dwells Utnapishtim. No mortal had gone further; Gilgamesh *had to* go further, for he was filled with fear and avid to experience how everything is connected to each other and how one can attain eternal life. So he managed to persuade the ferryman Shanabi, to take him over the water, which cost more anguish, efforts and privations than a man had ever taken upon himself. This man bore them because he wanted to know.

His first question to Utnapishtim, who received him with dignity albeit astonished, was: *What is Death?* The Initiated One answered with reserve: 'Death is furious; he knows no mercy. It has always been so that nothing lasts.'

Everyone saw Alexander make a movement, as though he wanted to command the storyteller to stop. Only Clitus seemed to notice nothing; on the contrary he went into ever more detail.

'Instead of going into Gilgamesh's excessive questions any further, Utnapishtim told his own story, which was miraculous, for he was the only one who had survived the great flood, with which the gods had once chastised human beings for getting too excessively and criminally out of control. As Adad broke the broad land as though it were a piece of crockery and raged so terribly, that even the gods crept away like dogs, this very, very clever being escaped with his family and some animals into the vessel, the measurements of which Ea himself had given him. How barren and solemn the silence appeared to him when he left his vessel again and saw: The whole of humanity had turned to dust. "Tears ran down my face," concluded the old man, to whom the gods had given immortality.

'Gilgamesh listened breathlessly, but his eyes begged and implored him for what was "essential". The very, very clever one felt sympathy, and so revealed to him the secret: if he were willing to descend to the bottom of the sea, then he would be able to find in the depths the plant, which was the promised, life-giving one. In his great desire Gilgamesh tied a rock to his feet and went down into the depths. Down there he found the plant which he had been looking for. It felt prickly. So he was able to make his way home. Out of gratitude he took Shanabi, the faithful ferryman, with him.

'While he was bathing himself on the way, a snake smelt the miracle-working plant, which he had hidden on the bank, but not carefully enough, for the snake stole it from him, while he was splashing around. So he had wandered in vain all those long years, and he returned without the secret, as he had set out, but just much older, and almost an old man. He reigned in Uruk, but without much pleasure. The valiant Shanabi stayed there as his minister.'

As Clitus became silent, there was also an oppressed silence in the circle. His grief had cast a spell over everyone. Only Alexander reacted against it. He laughed suddenly, while everyone else was gazing depressed into their goblets. This laughter, which had begun harshly but in a careless way, was silenced under the gaze of Clitus, which met the grimly aroused one of Alexander with cruel calmness.

As he told the end of his story, Clitus did not let his eyes stray any more from the king, those icily still grey eyes, the black pupils of which seemed to become bigger and in doing so become fixed in a very rigid stare. He turned only towards him, with a sorrowfully muted voice which had at the same time a silvery muted clarity; the rest of the company was forgotten.

'Not until several years later did Gilgamesh achieve a meeting with Enkidu's shade; he succeeded in doing it through the King of the Underworld, Ereshkigal.

'It did not come to real conversation between the two of them; they remained remote from each other. Gilgamesh, in whose heart there was nothing more than a thirst for knowledge and the fear of death, yearned to hear what was "essential"; Enkidu found no comfort, and also no sign that there was still some love between them. The only thing he said was how awful it would be to be dead. "Look, the friend, who made your heart rejoice when you embraced him, is being eaten by worms, just like an old piece of clothing." That was actually their entire conversation.

'Gilgamesh hastily asked a few more questions, but the shade, full of pain, answered only "If I told you about the way things are ordered in the Underworld, as I have seen it, you would have to sit down the whole day and weep." Already Gilgamesh was weeping. Finally he only wanted to know one thing: what fate was due to the spirit, who has no "carer" on the earth; for he had no "carer", with all his magnificence. "Did you see such a man?" he asked therefore fearfully. The shade answered:

'"Yes, I saw one. He had to eat the dregs left in the pot, morsels thrown away in the street." With this he disappeared.

'Soon after that the Prince of Uruk died, although he was two thirds a god. His whole life long he had been at a loss, immoderate and with a troubled heart.'

The sorrowful brows of all of them were lowered, and huge tears ran down Hephaestion's gentle face. Clitus did not let his mysterious eyes, which gleamed in the darkness, leave the king.

The latter ordered wine, striking the table with an exaggerated gesture. 'You know some unpleasant stories,' he said to Clitus; his words were unnatural, as was his movement. Clitus only smiled.

The king drank, became noisier and encouraged the company, by letting himself go, to coarser and coarser merriment. As he urged them all, with a reddened and bloated expression, and eyes which were already glazed over, to drink more plentifully, many stated that he reminded them of his father.

Although many found his behaviour weird, they all bawled out with him. After half an hour the only men left were drunk, or behaved as if they were. In this throng of men, shouting, cracking smutty jokes, staggering around, and spitting, there sat

Hephaestion and Clitus, the only ones who had remained quiet: the one worried, restless and uneasy, the other with a gentle, dreamy and distant cheerfulness.

At the end of the dining table one of the men of letters, one of those who had learned the art of flattery, hit upon an idea, that was generally felt to be excellent: it was decided that everyone should hold a speech praising and glorifying Alexander, about his deeds and glorious personality. Whoever did it best would receive some gold object. The plan seemed to please the dazed Alexander; lower down the table someone was already beginning with his tirade.

He really laid it on thick. For too long, said the windbag, the accomplishments of the older heroes had been praised, of Heracles, Perseus and Theseus; yet Alexander, the Macedonian, had outdone each and every one of them considerably, and even put Homer's heroes in the shade: 'Thus the grandson has surpassed his ancient forebear: Alexander became greater than Achilles!' The liar thundered out his final point with smug pathos. He was applauded. Alexander also clapped but only briefly.

For suddenly he directed his gaze, which was no longer glazed over, at Clitus. With one hand, which only trembled very little, he pointed at him: 'Now he shall give a speech glorifying me,' he said slowly and threateningly in a slurred voice. Everyone was quiet and looked at Clitus.

The king said again with grim persistency: 'Now he shall give a speech glorifying me.' And as Clitus was still smiling, and did not even look over at him, he added, with his angrily lowered brow beneath which his eyes were burning black:

'Here at this table there sits one person, who despises me and who will not speak to glorify me. He finds that I have always been at a loss, immoderate and with a troubled heart. And I should eat what's left in the pot. That's what he's offering me.

Shall I reveal to you why? I once disturbed him very much. I once almost spoiled the figures for him, and that he will never forgive me for. If he knew how he has disturbed me, since I have been able to think, since I have been able to breathe – oh!'

As he lay back his head and screamed, no one could tell whether the sight he presented was of a wailing or an angry man. He stood there, a desperate god bringing disaster, surrounded by fear and cold curiosity, alone as never before at the top of his festive table, with his head cast back, painfully gaping mouth, and hands tensely intertwined.

Meanwhile friends were harassing Clitus: he *must* speak, otherwise some calamity would befall them. As Clitus stood up, his face was as cheerful as ever, though it is true a tone paler. It had exactly the faded shimmer of pearls. Above all a gleam emanated from the smooth brow, and below it his eyes, which looked cruelly as well as cheerfully and peacefully, were dominated by the dilated pupils.

He began to speak, very softly, but with a silvery clarity and quite distinctly. Alexander, with an ear cocked expectantly, and a half-open mouth, listened ardently, as though it was a question of learning here and now from this mouth the decision of his life, on which his happiness or eternal sorrow depended.

'It is generally said, that you have accomplished great deeds,' he heard the voice of Clitus saying. 'I don't understand anything about that. Also I did not pay any attention to them, as I had other things to think about. In the world, in which *I* live, Alexander, you have not been able to change anything. You have not even disturbed me. *I do not know you,*' he said slowly and looked at him, merciless in his contemplation. 'Whenever I thought about you, I felt only pity. Didn't you lay at my feet?'

He did not get any further, for Alexander had torn the halberd from the fist of the guard, who stood behind him. He brandished it, and before anyone could shout it was already in flight.

Clitus sank down slowly. Nobody had heard a sound of pain or horror from his mouth, which became white like his gleaming brow.

When Alexander had been alone for three days and three nights in the darkened tent, he believed the gods would be merciful and take away his reason. Thousands of times he had thought through to the end the fate that he himself had taken on, and now he hoped that even *his* capacity for suffering was at an end. 'Give me darkness,' he beseeched the mighty powers. But the light remained and with it the consciousness of his loneliness which became unbearable.

He allowed Hephaestion to come to him, and received him gently and calmly. 'Kill me!' he begged him tenderly. The other hesitated, did not know what to do, and grasped helplessly, as once on the ship, at his hand. 'Kill me!' Alexander begged once again. 'Here is my sword.'

With a gesture, in which there was all the weariness, which had come over him after those three twenty-four-hour periods, he indicated the weapon, which lay next to him. 'Do it!' he demanded gently. With a look which slipped down sadly he added, 'If I do it myself, it means I don't have any carer – '

As Hephaestion did not want to take the sword that was held out to him beggingly, Alexander turned away, more disappointed than ever. After a long pause he said thoughtfully: 'Did I love him then, Hephaestion?' Hephaestion, choked with tears, nodded.

'Yes, I loved him,' decided Alexander, full of melancholy. Now he also wept; more from weariness, it seemed, than pain. He wept, without contorting his face, and the tears flowed gently and abundantly from his eyes, which were no longer used to such relief.

'Do take the sword!' he begged once more, but, as he did so, finally giving way, he let himself sink into the arms of Hephaestion, who closed them firmly round him.

'Instead of killing me, he kisses me. You kiss me, instead of killing me.' Hephaestion, who cradled him like a child, did not know whether Alexander went on babbling these words again and again out of gratitude or was really accusing him, until he fell asleep.

4

As some soldiers of the great army, while on scouting trips, had unwittingly entered the territory of the Amazons, the latter sent women envoys and declared war, so insulted did they feel.

At first there was much mockery and laughter in the camp and the incident even made Alexander cheerful. He thought it would be amusing to fight against these armoured women, and it would finally provide a change. The mood of his body of soldiers would get better after they had beaten this unusual enemy and had the prisoners in the cells. If the others could be judged by the women messengers, then the women warriors seemed to be as pretty as they were energetic.

They did not have much feminine plumpness to offer, but they had had enough of that in Babylon. It was said that they had had their breasts removed by an operation, and the Greek-Macedonian soldiers, used to pederasty, found this very fact very attractive: the firm, slim, trained bodies of boys with a woman's sex. And the way they held their heads! The eyes of a Greek, Persian or Egyptian woman did not sparkle so bravely nor so merrily and wild.

They raised their spirits with this fighting sport, which they regarded as the especially urgent wooing of a stubborn but very desirable mistress, who denied herself to all men with stubborn coquettishness.

Surprisingly matters became serious. The beautiful hermaphrodites would not let anyone take liberties with them; on the contrary they fought cruelly and inexorably. It was noticed that they were furious, indignant and vengeful to their innermost being. For decades no man had entered their territory, and even the King of the Persians had not dared to. And now there came these people of the interloper Alexander. Especially the young queen and supreme commander, Roxane, seemed to be possessed with rage. The arrows which she shot struck home best and they poisoned the worst.

Alexander's soldiers realised already on the first day that it was not a matter of erotic fun but of bloody battle. There were many dead. No enemy had been so furious as this one. They were surprised by weapons, stones and projectiles flying out of hiding places, and a glittering being leapt from a rock onto the shoulders of a speechless man, choked him, bit him, and thrust a short sword into the unfortunate man's neck, when he sank down. When a careless man wanted to take his revenge on one of the women he had captured, an especially wild and especially beautiful one, by raping her, then twenty others appeared, as though produced completely out of thin air; they tore him into bloody pieces.

Then the men pulled themselves together. If there had ever been a time when it was a matter of their honour, then this was it. They had coped with Darius and Bessus, then why not with these armoured furies? Now they also learned how intoxicating cruelty could be. They did not violate the ones they caught any more, but throttled them, cut up their faces, breasts and the sexual organs, which they had not willingly yielded to them. If only they had the queen! Alexander himself should murder her.

What a triumph, as the army of women began to retreat! Still fighting, and still venturing small advances they tried to reach their fort. This was considered completely impregnable. It was said of the rock on which it lay that only winged soldiers could take it. Even if one could take the rock, there remained the iron gates and thick walls, and out of the small window slots the women poured boiling oil and hurled their lethally prepared arrows.

Into this infernal fort the last thing they saw disappearing was Queen Roxane. She greeted them scornfully, waved to them and shouted out something coarse; at the sight of her raising herself up, ice-cold shivers ran down the spines of the soldiers down below.

In the army the grimmest rumours about her excesses and cruelties were spreading. They told each other in hushed voices of the small children, which it was her habit to slaughter, of the beasts on which she rode, and of the spells, magic, and the in-decent cults, with which she was familiar. Many compared her with Olympias, but she was unquestionably much more terrible.

When Alexander was told such things, he waved them aside. She was an enemy like all others. Enemies were there to be beaten.

He had not discussed with his generals so intently even before the battle of Issus. They were familiar with that black gloominess in his eyes, that determined play of muscles around his mouth. But his voice had never before sounded so full of energy and cold.

The plan of attack which he presented to his leaders, was as cunning as it was bold. It was certainly the most daring which he had ever designed.

Two days later Alexander's army had stormed the fort of the Queen of the Amazons. They were already forcing their way into the rooms; a part of the walls was burning; and from the smoking ruins came the women's cries of anger and despair.

All the rooms were piled up with disfigured corpses; even these soldiers had not wreaked such havoc before. The king could be seen constantly pushing his way through twisted together heaps of struggling, bleeding, resisting, falling bodies, through all the rooms, as far as the last chamber. He stopped at the door, with his weapon still raised, spellbound, when he saw Roxane standing alone, upright, and armed in the middle of the room. She looked towards him calmly and solemnly; under her reddish-silvery enamelled eyelids she had greenish-black, deeply serious cat's eyes.

Thus they looked at each other, having known each other already for a long time, without being aware of it and suddenly realising with great astonishment: we belong together. We still have to prove ourselves only to each other, for we have always been intended for each other, unconditionally, inexorably. There is nothing more for us to do, but approach each other and give each other our hands, if we dare. They approached each other with small steps, like sleepwalkers, the way people do who are hypnotised. When they found themselves all of a sudden standing opposite each other so closely, that their foreheads almost touched, they both became alarmed. They did not dare to lower their eyes in front of each other, although the eyes of the one caused pain for the eyes of the other.

The wedding of Alexander with Queen Roxane was prepared with great pomp in the camp. Alexander had made the soldiers give their word of honour, to treat all of his wife's escort with the most refined politeness. Nevertheless no real cordiality manifested itself between the troops and the armoured ladies. Painful incidents were all the same avoided, and everything ran with dignified ceremoniousness.

A division of women accompanied Roxane to the throne. All the ladies walked in a dignified way, but most dignified of all was the garlanded one in their midst. The young queen had been delightfully adorned. Her hairdo shimmered with a golden-violet colour from the coloured powder, and her face was also brightly coloured. The carefully trimmed eyebrows curved up majestically, and below them the lids appeared to be even more artistically enamelled than usual. Most impressive of all was the long, solemn, curved nose, which, with its bluish-white make-up, and crimson nostrils, stuck out prominently. The young keen mouth with its magnificent teeth, and narrow, blood-red, seductively firm lips, had a rigid smile. As she approached the throne, everything about her jangled, the pearl decoration on her head and the metallic dress. Her smile also seemed to jangle, so coldly, precisely, and inexorably did it lie upon her face.

Arriving at the throne she lowered her brow solemnly, as the maids of honour threw themselves onto the ground. Alexander offered her his hand, so that she might rise up to join him.

At night, in the tent, she appeared differently. She squatted silently on the bed, and Alexander leaned back at some distance. She had combed her gold-coloured hair down over her forehead, below which she looked with her cat's eyes, which had become saddened.

Out of the darkness, Alexander said softly: 'Your eyes glow in rings, Roxane. There's a red, a yellow and the innermost one is a black ring – '

She replied in an almost wailing flute-like voice: 'If only I was already mother of your son.' Suddenly stretching herself up she said ardently: 'So that I could compete with him in a fight.' She finished with 'For *that's the way I am*,' and sank back down, but in triumph.

As Alexander kept silent in the background as though he was afraid, she began suddenly to speak of his mother. 'You look like her,' she said, scrutinising him thoughtfully. Then she added that she hoped that Olympias' blessing for the marriage would soon arrive. 'Only then could I be happy with you,' she explained with that flute-like voice.

Alexander still did not move. Roxane's mouth, very famous in all eastern realms, and which had never been other than firmly closed or with an icy smile, was trembling. Her nose dominated in a movingly emotional way her face, which had become soft and willing. From her forehead there came a gentle gleam, and also from the silvery eyelids, as they closed. She knelt with bended neck, a humble woman. The arms which had shot arrows hung defenceless. Her body and her face became tenderly transfigured in expectation of her husband and hero.

Alexander raised his hands towards her; but he was standing too far away and he could not reach her. He thought, with his brow burning with shame: 'What law is it which forbids me to take hold of her? Have I forfeited the right to my own wedding night, because I have been chosen and blessed, to bring about a greater wedding?'

He noticed how the crouching woman raised herself up on the bed opposite him.

Her garment fell from her shoulders, and the nape of her neck was gleaming, as were her breasts. He stayed at the entrance, where the curtains of the tent were gathered up. His thoughts became more painful and confused. 'I can't,' he thought, 'or I may not? Why then may I not have a son? Why may I not touch her? Why may I only touch, in order to kill? Oh, the one I would most have liked to touch, I have killed – '

She heard him lamenting and called out his name once more in a voice which sang with pity. But he was no longer in the tent. The night had already received him with wind and solitude.

The Roxane, who had revealed herself to him that night, he did not see again. The one he was to see was only the stern, tense, ice-cold one. She carried her nose like a weapon, and beneath her coloured eyelids her look was that of a scheming predator. Towards the king she presented herself as crushingly polite, standing on ceremony in every movement: the way she walked, lowered her face, wore her complicated hairdo, and formed angry and exact words with her hard lips.

For a short time Alexander tried to woo her, asking her at the same time to excuse him. This proved to be an absurd undertaking.

Once she laughed horribly, when he wanted to kiss her. She laughed out loud, with her mouth wide open and her eyes closed. Still laughing she turned away and ran off

After this scene Alexander kept his distance from her. The adventure seemed to be a closed matter for him, and he turned his attention to strategic and political affairs.

As always after his most intimate defeats, he seemed to grow more extrovert, more domineering and inexorable than ever. He tyrannised his entourage, imposed harder punishments than before, ingenious oriental tortures.

In the evenings he ordered little Bagoas to come to his tent. He approached, with his narrow, cunningly sweet eyes in his painted little mask. Feeling tired, Alexander turned towards him.

'There you are,' he said weakly. 'Why don't you come nearer? Are you still afraid of me then?'

5

It was in a cellar which was semi-illuminated in an uncanny way, where the rebellious pages met together with Callisthenes at night. They were almost exclusively Greek boys, and their leader, the ambitious lithe Hermelaus, belonged to one of the most distinguished Athenian families. They greeted each other solemnly, with a kiss and a full handshake. None of them was older than sixteen years, many of them of a perfect beauty, so perfect that it was moving. They loved each other; almost everyone had been the friend and favourite of everyone else.

Outside their passionate alliance, Callisthenes, the man of letters, stood alone. But he was also their head. They venerated him on account of his accomplished Hellenic education, his bravura skill with words, and his relationship with Aristotle; above all they were impressed by his unyielding opposition to Alexander.

He came to join them, with a fiery look, like that of his colleagues in the market place at home, and his mobile, already somewhat worn-out mouth, which was reminiscent of that of his great uncle, opened to speak.

'He's going too far!' thundered Callisthenes, stamping his foot. The boys listened, with eyes of dark determination below those young brows. 'The concept of freedom, which was the highest we had, has become for him something to mock and laugh at,' explained their leader to them. 'That he demands even from us, Hellenes, that we kneel down before him, completes the dreadful picture. We can no longer just sit back and watch, my Greek boys. History expects action from us!'

Ice-cold shivers ran down the boys' backs and they pressed shyly against each other. What this *action* must be, they knew already. It was both horrible and uplifting.

Hermelaus was the first to regain his self-composure. He stepped into the circle, moving elastically like a dancer, and it is true to say that there was a lively glow on his cheeks. 'We must swear ourselves to silence,' he whispered with hysterical solemnity.

They performed the swearing ceremony, by all making cuts in their soft arms, and letting blood trickle into a dish, over which they murmured formulas and vows.

Some of them felt sick. The others crowded in awe around Callisthenes, who held the dish of blood with a grand gesture. 'My Greek boys!' he called out, and kissed each of them on the forehead. Huge tears ran down the children's cheeks.

They felt fearful, for a musty smell came from the walls, and the torchlight caused fantastic dancing shadows. And with shadows dancing around him Hermelaus began to develop his plan.

Every morning three pages served the monarch personally. It was to be decided by lot, which of them should strangle Alexander in his bath, 'who may be the murderer of the tyrant', as Hermelaus concluded, looking around him threateningly.

The boys looked severe and determined to the last. Over many years they had increased their hatred against Alexander, the Macedonian tyrant and tormentor of Greece. In the last few months the vain Callisthenes had done his part, to make them ardent. This hour of shedding blood for the bond between them, the great oath and the grim plan appeared to them to be the most splendid of their lives.

The lot fell to one of the youngest of them, a blond child with a sweet immature face. This poor, twelve-year-old face became chalky white, when the child stepped forward into the circle of the conspirators, who watched gloomily.

'Do you feel yourself capable?' asked Hermelaus. Callisthenes repeated the question with distrust.

The child nodded heroically; though it is true that as he did so his mouth trembled.

After a sleepless night full of tears and shaking with fear, of prayers and misery, the little boy ran to Alexander and gave it all away.

Alexander insisted on conducting the investigation himself; he interrogated every one of the young people individually and then all together. Hephaestion observed him anxiously, listening in the background.

This conspiracy had horrified the king and hurt him as no other had. So that was how the elite of the young people felt about him, his immediate entourage, almost his sons.

He investigated and asked questions in a quiet oddly cursory voice, and sometimes he laughed briefly through his nose, when the answers satisfied him. 'Aha, I can imagine it. You were lying together at night. But who had the idea first? That would be interesting to know.'

The boys stood with lowered faces in front of him. Not one of them dared to look up, for they knew that his look would hurt them. They let those hands, with which they had intended to kill him, hang down, as heavily as lead weights.

Alexander looked with his ice-cold eyes, which were black and had become wider, at their moving and beautiful figures. He examined, with a mercilessness, which horrified even himself, their slender hips, sinewy knees, young mouths, their young and living hair. 'All this I will have executed.'

One of them fell down, because his knees were trembling so much. Alexander thought with horror: 'You're all just afraid of me. But I wanted you to love me.' His questions they answered with soundless voices. What is more nobody lied any more. It seemed to them, as though he already knew everything anyway.

Hermelaus appeared with his hips like a dancer's and mobile shoulders. 'His head is good and very sleek,' thought Alexander, who looked him up and down. A long narrow skull, with a long somewhat bumpy nose. No eyebrows and a mouth which was drawn together coquettishly and had a distorted smile.

He was the first one who dared to look Alexander in the face: with a look that was cowardly in a sweet way, impudent, and malicious but colourless. 'Here I am, my king,' he said with affectation. On his cheeks there glowed an ardent redness.

Alexander assessed him from top to toe. He could see through him, work him out, nothing remained a secret to him. This one was vindictive and effeminate, mentally vague, but ready for anything out of offended vanity. Without question he had been neglected; usually a sensitive dancer, he would have liked to watch smiling, as his king was roasted over a slow fire.

'You are not harmless,' Alexander concluded his observations. The page lowered his gaze in a vain way. 'Stupid monkey!' thundered the king. At this the unhealthy redness faded away from Hermelaus' cheek bones, and his lean face became drawn and yellowish. Alexander turned away disgusted. He began to ask questions again, quickly, quietly, precisely. Along the wall the boys stood in a row in fearful silence.

'So you were the first to think of the plan to throttle me in my bath.' Hermelaus, trembling with an impudence that could easily tip over into a fit of weeping, said: 'It was me who thought of the plan.' 'Out of malice you have forgotten that all that you are, you are because of me.' 'I know very well that everything we are, we are because of you, O King: wretched, neglected, abandoned to Barbarians, whom you give preference to.'

'You prattler!' the king, his face going suddenly blood-red, shouted at him. 'You just repeat the lies that Callisthenes makes up.' Hermelaus had again his sweetish smile on his mouth, which he had unnaturally small. 'We have thought all that over very carefully for ourselves. We did love you.' Then, as the king hesitated, he went on with a tinny voice like a lyre, as one recites something learned by heart: 'For that very reason we hate you now most of all, for you have disappointed us most of all. Every one of us would have rejoiced in dying for you, if you were our leader, and we had remained your free soldiers. But you became a tyrant, and you trod everything under foot which was Hellenic, and finally you killed the best of all the Greek-minded men, our Clitus. Tyrant! Tyrant! – ' he shrieked, and at the same time wriggled like a possessed puppet, with bright red foam on his lips. His gaze had a yellow gleam, and his cheeks burned red again.

Alexander shouted between his epileptic whining to the soldiers, to get hold of him. 'Strangle him outside!' he shouted, his face turned away, for it was nauseating to see how the fettered boy danced around and showed himself foaming. 'But beat him first. He insulted your king.'

The soldiers dragged him away, and he hung in their arms, suddenly lifeless, like a rag, limp and dead; only between his half-closed eyes there was some bright green phosphorescence.

The boys stood motionless and pale, and waited silently to see what would be inflicted on them. Many trembled over their whole bodies, as though they were being shaken by a great hand; others had grim faces, determined to remain courageous to the last. The hysterically scandalous show that Hermelaus had presented to them, had on the one hand shattered them and on the other hand brought them to their senses: they should behave decently.

They looked at Alexander's broad, stone-like figure no differently than they would a supernatural being, which had power over them, and which could only with difficulty be credited with human feelings. He was a tyrant.

The tyrant nodded. The voice which came from him was no longer the angry and harsh one, which frightened the boys; rather it was sluggish, as though weighed down with pain.

'Go!' he said slowly. 'You're to go home to Greece. I don't want to see you again.'

He saw their faces in a row before him, a row of pale, young faces rigid with fear. He was overcome by tiredness, weariness and the feeling of great loneliness. He turned his back to them and walked slowly away.

As he passed him he said to Hephaestion: 'Send them home. I don't want to punish them. They're stupid.'

Only Callisthenes was executed. The executioners cut off his lips, nose, ears, sexual organs and hands, and he lived like that for weeks in a cage, decaying while his body was still breathing.

The air around Alexander became more and more severe. No one dared to approach him without inhibition. Since the discovery of the conspiracy amongst his pages he hardly appeared any more without being accompanied by Persian officers.

The Orientals, who surrounded him with their flattery and gravity, confirmed to him daily that he was the son of God. He could not be spoken to alone any more, for there were always a couple of worthy plotting men with long beards around him. They called him the offspring of Amun and sank down with complex movements on the ground in front of him. He allowed many to kiss him, which constituted the greatest honour imaginable for a courtier trained the Persian way. The fact that he had also introduced proskunesis[13] for his Hellenic-Macedonian entourage, had made him the most enemies.

The spokesman for the refractory group was Philotas, who had always been a braggart. His father had already years ago advised the high-spirited brown-haired young man: 'If only you would try to fit in a bit more, my son.' Philotas did not try to fit in at all; on the contrary he behaved even more audaciously.

In spite of his somewhat turned up lips this strapping man could almost be called handsome. The women went mad about his athletic body covered with black hair. His dark hair grew right down his arms and in between his fingers, and his well-exercised legs were shaggy. He had an effective albeit stupid way of looking, and the gait, strutting like a cock, of the military seducer.

The speeches which he held about Alexander were as disrespectful as they were silly. It was his conviction that only his father and he deserved any merit for the Macedonian victories. The king enjoyed fame which was not his due.

Such prattling naturally came to Alexander's ears; everyone could see the storm that was brewing over Philotas' head. But he went on blustering.

Alexander had him closely observed. Finally they had a reason for having him arrested. The suspicion which fell upon him was an embarrassing one: he had not informed the king of a plan by discontented officers to murder him, though it was notorious that he was acquainted with it. That was as much as to say that he himself participated in the plot.

However he might thunder and puff himself up, the monarch had him found guilty, and the next day, in view of the grimly silent army, he was executed.

Alexander attended the event on a raised platform in his ceremonial robes and surrounded by his leaders. There was no movement to be seen in his facial features, as the friend of his youth begged for mercy. He gave the executioner the sign with his hand, which did not tremble.

'I will sort things out,' he called out in a horrible way over the gathering.

On the same day, he sent messengers to Ekbatana, where Parmenion, the one with sideburns, was staying and suspecting nothing. He hurriedly admitted the king's legation, as he had not heard from headquarters for a long time. What they brought him however was no military news; rather the three authorised agents of the king stabbed at him with three knives: two struck him in the chest and one in the throat. This had been their master's order.

The old man remained standing, and all three men entrusted with the task drew back from him with horror, so dreadfully angry and complaining was his gaze. In a classic gesture of great pain he stretched out both arms, and his voice thundered, although he had the knife in his throat.

'Tell the tyrant, who sent you, that with me the last free Greek dies. My curse will be dangerous for the rule of tyranny. I am going to speak against him before the gods.'

The circle at Alexander's table became quieter. There were too many bad things to remember: the tragedy of Clitus, the feud with Roxane, and her childless condition; the conspiracy of the pages; and the executions of Philotas and Parmenion, who had been considered the most faithful servants of the Macedonian royal house.

The king however, at the end of the table, said, with a gloomy and ruthless contentment, as though he was enjoying sitting like that in a state of emptiness: 'The one who committed high treason has been got rid of. We can move on.'

It became known to the army, that this time they were to go as far as India. There was no open contradiction, but just sullen silence. 'He's taking us to the end of the world. What are we looking for there?' they scoffed among themselves.

But he stepped in front of them and said in that voice of his which was both threatening and enticing, and which still enraptured them:

'I'm taking you to the end of the world.'

Temptation

I

Riding towards them up to the very border of the country was Prince Taxila on a marvellously decorated elephant. The white animal wore pearls like bunches of grapes on its drooping ears, and on its back a small tower built out of gold, mother-of-pearl and silk, in which the rajah sat among nothing but cushions and precious things.

Taxila, and his supporters, were well-disposed towards the Macedonians, not only out of goodness, but mainly by calculation, for they were hoping for help from the strangers against their powerful neighbour Poros, who had a mind of his own, and whose strong capital lay on the Hydaspes River.

The regions this side of the Indus turned out to be for the most part peaceful, and only few still ventured to put up any resistance, such as the Aspasii, for example, whose cities had to be destroyed. It was also learned that the Assacenii were arming themselves. They had beaten worse enemies, and so their capital Massaga fell.

After the harsh adventures in the mountains, these areas appeared tempting like a dream to the soldiers. In a gentle and enticing region there flourished almond trees and laurels; they had never seen such blossoms anywhere else.

As mild as the beautifully cultivated land were the teachings of the holy men, who sat in the woods, to do penance. They were so gentle, that Alexander's soldiers were often frightened. They did not feel themselves mature enough yet for such wisdom, but nevertheless it moved their hearts in an odd way. They defended themselves against such emotion, which they felt to be almost a weakness.

They were already starting not to love fighting any more as they had done earlier. Earlier it had bored them, that they often gained their goals through peaceful agreements; nowadays they were thankful for it.

The friendly country, the capital of which was called Nysa, was ruled by thirty noble men. Here the Greeks were received with special reverence, for the inhabitants of Nysa claimed to be the descendants of Dionysus. It was believable, because they were big-built, brown-skinned and clever.

The Hellenes listened in awe, when these pleasantly built strangers, who claimed to be related to them, told them about the deeds and adventures of Dionysus. He was the only westerner, who had come this far into this magical country before them. Alexander's soldiers could consider themselves to be his successors, which made them feel proud and pious.

Their king, whom they had almost hated, they now loved again. It was the God of Greeks who was leading them. They understood his task as little as ever. But he was leading them into a blessed country, and they believed in him again.

Prince Taxila handed over his residence to them, which was considered to be the most beautiful city between the Indus and the Hydaspes. No other could be more beautiful: it looked splendid with its temples, in which wood carvings of gods, animals and plants intertwined with each other luxuriantly. In the extensive sweet-scented gardens blue water lay between the pink and violet-coloured bushes in the white marble basins of the pools. White peacocks fanned out their tails, and a shudder ran through their entire vain bodies as they did so. There were also other colourful birds with glittering plumage, golden bronze beaks and angry crimson eyes. Decorated elephants trotted through the alleys paved with white stones, from which there arose singing, pleasant smells and warmth. The successors of Dionysus believed they were no longer on this earth; surely they were in the promised paradise.

In the meantime Alexander received legations. Many princes sent gifts as a sign of their submission. Only Poros, of whom all spoke with anxiety and awe, remained defiant. He let it be known: he would await the king with weapon in hand at the border of his realm. They should therefore be prepared.

When the soldiers returned to the great army camp from their scouting trips, they told each other the wildest and most unbelievable things. They outdid each other with the most monstrous stories; everyone had experienced something even more fantastic.

Under the luxuriant plants they crouched in a circle; as the night was not peaceful, they could not sleep. There were fragrant smells and wailings from the thickets in the forests. The monkeys climbed about, and many had seen thick snakes, which, colourful and swollen, wrapped themselves around the trees. As the birds also cried and fluttered around, they certainly would have been afraid if they had been alone. So they preferred to camp in a circle and made all kinds of things up to each other.

Huge lions, great snakes, and elephants were no longer interesting enough. But there were scorpions, prickly and as big as dogs, which hopped and crept around horribly. It was impossible to escape from them, as they could also make great leaps. They killed only out of cruelty, because they did not eat human flesh. But near them there hung around great white foxes with red eyes; it was these which ate up the victims of the great insects; many soldiers had seen it themselves.

Others had met up with a six-handed ape-man, who was covered with hair and stank. He could strangle six people at once, each one with one hand. He laughed as he did so, but in a dreadful way. He laughed with a hollow moaning sound, like an animal, rumbling with amusement, so that it was disgusting to hear.

One had made the unpleasant acquaintance of the cursed fruit tree. It stood in the middle of a meadow, broad, beautifully formed and alone. The fruits which it bore gleamed so temptingly and abundantly, that even for India they were rarities. But if you wanted harmlessly to pluck one of these fat pears, then you got the most unfortunate blows in your face. The branches, brandished by a completely invisible hand, beat upon the unsuspecting wrongdoer, and in addition a voice called out with such a roar, that, paralysed with horror, you could not run away, but rather kept still, and streaming with blood as well.

Thus they could never guess what was holy in India and when they were committing a sin. Only the gods knew, what sensitive powers dwelt in these fruit trees. 'But after all,' said the offended Hellenic soldiers, 'in our trees there dwell deities, but they don't beat you the moment you want to pick something.'

Many also had nice things happen to them. Like the young knight who had caught sight of the gleaming palace on top of a mountain. Two thousand steps made out of sapphire led up to it; above he discovered that the palace was made completely out of precious stones, and hence the gleam. He forced his way in, partly because he wanted to rob things and partly because an incomparably profound and heartrending music enticed him. It had been the kind of music, the young gentleman reported, a melting and flute-like sound, a wooing for love, which was like a woman cooing. All the doors had sprung open, as though for a celebration, and even the bells, golden bells, had rung out in a charming way to receive him.

In the innermost part of the palace, where the music was the most amorous, he found an enchanting princess laid out, with a crimson cover, precious stones on her feet, wrists and in her dull hair. Only it seemed that this laid-out person was dead, for she was not breathing. But the music was emanating from her; there was no doubt that the sounds were pouring out of her resting body, so intoxicatingly that the horseman had to close his eyes.

'You've no idea what abysses I sank down in,' he told his comrades, still enraptured after the event. 'There's nothing else you can compare it with, such a confusingly pleasant infernal journey. Do you know how I awoke? A cold, delicate hand touched me: delicate, as you can imagine, but icy cold. When I opened my eyes, the princess had raised herself up, stiffly, as the dead raise themselves. She reached towards me, and she had already almost pulled me to her. What a marvellous death it would have been in her arms! How did I tear myself away from her, and how did I come down the stairs of precious stones? There was such magical singing following close behind me. I'll never forget the pressure of that sweet magical hand.' Thus he concluded dreamily; everyone noticed that he secretly regretted not having followed this pressure and having missed a marvellous death in her arms.

The young blond youth, whom they all treated affectionately as though he were a child, knew of the most charming thing of all. Music also featured in his story; it was also about girls, but about many and they were still alive. It is true they lived and indeed thrived differently from the majority of earthly girls. They were to be found in a forest; again it was singing which drew him on. But this time it was not luxuriantly amorous, but rather a clear babbling. 'Like a mountain spring,' said the blond youth, smiling at the memory. It turned out later that the girls lived in the calyxes of flowers. They were tied to the calyxes of flowers, growing together with them. But this did not restrict them, for they enjoyed their existence.

They were as delicate as blossom, white and completely transparent; and besides this they were naked, with very tiny, pointed and charming breasts. They laughed to each other, joked, played, had fun with each other, sang and threw balls.

They received the young stranger with shouts of joy and twittering.

'I was with them for three months and twelve days,' said the blond youth quietly and blissfully. They all knew, that he had only been away for two days, but they nodded thankfully, because his young voice, husky with emotion, pleased them. 'It was the happiest time in my whole life. And will always remain so,' he concluded with melancholy.

He related also, but choked with tears, how his friendly marvellous girls met their deaths. 'They can only breathe in the sunlight, and cannot bear the shade. Oh, as the shadows of the trees crept nearer and nearer, they became paler and paler and more worried. They did not laugh any more, and many of them clung to me anxiously.' Thus the adventure of the blond youth also did not end cheerfully.

But those, who came home and claimed to have been to the end of the world, Alexander himself had brought into his own tent.

He was resting in the background on his bed, as the two infantrymen came in awkwardly; from the semi-darkness he looked at them with that look of his, both soft and imperious, which seemed to draw you in: 'You claim to have been at the end of the world?'

The soldiers muttered and broke off. Alexander, suddenly upright, asked with a childlike and bright curiosity: '*What did it look like?*' Both of them grumbled something into their beards. Alexander ordered them, feeling already impatient and with a dangerous sharpness: 'Speak clearly, when I ask you something.'

The two bearded men stuttered even more speechlessly: there had been, they said, a great storm, such a dull roaring – Alexander waved them away in disgust. 'You don't know anything either,' he said feeling tired. And as both of them still stood there he added: 'Why don't you go? Push off!' Blazing with anger, and having raised himself up to his full height, he shouted at them: 'You have lied to your king! Be thankful, that I don't have you whipped!'

After they had both plodded out, he collapsed again in the twilight. 'They don't know anything either,' he repeated.

Tormented by his enormous curiosity as though by an illness, he groaned, with his hands pressed against his temples: 'Who would know? Who would have seen it?'

2

Those that were doing penance were sitting in the remote groves. They squatted there gaunt and naked, and their infected skin was completely the colour of loam. They scraped at their leprosy and sought knowledge. When they found such men, Macedonian soldiers looked at them as much in disgust as in awe.

They had already seen many a wise man in excrement in this way; at home they were called cynics,[14] because they behaved like dogs. Here they were called gymnosophists,[15] for they were unclothed and strove to attain truth.

They tried to mock them, but their gaze remained mild, and even proud for all their humility. When the soldiers tickled them with sticks and stalks on their tangled beards and crusty ears, they smiled indulgently and encouragingly. They threatened with their fingers: no one understood what they were murmuring, but it was bound to be modest and pious.

Alexander arranged to be taken to some of them, who had a special reputation. They greeted him with quiet, unmoved friendliness, as they had also greeted the common soldiers. The king was startled at their eyes: there was a look of blissfully painful reverie in them. In their mouldy faces, rough from dirt and rashes, those eyes gleamed with a more than human power.

'Teach me!' was the request made by Alexander, who was used to listening to strange revelations. One of the old men replied in a friendly but unyielding way: '*You cannot listen to us.*' 'Why not?' asked Alexander, somewhat hurt. 'Instruct me!' he requested of them fiercely once more.

They shook their withered heads with gentle severity: 'Your spirit is restless. You must enter into yourself. Sit on this tree stump and do not speak a word for twenty-four hours.'

All three pointed with their shrivelled hands to the place where he should sit. His thirst for knowledge was stronger than his obstinacy. He hesitated for a moment, and then wanted to leap up. But then he sat down and kept silent.

It was difficult, because he was used to everything, except quietness. Thus thoughts came to him, which were almost unbearable; above all he thought about Clitus.

'Console me!' he asked after twelve hours. But the mouldy old men shook their heads, silent and unapproachable. For twelve more hours he had to look into his inner self, which he was afraid of knowing. He noticed that it was unfathomable and he felt dizzy. 'Where am I looking, when I look into myself?' he asked in horror.

Finally they indicated that he could ask a question. He asked hastily, for he was as in need of consolation as a man whose wound is bleeding needs a bandage. 'Have the actions been good ones, which I have accomplished?'

They replied with a riddle, as they knew all his thoughts. 'The essence of an action is as profound as an abyss.' After a long pause they added:

'He who perceives the inaction in action and in inaction particularly the action, he is a man of insight and will perform every action devoutly.' After an even greater pause, one of them said with a look that wandered away dreamily: '*For him the concept of action is completely dissolved.'* At this all three closed their eyes and remained silent.

The effect of their speech on the king was both peaceful and horrifying. He felt, for a few seconds, everything that he had done and achieved dissolve into nothingness, saw it annulled, and also that which he would still do. While this alarming peace touched his brow like a breath of air, the three dirty wise men were also already talking about the breath which they called the highest principle, the first of the gods.

'It is the wind, which draws everything unto itself,' began the first with an enticing singing intonation. 'When the fire goes out, it goes into the wind. When the sun goes down, it goes into the wind. When the waters dry out, they go into the wind. The wind draws all of these unto itself.'

When the first one had finished his dreamy sing-song, the second began his just as sweetly and just as monotonously. 'It is the breath, which draws everything unto itself. When one sleeps, then the voice goes into the breath; the eye goes into the breath, the ear goes into the breath, the manas[16] goes into the breath, the spirit – '

Alexander, who had been awake for twenty-four hours and looked into the abyss, was already asleep. He heard the third man, with his droning seductive voice:

'Prāna, breath, is Brahman; kham, joy, is Brahman; kham, ether, is Brahman.

'The breath of life, space, the heavens, lightning – that am I, reveals Brahman.'

In deep sleep, so said the teaching, the individual joined with atman, which is the universal soul. Not until Alexander was tired did he become receptive, and the recitation of the initiated ones reached the sleeping man. To the gently breathing man they could sing and drone on about the secret of the infinitely formed, never revealed, mild, peaceful and immortal bosom of the Brahman; only the completely calm person was receptive.

They took it in turns in a solemn alternating melody.

'Brahman is food,' said the first.

'Brahman is breath,' said the second.

Then the third: 'Brahman is spirit.'

The first spoke again, with great emphasis: 'Knowledge is Brahman.'

The second was silent, at which the third completed it proudly:

'Bliss is Brahman.'

It turned out that Brahman was *everything*, the essence of all appearance, which consists of thought and bliss. He bore many names; but if you looked at him piously and thoroughly, he was always the same.

The sleeping Alexander learned how humans could be most sure of approaching the Brahman. Oh, he himself had started in the completely wrong way; the clever voices did not recommend one's descendants, wealth or pious works, let alone warlike deeds, which were bloodstained, as the path to redemption; they recommended renunciation. This was the very thing he had never practised.

When the sleeping man asked the old men what redemption was, all three of them were silent and looked at the earth with impenetrable smiles. But from their silence there wafted peace, which was as strange as it was tempting.

Instead of an answer they began their teaching again, on how one can approach Brahman. What a precisely prescribed and mysterious approach!

'The wise man enters into the flame,' the first one began in a singing, complicated way. 'Out of the flame into the day; out of the waxing half of the month into the six months when the sun goes to the north; out of those months into the year, out of the year into the sun, out of the sun into the moon, out of the moon into the lightning. There he finally meets the spiritual man, who is no longer human, and who leads him to Brahman.'

After this the third one said in mild confirmation: 'That is the way of the gods, the way of Brahman.'

The third one concluded, full of promise: 'Whoever reaches it, will never return to the human vortex – Never return,' he repeated in a charming and empty way.

Now the sleeping man had an inkling of what redemption meant: not returning. 'Not suffering rebirth any more,' they called it. His self wanted to rebel but the temptation remained stronger.

He felt as though he were floating down a stream, on a boat, which was rocking lightly. Fragrances came to him, both from the water and from the banks, which were full of blooming bushes. He had never been rocked so enchantingly before. Around him colours and forms dissolved. What he had regarded as matter, proved to be illusion; he saw with feelings of pleasure how it evaporated. Nature, dream and spirit, all blended into each other, everything became the deity, and finally the deity became nothingness.

The sea which they were drifting towards with such sweet rocking movements was nothingness; the man travelling down the stream knew it without admitting it; it enticed him with its formlessness, bottomlessness, endlessness. First came the recognition, then the bliss, then the dissolution, which frees one from all bonds.

The voices of the teachers whispered and beguiled him; how long did the king rest with the three old men? If he had stayed in deep sleep a little longer in their midst, he would probably never have stood up again.

For the sea was already near when with one last effort he opened his eyes. He noticed that he was freezing, which had brought him to consciousness. It had become cold, and it was raining as well. Over the trees, which stood in darkness, the water poured down softly. At first Alexander believed he was alone; then he noticed that all three of the old men were squatting next to each other by a tree a few metres away from him; their eyes had a dull gleam, like damp wood.

They waved childishly as the king leaped up and shook himself. He felt as though he had been freed from a spell. The three of them could do nothing more than babble under their crusty beards.

But not until now did they tell him their best and most definite piece of wisdom.

'He who sees himself in all beings and in all beings himself, will enter, not for any other reason, into the highest Brahman.'

Their voices had no seductive power any more, but were only warning and weak. Alexander was already rushing away, bending the branches violently apart and treading on flowers and small creatures.

With painfully glowing eyes the three old men watched him as he went off through the rainy night, and saw how he offended the animal world and distanced himself from the way of knowledge, bliss and redemption.

The breath, which Alexander offended, took its revenge: when he faced the might of Prince Poros with his army at the River Hydaspes, a cloudburst and a hurricane were raging. Outraged nature was itself against the intruder.

The swollen river made its waters rage and roar, the rain blinded people's eyes, and struck them in the face; even the elephants seemed to be cruel and wild beyond what was required of them.

There were two hundred of them, separated from each other by fifty feet and they controlled about a mile of the terrain. When they trumpeted and struck out with their trunks, the Macedonian horses drew back in complete panic. The foot soldiers, who ventured close to the furious giants, were immediately pierced by the tusks, or grabbed by the trunks, thrown up in the air and stamped on.

On the greatest of the animals sat Poros, who was also the greatest man; above his white costume his face looked black, and with his thick lips and golden eyes, almost like that of a Negro. Although those eyes which were both dark and gleaming, seemed to be sightless, the prince could aim with awful accuracy. Every one of his long poisoned arrows struck a Greek soldier between the ribs or in the throat. Poros still took aim, even when he was already bleeding from several wounds. From the body of his lord, who was insensitive as though made of bronze, the elephant pulled out the enemies' arrows and missiles with its trunk.

The battle remained longer undecided than any other, of which Alexander had been its leader. His soldiers almost sank in the softened ground. They were fighting at the same time against the enemy, the swamp, which hampered them in their attacks, against the endless rain, which hurt their tired out faces, and tortured their nerves, and against the elephants, with the trumpeting noise which tormented them and made the horses shy, and the teeth and trunks of which were more dangerous than all weapons and brought about a worse death.

If Alexander had yielded for just a moment, it would have been the decisive and final defeat. The example which he set, and which was superhuman, saved the day. At last the Indians gave way. Prince Poros' elephant sank down and all the other elephants gave everything up for lost.

3

Already for some time there had been whispering and gossiping around the camp about the fairy-tale wealth of an Indian queen, called Kandake. So a certain satisfaction prevailed, when finally her envoys appeared before Alexander.

The splendour with which they appeared, confirmed all rumours, which were in circulation about the considerable wealth of this princess; above all there were the gifts, which were carried past the Macedonian king in a solemn procession. There were small golden deities with diamond eyes, and ones made of ivory; in cages made of fine metal there were five hundred birds of the most colourful kind, which could sing but also chatter, and parakeets and sphinxes; black slaves, who were half-naked, led tamed tigers, lions and leopards on coloured, prettily plaited leads, and which smelt of the wilderness and crept by in procession with subdued grace but ready to leap. These were followed by twenty-five white elephants, solemnly decorated, on which Moorish children sat: all the soldiers had to laugh, because the dark little ones had such frightened looks on their swollen faces and had such large hanging ears. An artist had also been sent with them, who made a very artistic portrait of the king on a wooden board.

A lady who introduced herself with such gifts, was at least as powerful as the boldest legend had supposed her to be.

The envoys took their leave after several days, and after they had received gifts in return, which were certainly tasteful, but would not bear comparison with those that the foreigners for their part had brought with them.

A few days later another gentleman appeared with a great retinue, who referred to the lady Kandake, claimed to be her son and to be called Kandaulus; he said he had to talk about an important matter with the king.

Alexander was in the mood for masquerades, and was in a state of rather dubious amusement, which bordered on silliness. He decided to make a fool of the prince, and expected to have some fun with him.

He received him alright, but his bodyguard Ptolemaeus had to play the role of king, and Alexander took on the name of Hephaestion. The real Hephaestion, who was disturbed by the joke, stood in the background with a worried expression.

Kandaulus sank down onto the ground in front of Ptolemaeus and handed over to him a present. The false king, all clumsy gravity, received the gold-plated little basket, which was daintily filled with fruits and precious stones, with an embarrassed grand air; the prince, who found the Macedonian king very dignified and reserved, presented him his request on his knees.

It concerned his young wife, who according to the description he gave, must be desirable, and who had been abducted by the captain of a band of robbers and was in a mountain fortress. Kandaulus, by nature unwarlike, weak and philanthropical, did not know what to do. He had heard that the Macedonians were both brave and noble, so he was asking on his knees if they would be willing to help him.

Ptolemaeus cleared his throat uncertainly and with affectation, and finally he said haughtily, that he, as a monarch occupied with many different things, could not of course bother himself with such a private matter, and that he left such matters to his general, the valiant Hephaestion.

Alexander stepped forward, charming but modest; he bowed deeply. It would be an honour for him to be allowed to help the prince – if his lord allowed it, he added respectfully. Ptolemaeus nodded, embarrassed and graciously; it was painful for him to have Kandaulus cover his feet with kisses yet again.

They set off with a small detachment of able soldiers, to overcome the defiance of the captain of the robbers. Alexander had everyone call him Hephaestion, and he ended up believing himself in the transformation, which he found strangely flattering and confused him in a pleasant way.

'It's so easy then to lose yourself,' he thought, in a dreamy daze. 'How carefree I feel.' He gave himself up to this freedom as to a sweet and forbidden pleasure. In Bactria such a game would have still caused him nothing but disgust; India had very much cast a spell over him.

The robber captain, who had behaved so fiercely, was not difficult to overcome. When he saw the Macedonian cavalry, he became afraid, and Kandake's son had his beloved again. With tears in his eyes he thanked the general, who remained humble and reserved.

'Alexander has faithful servants,' said the prince tersely, shaking the officer by the hand. In his great joy, he made a suggestion to him, that he should spend a few days at his mother's castle. 'She will be pleased to get to know, if not the lord, then at least his best vassal.'

On the way to his mother's palace Kandaulus asked the general about many of Alexander's peculiarities. The false Hephaestion answered in a bright and precise way. 'Is Alexander very pious?' asked the inquisitive man. 'Does he believe in all the gods?'

'In all of them,' said Alexander in a lively way.

He had to inform him how long Alexander usually slept, what he ate, how he treated his friends. He answered everything in impartial detail. What a charming game, he thought, as he reported about himself. Without any pangs of conscience he enjoyed the impermissible, frivolous aspects of this situation.

Kandake was no longer a very young woman, but she was incomparably magnificent. The gathered up dress with its train, which she wore, was made of a soft, embroidered glittering material; flowers, birds and figures decorated the wide dress and the puffed sleeves. From her hair-do hung bunches of pearls like grapes and diamond roses, and her white hands were also heavy with diamonds, and blue and red jewels. She was rather broad, and strictly speaking almost fat; but you willingly forgot that, because she proved to be graceful. Her milky tender skin seemed to be immaculate, admittedly not fresh, but of a mature, intelligently handled beauty.

Opening her eyes in an enticing way she greeted Alexander, who was introduced to her as a general. 'My son is very much obliged to you, and therefore I am too.' She sat in a delightful but seductive way. In the great hall of her palace a meal was served up to receive him.

In there the aromas were such that you had to close your eyes. The gods only knew, what was being burned there. From coloured little pans there arose silver and blue clouds of steam.

When you had got used to the semi-darkness filled with pleasant aromas, you noticed that you were in a magical room. Palms and blossoming bushes grew out of the walls, and the sun, the moon and the planets circled round in their crimson-golden light below the ceiling, with its vault which seemed infinite. Black parrots sang from cages like nightingales, and among all the utensils monkeys climbed about, who could speak and quarrel. The prettiest were the little yellow, red and green cats with gilded paws.

At a round table full of fragrant drinks sat Madame Kandake, and Alexander also had to sit down. They were served by dwarves, at least a hundred of them. They were all wearing nice little fur coats, either grey, patterned or coloured; and they toddled by with their wrinkled, devout faces. In the bulging bowls which they held unheard-of dishes were steaming.

Alexander ate with pleasure, and his hostess held up her heavy face, shimmering like silk, in her hands, heavy with rings, and watched him with drowsy tenderness: 'What does it taste like, my dear General?'

Afterwards, in the little ante-room hung with tapestries, into which she had led him, she handed him a long silver pipe: 'Let's smoke!' As she said this she leaned back and stretched herself, so that the jewellery on her bosom and hairdo tinkled. She handled the pipe with careful grace, as a shepherd does his finest flute.

'I have never smoked,' claimed Alexander, still rather stubborn, although he had eaten and drunken a lot. She rocked to and fro, to charm him. 'My dear General,' she begged with purring, guttural sounds, 'It will do you good, my dear Hephaestion.'

It flattered him again that she called him Hephaestion and made him pleasantly confused. 'I don't want to,' he contradicted her only gently. '*You are not you*,' she said suddenly, and at this he had the feeling as though the ground was giving way under his feet.

With perfect circular movements she heated the brownish poison over the small flame, which was burning in a small lamp. The preparation smelt delightful, and she put it into the pipe with silver instruments, which he had to draw at with all his might, bent over the flame.

After the first breath he felt sick; but he heard her sonorous, flute-like voice comforting him: 'It's harmless.' And as she spoke she lay her cool fleshy head on his burning brow. 'Close your eyes!' she advised in a sing-song voice. He preferred to keep them open, for he liked seeing above him her large face with its broad dull-white cheeks, its sleepy eyes, and the wide indecently half-open mouth.

'Don't you like being you?' she asked lustfully.

'Very much,' babbled Alexander, who was sinking into some unfathomable depths.

'Shall we sleep together?' she asked and made a sign to him with her misty eyes. 'I don't sleep with women,' the false Hephaestion said defending himself. 'Not you,' she teased him, 'but it's you alright – not you, because not you – yet it is you, oh, how much – '

The moist kiss, with which she stifled his answer, smelled of spices. 'Don't kiss me in such a sloppy way!' he said resentfully. But now he had closed his eyes.

He took a few deep puffs from the silver pipe; the ceiling moved away, and the walls moved apart. Circles and figures came towards him from the dreamy blueness.

That which the three old men had taught him was becoming a living adventure in a sweet way which it was impossible to escape from. With them flight had been possible; here it was too late for that.

The struggle of the self did not matter any more, and what bliss it was to let yourself fall. Above all action did not matter any more, and if action was anything it was sin. It distanced you from knowledge, but with the tempting dream stories knowledge streamed in upon him from the stirred-up darkness, a very vague and general knowledge it is true, but this it was which led to the innermost part of the universe, which those Indians who had presentiments of those things called Brahman.

'Not you, because not you – yet it is you, oh, how much – ' purred Kandake above him, making guttural sounds. He sank powerless into her wide embrace, which was cool and soft and enclosed him.

'She has given me the Indian love potion,' thought Alexander as his senses faded. 'With that Queen Kandake already defeated Heracles and Dionysus.'

She asked him to say the syllable 'Om'. He did so, for he wanted to approach as closely as possible to the great intoxication of knowledge. 'Om – Om – Om – Om – ' he babbled monotonously, a hundred times. He lost the consciousness with which he normally lived; but instead he moved towards another, limitless one, of which he was a nameless part.

Dissolving within the wind, that was the doctrine; to become a component part, as it comes to rest, of the –

How did this immoral fairy tale end, which offered the bliss which comes with giving up consciousness? Wasn't there a grotesque epilogue, which one could later remember only vaguely?

A man hurried into the chamber; it was Kandake's younger son, Karakter. What did he want? It seemed, that he was a friend of the conquered Prince Poros, for he wanted to revenge him, by killing Alexander's general. Did blood flow, or would it only almost have flowed? Did the queen stretch out her arms? Was there the clank of metal, and did Kandaulus rush to save the threatened stranger, who obviously could not defend himself?

The next morning Alexander awoke with pangs of conscience. What he had allowed himself the previous night, had been the very thing, that he should never have allowed himself.

He felt guilty above all towards Hephaestion: had he not abused his name and his friendship abominably? For that very reason he was annoyed by the silent reproach with which the other man met him; it made him defiant.

'I have to think about myself more completely than ever,' he said to himself harshly.

So he summoned a gathering of the whole army, to inform it of his will. 'We are moving on,' he explained in a brief speech, which started oddly. 'The whole of the Orient awaits us: the land of the Ganges with its incomparable treasures, beyond that China, and beyond that the End of the World. The limits of this earth will be the boundaries of our empire. We still have much to conquer.'

He spoke as enthusiastically as ever, and his eyes were radiant; but the troops who were sure of their instincts noticed that he was weakened. This gleam in his gaze was feverish; he stretched himself up with an exaggerated gesture. So they dared to contradict him, and his speech was answered with grumbling.

Even further? And still not going home? What did they care about the End of the World? They muttered that they had seen enough. What concern of theirs was the Ganges, or China? He shouted furiously: 'Who's that speaking there?' And they all answered together: 'We are! We are!'

That a communal group which he had despised as dull, could ever be stronger than he, the individual, who had the passion and the will, seemed incredible to him. What he was experiencing here, facing this yelling crowd, meant for him the direct punishment for the impermissible pleasure which he had allowed himself the night before.

So he did not contradict them any more, withdrew into his tent without speaking in silence and did not appear again.

This time the soldiers noticed that they were the stronger ones, and they even put up with him not showing himself for three whole days. He had to give in, renounce and adapt himself to their wishes. That was unprecedented, and he did it, grinding his teeth.

The River Hyphasis, which was to be the starting point for new eastern campaigns, became the endpoint. Here they turned back.

4

On the rivers the pious patient inhabitants, working in the paddy fields saw ships which created a surprising effect with their colourful sails. There must have been thousands of them. Many were fitted out in a threatening way as warships, and others were uncovered for the transport of horses. All the men, who were in the ships must be armed, because you could hear the clanking of swords, lances and shields.

Thus the wild hunt, bringing with it diabolical misfortune, made its way, colourfully and clanking, down the rivers to the sea. Thus they rattled, these nothing but evil men, towards the ocean, which was welcome to swallow them up. The pious and patient inhabitants watched them go from their paddy fields, horribly moved; they shielded their eyes with their hands and turned their gentle brownish faces away in horror.

They knew about so many awful things, which these bloodthirsty fellows had brought about in the great and peaceful country round about. How many good elephants had died from their poisoned arrows. The pious and industrious people in their white shifts watched the ships go, shaking their heads, as they swayed down the rivers. Sometimes the ships jumped and bobbed around, so that it was horrible to see. That happened when they passed over whirlpools and rapids. But they always escaped. They must have supernatural powers.

Their young leader was unquestionably the son of the gods, but an evil one. The story was that he could kill with his eyes. His eyes had a gleam which brought about death; they seemed to consist of circling rings, red, green and black ones. It must be horrible.

Even when you thought you had him, he escaped with a big noise and through magic; that's what happened for example in the capital city of the Malli. There he suddenly flew from the city wall right into the middle of the market place, where he was surrounded and they thought they could overpower him. But he ground his teeth so that it sounded as though fifty shields were being struck against each other. Sparks came from him, and he spread himself out, killed a few with his eyes, and fluttered off in a frightful way.

This story had spread out from the capital city of the Malli over the whole country. An evil god, without doubt. Since then nobody dared to attack him any more, although many advised it, above all the priests. For it was they who hated him specially. They implored the people, to punish him and to attack him, but they were afraid.

Alexander managed to travel down the great rivers un-impeded to the sea.

The soldiers talked together in the evenings by the fire.

'Alexander dared to venture on the journey into this unknown ocean almost alone. There's only a few sailors with him.'

'What's he looking for on the ocean?'

It was the blond youth: 'He's looking for the end of the world.' They nodded, shaken

'He'll have to fight with monsters,' someone said. 'There are supposed to be sea-dragons.'

'But he's stronger than them,' the blond youth concluded, full of trust in him.

'This sea is different to all other seas. It's the World Sea. No Greek has ever travelled on it.'

And again the blond youth said in a voice, which was so clear, that all turned towards him: 'He is more than a Greek. His father, who lives in the oasis, will help him, to be able to walk on the water.'

His face radiated with so much belief, that they all looked across the ocean. They believed they could see their king walking on the horizon.

Alexander was travelling towards the same horizon. After two days the sailors asked him to be allowed to turn round, because supplies were becoming short. But he shook his head. 'We have not got nearer to the horizon yet.' They discussed together in whispers: should we turn the ship round against his will? But then he looked at them, until they noticed that his pain, his anger and his inexorable curiosity were worse and more dangerous than all the restlessness of the sea.

He stood at the bow, with his hands on his back, and with his defiantly lowered brow, as though he were pressing it against an impenetrable wall. Thus he stared out towards the horizon.

It changed its colour; that was no use, for it did not come any nearer. It paled down from a deep blue to a mother-of-pearl grey; it became dark, hid itself in the surging blackness, to let its cold, light-blue line rise up again after wretched hours of waiting. But it had not come any closer.

'It has not come any closer,' the man at the bow of the ship confirmed bitterly.

And what about when sea monsters came snapping and playing around and teasing him in his solitude? But he remained stubborn and never smiled. The clouds put on their prettiest performances for him; they formed rosy-coloured groups, making stairs and gateways, as though they were inviting him to fly up and settle down on them. He did not fly, although he certainly could have done.

As the sea could not tempt him, it threatened him. During the night a storm came up, and the black waves threw the small ship about and struck across the deck. The silent man with the defiant brow stood there soaked with salty water, and it would have almost washed him away, but he did not move.

He stared out into the interminable distance, which was in a wild state. 'Infinity rebels against me,' he said scornfully between his teeth. 'It will not allow me to conquer it, and rears up in hatred. It will not submit to me; so what have I achieved?'

After six days those on the shore, who had already given up the king for lost, saw the ship with the brown sails finally returning. It emerged from the evening calm of the sea, a silent, sad apparition. There was a quivering, silvery quality to its contours, and the brown sail stood out against the solemn palely transfigured sky. Slowly, not seeming to move, it came nearer. At the sight of it those on the shore felt they had to weep, without knowing why.

The man, who was crouching down in a corner on deck, had tired, bloodshot eyes. They could hardly recognise their king. His head was sunk forward.

'Again he has not found what he was looking for,' the sailors said to each other in shy, whispering voices. 'The whole night he did not talk to us, but to others, whom it is true we could not see.'

A few days later Alexander called the whole army together. He proclaimed his will.

'I have decided to split my army into two parts for the return march. I will take the land route with one half of the army via the country of Gedrosia. My admiral Nearchos will return with the fleet via the sea route.

'There is much that must be found out. A connection between the mouth of the Indus and the mouth of the Euphrates must be possible. We will provide humanity with this connection. A little bit less of the earth will be unknown, and more of it will have been conquered by us.'

5

At first there were still myrrh bushes, which had a strong fragrance in the sun. Near the rivers and small lakes tamarisk and spikenard thrived. Here there were still people living, even if they were only the dull Ichthyophagans.

The way they squatted down and babbled, they were poorer and more degenerate than animals dying miserably. They fed on stinking fish and foul water, and their huts were built out of fish bones. They could not show you the way. If you asked them, they just grinned stupidly. The more gifted ones among them pointed out into the wasteland with an idiotically trembling gesture. Their faces were disgusting, and it was better not to look at them. It horrified the Hellenic soldiers that human creatures could become degraded to such a wretched state.

They left those foul-smelling huts behind them; and only now did the hell of the sands begin.

This time it really was hell, through which their king led them. It had been bad in Bactria, and also in India, when the cloudbursts came. But here was the haunt of the damned.

Alexander stared into the interminable distance of the sand with the same hopeless craving with which he had stared into the interminable distance of water. The eternity teased him as mercilessly as the other had done. This horizon also escaped him.

It flickered with a yellowish-reddish colour, and in the evening it hung heavily and brownish, drifting away in a deep blue at midnight. The desert created violet waves, which also rustled, softly, but penetratingly. From the sharp, black shadows that they cast repulsive little predatory creatures looked out with calm but sneaky eyes. Larger animals, gentle and long-haired, trotted in herds across the surface. A moon of rosy silver wandered across a sky of green glass.

A wind came up with a strong rushing sound, a desert wind, with a great beating of its wings like a sea wind. A shudder went through the unyielding landscape. The sand trickled. The evil little animals whined, and the gentle long-haired ones trotted away faster.

'Still not stared long enough into the interminable distance?' scoffed the desert wind with a fluttering sound.

As Alexander did not answer, it made a rushing sound which sounded like huge laughter: 'Even in hell you are still proud, you stubborn man. Don't you know where you are?'

From the horizon there came an echo and the animals whined with it. In the green sky the moon had disappeared, and the gentle long-haired ones had risen up and formed the wailing cloud in which the moon hid itself.

'Stubborn fool!' came the rushing sound of the eternal wind, already flying away. The landscape lay there unyielding again, but, as the moon was no longer shining, in a still paler, greener and colder light.

Did this stubborn and extremely wilful man on his worn-out horse finally open his eyes? For so long they had seen nothing, from sheer staring at the horizon.

How long was it since the food provisions of his army had run out, and how long since the water skins had become empty? How many had remained in the sand? Half or three quarters of his troops?

And were there not men who had strangled and fought each other among the camels, for the privilege of being allowed to drink the animals' urine? And others who had gone mad and stuffed sand into their mouths, spat, yelled and laughed?

Everywhere there were men groaning, sinking down and dying miserably. There was a great stench, with everyone drying up and dying in a state of misery everywhere under the scorching sun. Certainly it was not for nothing that at the entrance to the Plain of the Damned, the dwarfish Ichthyophagans had grinned and pointed into the desert. Those little heaps of filth had been the last warning. They had ridden by them. They had thought: can this desert of Gedrosia be worse than other deserts? The Desert of Gedrosia indeed! Let's just see.

The head of the stubborn man on the languishing horse sank down. 'This is the paradise I set out for.'

His eyes met the deathly tired eyes of another man, who lay in the sand. It was a miracle: the eyes in this starved young face were shining, while all others were complaining.

'What are you thinking about that makes you so happy?' asked Alexander, who made his horse come to a halt.

The only thing the blond youth could do was whisper. His lips and tongue were dried up. 'I believe,' the blond youth whispered.

Alexander bent near to him: 'But you are dying – '

The blond youth nodded and smiled. 'You walked on the water,' the transfigured youth whispered. 'You will lead them out of hell... home... to your capital.'

The Angel with the Bound Hands

I

He issued the order to General Hephaestion in just a few words: he should march with the greater part of the land army along the flat coast towards Susa; Alexander himself chose the closest route through the mountains, via Pasargada and Persepolis. Hephaestion accepted the order with a slight and solemn inclination of his head; he expressed thanks to His Majesty for the trust that was vouchsafed to him. While he was dictating these polite modes of expression he thought: that means being separated for weeks; and also in the last few weeks he has hardly seen me. He must have already forgotten my face.

Wherever Alexander went, all those who had run things unfairly trembled. He did not get involved in negotiations, but established the facts and handed out punishments. His decrees were unsparing, precisely formulated, and everyone felt that they were final.

First of all the satrap Astaspes of Carmania was deposed; he had oppressed the poor, instead of protecting them and thus brought dishonour to the holy name of the king. After him the Persian Ordanes fell, who had controlled inner Ariana. From Media the following men were summoned: Cleandros, Sitalces and Heracon. Particularly bad things were reported about them. The army, which they had equipped, was intended to fight against their own king. Suspiciously enough they arrived with six hundred soldiers to start with. His Majesty had the three generals together with the six hundred soldiers executed. At the same time the order went out, that all mercenaries, in so far as they had not been recruited in Alexander's name, were to be dismissed immediately and without any ado.

The further he moved into his empire, the more threatening his gaze became. He was no longer recognisable; earlier he had been violent, but this cruel calmness in his face was strange.

He did not ride any more; wrapped up in his severe state robes he sat enthroned in his carriage. He was followed, as formerly Darius Codomannus, and Xerxes were followed, by the executioners, to whom he only needed to give horribly gentle nods.

In the grove of Pasargada the grave of Cyrus had been awfully neglected, and, as it turned out, even robbed. The king took this as an opportunity to hold a terrible criminal court. Magicians were painstakingly interrogated and tortured, and everywhere suspicious men were arrested. No Achaemenid could have avenged an offence more cruelly; Alexander felt consciously that he was their successor.

The man who had appeared to the country as a bringer of freedom and as a much-loved saviour now came as nothing other than an affliction. The gleam had disappeared from his face, which had grown larger and fatter; it had gone, and with it his youth. The king seemed to have aged astonishingly in the few years of the Bactrian-Sogdianian and Indian campaigns. He was no longer supple and soft, but heavy, and hard as well however. At his arrival officials fled, for he even condemned many, who had not been guilty of doing anything. A great laxity in morals had caught on everywhere, while the one they feared was conquering in Fairy Land. Not everyone considered himself immediately as a criminal, if he had embezzled something here, or had collected a little too much there. Such things had become common under the rule of Alexander at a distance, as they had been common under Darius Codomannus close at hand.

Admittedly the dull Harpalus had done things a little too impudently. To trust the state treasury to this pleasure-seeking, vain person had been an experiment of Alexander's, which one could describe as careless. As the treasurer found oriental women too sluggish he had one of the best-paid courtesans brought from Athens; she was called Pythionike and had a slim figure with a tough charm. With her he organised such extravagant orgies, that her weakened health could not bear it. During a specially solemn festivity she died, and a monument was built for her of inestimable value. Her successor should be no less a person than Glycera; any other would have been too cheap. Straightaway she had to be worshipped as a queen; Harpalus would have it no other way. The parties which he gave for her offered even more exceptional pleasures than those at which Madame Pythionike had presided. Things had not been so wild even at the court of the Great King.

When news came that Alexander was close to Babylon, the treasurer was up and away, taking with him: Glycera, five thousand talents in gold and a three-year-old daughter, who had been left him by Pythionike. He turned to the Ionic coast.

He used his state capital to hire mercenaries, six thousand men in fact. He appeared one day in Athens, where he was able to stay at first, by the special intercession of Demosthenes. But only until Alexander very emphatically demanded his arrest. Then they let him run, for they did not want to have such a proven enemy of the king. The jolly man, driven hither and thither ended up in Crete, where his bosom friend, the Spartan Thibron, murdered him, probably to take possession of the few talents, which, after all his swindling trips, remained from the whole robbery.

Only after his death did he truly move to the centre of interest, for now the scandal surrounding his name flourished as fully as he could have wished it to. Athens had a nice big affair once again, and this time even Demosthenes was accused. It did not help at all, that the pathetic old fox dragged his children before the tribunal, sobbing as he displayed them, in order to move the people. The fact remained that he, whose voice had quavered for decades with civic virtue, had been bribed by the adventurer Harpalus. Why else had he spoken so heartily in favour of accepting the defrauder within Athens' walls. It was inappropriate philanthropy, which must yield the most fatal consequences politically. All his summoning up of great gestures, oaths, tearful outbursts did not help the experienced old wizard any more. They were unmoved and stuck him in prison, though admittedly they let him escape the next day. With him many others were arrested, nothing but highly respected men. The mob on the streets had not been granted such a sensation for a long time. They were thankful to the lively treasurer beyond the grave.

In Susa Alexander met Hephaestion and his army unit again. He asked the general to come immediately to a private audience.

Hephaestion was led into the king's private chamber, not into the official reception room. Alexander stretched out his hand cordially to him, as he had not done for a long time. The man who had been neglected for months blushed slightly with grateful joy. As he bowed he smiled, revealing his beautiful teeth. While still bowing he said in his pleasantly hoarse voice: 'It's marvellous that you still have some time for me.' Above him the king turned his face away, already feeling weak. 'Yes, really, I am quite busy – do sit down!' he asked him cursorily, as Hephaestion was standing with a disappointed expression.

'I'm preparing some festivities, which are politically of the utmost importance,' said Alexander, who was walking in a harassed fashion to and fro. Suddenly he stopped, with his hand on his forehead, as though overtired: 'Excuse me, if I talk to you of public matters, instead of our personal concerns, which perhaps interest you more.' He hesitated, but went on immediately:

'Ten thousand Greek and Macedonian soldiers are to marry ten thousand Persian women. I'll pay a dowry for each of them, and one silver talent in addition. I will provide an unusual celebration for the young couples, for on the same day I will also get married again, and in a more appropriate manner than the first time.'

Hephaestion looked up with his eyes completely full of dark astonishment. In the middle of the room his king was shouting boastfully, with a raised arm:

'Her Highness, Princess Statira, oldest daughter of the Great King and Achaemenid, Darius Codomannus, is already on her way from Babylon. With her is her younger sister, Princess Drypetis, who I thought of for you.'

He grasped the shoulder of his friend, who turned away hurt however.

'Leave me out of the affair!' he pleaded, in a warning and imploring way.

Only now did he come to hear Alexander's new voice, which bellowed out, admittedly not with enthusiasm as in battle, but rather, harshly, cutting and in anger. 'Have you forgotten everything then?' he shouted at him, his brow sunk down in anger. And then, stretching up tyrannically, with a gesture which was both imperious but which also slipped vaguely away:

'*The wedding!!* The goal –'

He let his arm sink down, and stood there with his hands hanging down heavily like someone ashamed or who has had an accident. For a moment Hephaestion thought: 'Someone who's organising a wedding doesn't look like that.' But he regretted the thought at once.

Meanwhile Alexander had taken refuge in a rasping military tone: 'I am not used to discussing my orders.' Hephaestion heard this strange voice, which reminded him of that of Philip, saying, 'You are provisionally dismissed.'

Hephaestion, already at the door, bowed silently. In despair, his eyes, which were swimming with tears, showed him a distorted image of his friend.

At the top of the dining table the king sits on his throne next to his veiled bride, who, above the veils worked with gold and silver, reveals the eyes of a sadly surprised animal. The next couple are Hephaestion and his Drypetis, who gazes with the same solemn lack of comprehension as her sister; then, in a long row, all dressed-up, come all the other Macedonians – Greek generals, princes and officials with their Asiatic ladies. Although the jesters burped, hopped and tumbled around, and the slaves hurried diligently to and fro with the wines and delicious foods, the mood did not become really lively. Toasts and humorous speeches seemed disturbing and uncalled-for in the often painful silence. Nobody could laugh at the conjurors or only in a way that did not seem quite natural. The men ate and drank a lot, in order not to have to talk with their new spouses, whose names they hardly knew. They had reached dessert; there were sugared locusts, dates, pears, pomegranates, and almond pastries.

Alexander could not stand the reproachful silence of Hephaestion and the dull gaze of the little wrapped-up princess. He leaped up and beckoned to Bagoas to follow him. He excused himself to Statira. She gave an empty ceremonial smile from under her delightful veil.

Outside the night was enticing with its smells and noise. There were only drunks around, and in between clicking, wailing and tootling sounds of music.

Alexander fled past squares, where snake charmers were showing off, and Greek storytellers were declaiming their great fairy tales. Brownish-coloured dancing women shook their well-trained bellies, and fat men drank to them, squatting on the ground and taking meat out of pans in fistfuls. Other soldiers forced themselves on other women, and the king hurried on, so as not to have to see, how the couples sank down, closely intertwined.

There was a huge sense of joy, for His Majesty had granted the troops the most substantial privileges: apart from the silver talent and the dowry every young married man had his debts paid, which he had accumulated throughout the whole campaign, if he just presented his bill. The whole day the tables had been set up in empty squares, from where you could collect your gold pieces. The evening followed with a big public festival and enormous feasting, and which was to end with the wedding night of the ten thousand. For the following days tragic and light-hearted theatre productions were planned; it was said that more troops had arrived from Athens.

Alexander rushed past boozing, bawling groups to reach open country; he was followed by a skilful shadow, the hermaphrodite. They were already stumbling frequently over bodies, which were rolling about on the ground, intertwined with each other and groaning. The king ran, not understanding his own fear. It seemed to him that there was no more escape, for the further they came out into the open, the more frequently there were bodies lying on top of each other. So he stopped, felt that he had to sink down, closed his eyes and sniffed.

He sniffed in the air, which seemed to be saturated with smells of many different kinds. It smelled of wine, fried fish, the juices of ripe and burst fruits; and also of sweat, blood and vomit; but also of something else, which Alexander endeavoured to guess through sniffing it.

He drew Bagoas closer to him: '*What does it smell of?*' And at the same time he closed his eyes like someone stunned. The cool and obliging creature at his side snuggled up to him more tenderly. 'I'm afraid,' whispered the indefatigable Alexander. 'It was never as bad as this on the battlefield. Twenty thousand people mating in the open air – it smells – ' He sniffed again, with an expression on his face, as when yielding to a vice, which you know does not agree with you at all. 'Don't you see, little

Bagoas, how the women open their voracious mouths wide when they kiss? How they let their fat tongues loll around? How the men grab them by the hair? It's horrible, how they bash them around – '

The whole country was covered with stinking, jerking bodies, as though it were leprosy. They hung from the trees, climbed about on rocks, strutted about and showed impudently what they had, both thighs and bellies. Alexander, with the whole force of his body supported on the supple child, whispered with lips which became sluggish with horror: 'Tonight ten thousand new human beings are being produced – and it will go on.'

Finally he threw himself down, and pulled the obedient child down with him onto the ground.

2

In the city of Opis the great army route divides westward and eastward, to the West and to Media. On the march of the great army from Susa towards Babylon a period of rest for several days in Opis was ordered, and the camp was set up in front of the city, while Alexander with his circle moved into the royal castle. This circumstance aggravated the bad mood, which had been felt in the army for months. They could not forget the horrible things they had suffered in the desert of Gedrosia: no joyful festival could erase the memory. The behaviour of the king hurt them, and they considered it to be ungrateful. They had got used to his wearing Persian clothing... and the oriental ceremonial, which he had introduced. But it still hurt them that he was becoming more and more friendly with Asiatic dignitaries and officers, and cooler and cooler towards the Macedonians.

'He's tired of us,' they grumbled, when they sat together around the fire in the evenings. 'Since he's had his Persian princess, he feels that he himself is like an Achaemenid. He is ungrateful, as his father was, who always loved Athens more than Macedonia. This one loves Asia more than Macedonia and Athens together. He wears the embroidered monkey's costume and sleeps with the Babylonian hermaphrodite. Us he just chucks away when he has used us.' They grumbled bitterly into their beards. When Alexander summoned them all to a great gathering, they all felt themselves to be in a wilful mood. They muttered rebelliously, when Alexander stepped out onto the platform in his magnificent robes surrounded by Persian military figures.

On the platform he sensed the defensiveness which emanated from them. Nevertheless he spoke with a cool kindness, in which there was a trace of pride. He had even a slight nasal quality. 'My dear friends,' he said smiling strangely, 'what I have to tell you is something really pleasant. I know that many of you are tired, exhausted and worn out.' Those down below muttered self-pityingly, and their strange lord above them smiled the more distantly. 'I used to settle the veterans and those incapable of fighting in the newly founded cities. For you, dear friends, things will be better! I know that you yearn to be nowhere so much as at home. My friends, my veterans, you shall see Macedonia again!' He spread out his arms theatrically, and his voice had an unnatural tremolo in it. 'In thanks for all that you have done and suffered, I release you all, so that you can go home, where it will be really great for you!'

At this they started to shout. He persisted still with this emotionally patronising gesture, but those below were already shouting with rage. For a few seconds he listened, not dismayed but astonished, to their accusations and curses. 'Now we know you. We've just been waiting for this! He sends us home, after he has sucked all the strength out of us! What did we shed blood for?' they asked threateningly. 'So that you can vainly put on airs, you Persian peacock! And chuck us away! What kind of work can we do, as you've left us no strength? Eh? Eh?' they asked again and again, shaking their beards furiously, and their fists, which they claimed had lost their strength.

Into their dull disorganised noise Alexander's voice, jangling with anger, struck like lightning. 'Quiet!' he bellowed, but they did not stay quiet. Then he leaped into their midst.

Unarmed he sprang from his platform. Around him a circle opened shyly: his eyes made them afraid. He grabbed hold of some of them, who had been especially vocal. 'He'll be executed! Him, him and him!' he snorted, shaking each of them. Now they were all silent. He, already back on his platform, stretched out his arm, threw his head right back, and shouted out across them.

None of them had heard him speak like that, and the Macedonian army sank their brows at the impact of his monstrous speech, as a man does in the face of a whirling storm. In a voice, which was rejoicing with pride, he related to them the incomparable story of his life. What spectacle had they taken part in? For what purpose had they been allowed to serve as a tool, even if only an imperfect one, a weak one? 'I have conquered the world,' he shouted with joy, so that they ducked down even more frightened. 'You, my creatures, dare to oppose me?!'

He reminded them about what they had been. His father had turned them from ragged shepherds into plain soldiers, but he had turned them from plain soldiers into the lords of continents. 'What have I been fighting for, if not for you?' he asserted suddenly, when his pride had exhausted itself. *They* were the ones who profited from his conquests; while *he* only had the nerve-racking worry about his neighbour. They slept better than he, they enjoyed women, and they ate with more pleasure. He did everything for them; and how did they thank him for it? 'Let the man come and show himself to me,' he demanded, almost weeping, 'who has more wounds to show than his king! I have been wounded by the projectiles of all peoples!' He tore open his luxurious garment so that they could see his chest covered with wounds.

As he had softened them, he became aggressive again. That's the way it was, and now they knew what they had done to him. 'I have loved you like my own son!' he cried, with his arms spread wide again; they were all already sobbing anyway. 'Those of you, who have become incapable of fighting while serving me, I wanted to send covered with honours back home, which I thought you loved and yearned for. Now all of you go! All of you, all of you! – *You are dismissed!*' he shouted, stamping his feet. 'Out of my sight! You are no longer Alexander's soldiers!'

As he was already turning to go, he scoffed at them backward over his shoulder, having gathered up his train: 'Just boast at home, that you have left your king in distant lands! It will doubtless be sufficient honour for you, if I surround myself with an Asiatic bodyguard, Persian officers, from now on. The history of the world will praise you for it!'

He hurried away, his cloak gathered up violently, a vein swollen with anger on his forehead. A few officers followed him in dismay. He shut himself up in his small chamber and gave an unconditional order that no one was to be allowed in.

Behind him everyone was at a loss. The army which had conquered India, Persia and Egypt was in panic. Speakers gesticulated from small rostra, but nobody listened to them. One advised them to go home as a private group; another that they should ask the hurt king's forgiveness; a third suggested they should attack Alexander as an enemy in his castle, defeat him, and make him their prisoner.

In the meantime news came from the king's chamber which was alarming. Alexander dictated to Bagoas his merciless orders, which were to be passed on to the army and the generals.

The army was informed, that they were to consider themselves as definitely dismissed. If they did not clear out of their quarters within forty-eight hours, the king would proceed against them with Persian troops. Orders were given for the urgent formation of an Asiatic bodyguard for the personal protection of His Majesty, and all honorary posts were to be filled by Persians, as were the posts of generals, who provided the most intimate service for the monarch, were called 'the king's relatives' and enjoyed the privilege of kissing the man who wore the crown.

No Greek-speaker was allowed into the royal apartments, not even Hephaestion; the Persian dignitaries thronged the anteroom. The king received some of them in his chamber, which he did not leave for a second. He ran to and fro issuing dictations, and little Bagoas could not scribble quickly enough. His face had the rigid seriousness of a mask: it seemed inaccessible to any human feeling any more.

It was announced that Hephaestion had been already waiting for several hours. He shook his head and rejected him. Then suddenly Hephaestion was standing in front of him, without having been given permission to enter.

Alexander looked him up and down, strangely astonished. Hephaestion cried out in a worried and warning voice: 'Alexander! The army is weeping!' Tears could be seen flowing down his face. 'They have all gathered in front of your castle! They are all weeping. They ask for forgiveness!' Here he sobbed so heavily that he had to turn away, with the tears glistening on his cheeks. Alexander stood still, and stared at him, with his hands resting on his back, and with an angry lowered brow. 'What does my forgiveness concern them?' he scoffed, laughing at the weeping man to his face. 'They're afraid that they won't find anything more to eat tomorrow.'

That was too much for Hephaestion. Now he raised his head imploringly and horrified: 'It's sinful, what you do, Alexander! They have served you faithfully and made you what you are. You cannot leave them here!' He sobbed again, so that he had to turn away.

Alexander stared at the weeping man with his black gaze which, below his furious brow, offered no comfort. As he began to wander around again, he said curtly, through his teeth: 'I must reserve myself the right to all my decisions. Please leave me alone.'

His soldiers had to weep for twenty four hours. They whined in front of the gate of his palace. They had thrown down their weapons, and were beating their bared breasts in misery. Their remorse made them ready to do anything: 'We'll stay with you without pay, Alexander! We'll go wherever you send us! Just let us remain your soldiers! What can we do without you? Let us be your bodyguards again!' they implored him and lamented in a heartbreaking way. 'Allow us also to kiss you!'

They wailed, the way a lover does for a desired woman. To be allowed to kiss him, seemed to be the highest of all joys conceivable. They kneeled down, scattered dust in their beards, on their heads and hairy chests. They did this for a night; and the following day, as well as the second night found them doing the same thing.

Then the palace gate opened up before them from within, and in the middle of the brightness stood Alexander. He was alone, without weapons, and like a messenger of peace he wore a white garment. He sent a smile of blessing over them: they did not notice that his smile was cold and overtired, that his gesture was calculated and artificial. They just cheered. They wept again, but with joy. They had never been so blissful after any victory. They loved Alexander, and had never loved him so much. Didn't he notice it? Didn't it give him a warmer feeling? He seemed to be freezing, though encircled by the deep warmth. They called him their leader, their young god. They surrounded him, and now carried him on their shoulders.

At the reconciliation dinner which he gave them, he allowed those sitting close to him to kiss him. They did it in a rather embarrassed, complicated and detailed way. When they laid their rough cheeks against his softer ones, he was seen to be tickled and to laugh fleetingly. After each of these little moments of laughter he closed his eyes for a second, as after a hastily enjoyed pleasure.

Politically nothing had been changed by the whole moving and disturbing incident. The veterans were sent home, and they were given Craterus as their leader. It was said that the general was to stay in Pella as Regent of the Empire, while Antipatros was ordered to Babylon with new troops.

The Persian officers stayed in their new honorary posts, which had been granted to them at first provisionally during the insurrection.

Both the new laws, which Alexander sent out to Greece, aroused general dismay.

He claimed that he should be personally honoured as a divinity among the Greeks as well. At the same time he antagonised the nation which he forced such humiliation upon; he did not even show consideration for the apparent freedom which he had left them. He demanded that the Greek cities allow those banned for political reasons to return, and accept them again as citizens among them. The king's envoy, Nicanor of Stagira proclaimed both laws to the assembled peoples of Greece at the festival of the Olympiad. He was answered by an icy silence.

Who was it sitting there on a throne in Asia, who called himself the Son of Zeus and dared to give them such orders? Were they not, today as ever, the free people of this Earth? Had they not beaten Xerxes?

Almost all the men hated him. But many a woman, and many a boy began to love him. Many dreamed about him.

Who was sitting there on the throne in Babylon? The envoy of the divinity, the sevenfold beloved son of Zeus-Ammon-Ré, who had been sent to bring salvation to humanity. He wore the silver cloak with the great train, and the royally adjusted hat, below which his face gleamed mildly. To fall down before him was bliss, for he brought good fortune. He fulfilled truly what had been promised: the Golden Age came about, in which predatory animals became gentle.

They dreamed of him as the Greek-Asiatic deity, with the athletic body of youths whom they loved, glittering in the mysteriously consecrated make-up of Egypt, Persia and India. He was called: Hermes-Osiris, Apollo-Tammuz; his brilliant voice came across the continents in giant vibrations.

'I rule the seas and the mainlands, the islands, rivers and mountains. I govern the realm of this Earth, so that there will be happiness and so that the promise will be fulfilled.

'I am the Son of God and the Beloved of Mankind.

'I am the bridegroom.' Thus his voice rejoiced across the lands, of which he was the worshipped lord.

3

Eumenes of Cardia was by far the most unpopular of the king's entourage. He did not seem to be even respected, although it was known that he was indispensable to Alexander as a secretary. The way he squinted and smirked was found to be generally repulsive. He was impudent and at the same time humble, and this was the very mixture which was least liked.

Alexander also found him unpleasant, but on the other hand he was useful. No one else had a memory like his. Eumenes noticed everything and knew how to remind you of it at the right moment. It is true that this flattering, hand-rubbing, stooping being got on your nerves, but sometimes he was amusing, for this inferior human being could make up droll and sly expressions of devotion. Also you could treat him badly, which was very useful, without a murmur of complaint from him. In India, to punish him for his excessive meanness, the king had allowed himself to play quite a serious joke on him.

At that time the fellow had behaved in a specially unpleasant way. Although everyone knew exactly how well off he was, he had, when the king himself was collecting from his leaders for the construction of the river fleet, given not more than a hundred talents and in addition remarked solemnly: that he was not at all blessed with the spoils of good fortune.

He should not have allowed himself to be so shameless. For the king himself it was also going too far. They thought up a cruel way of making a fool of him: at night his tent was set on fire, and in fact on Alexander's orders, so that the whole camp would have the fun of seeing the miser ducking out into the open air with his treasures, which he had withheld from the goal of providing something of benefit to all. The affair worked out rather badly, not only because the harebrained gentleman from Cardia himself was almost burnt in the process – that would have meant just one more bit of fun for the army – but because various chancery and state documents were lost through this, which could only be acquired again with great difficulty. Still, for all the enemies of Eumenes it was a nice triumph, that they found in the heap of rubble, which was the remains of his tent, more than a thousand talents in molten gold and silver.

Annoyingly even this affair could not break him. The king, who for some reason seemed to need him, kept him close at hand.

No one would have considered it possible that it would come to a serious argument between Hephaestion and this worthless old uncle. Nevertheless it came about.

On some occasion or other Hephaestion had received a gift from the king, a necklace, which was certainly expensive, but had been selected without love. Alexander's friend, who was used to more intimate gifts, was not especially pleased by the rather tasteless object, but he still wore it, if only not to hurt the giver. It was this necklace that Eumenes took as the occasion for scolding him.

That's the way things were: the favourites received golden jewellery, while faithful workers had to be satisfied with meagre rewards. Why were they slaving away? So that the favourites could live in splendour and joy; the others, however able they might be, were neglected, ugly and small.

It seemed that long hidden jealousy was feeling that the time had come to reveal itself. Hephaestion lowered his eyelids in disgust at this outburst of a mean temperament. But the other man went on grumbling. Repeatedly he asked what certain lords had achieved, with more and more forceful emphasis, as though he was really and absolutely demanding an answer.

As the scene took place in the anteroom of the king, Hephaestion still said nothing in reply. He just went pale, because he was thinking: how secure this creature must feel himself to be, as he dares to make such a noise in close proximity to Alexander, and to make such a noise against *me*, against *me*.

All the while the scribe was yelping in a voice, which became grotesquely clouded with anger. 'As for you, my fine Lord Hephaestion, what have you achieved? If you won't say it, *I'll* say it. You have slept with the king, that's what you've achieved.'

As Hephaestion still stood there as if turned to stone, Eumenes added, revealing yellowish teeth as he grinned: 'Admittedly others have done that too. Little Bagoas for example.'

Finally he felt the other's fist in his face. Hephaestion struck out at him, in the mouth, and on his nose, from which, giving him a wretched appearance, bright red blood shot out. And only when Alexander's voice came from the doorway, did he stop hitting. The king shouted 'Break it up!' grasping both of them by the shoulder. Hephaestion had never been handled by him so roughly before.

Eumenes was still whining and rubbing his smashed face, while Hephaestion was looking in disgust at his hands, which were bloody. Alexander asked brusquely what had happened. As Hephaestion remained haughtily silent, the whimpering secretary lied, saying that he had envied the favoured general his marvellously beautiful chain, and that the other had immediately become rough with him. 'But that's what the noble officers are like,' sobbed the beaten man, from whose nostrils blood was still running. 'And my Lord Hephaestion is the most brutal of all.'

Alexander said to Eumenes with a cutting friendliness: 'Calm down, my dear friend, you'll get the same chain as the general. You have richly deserved it.' While the man so honoured was already sobbing, bent over the royal hands, Alexander remarked further, turning halfway towards Hephaestion, but avoiding the look of dark horror, which the friend was directing at him: 'I will not tolerate, by the way, your starting a fight with my official.' He jerked his head and went quickly away. The scribe followed him subserviently.

Hephaestion, who tried to hold the king back, with a gesture which expressed the fact that he was still completely bewildered, let his hand drop down. At the same time, first his face dropped, and then the upper part of his body, as though becoming suddenly weak.

This incident occurred a few days' journey before the arrival of the army at the royal camp in Ecbatana.

Hephaestion asked to be excused from attending the official festivals in Ecbatana; Alexander attended them mostly in the company of little Bagoas. It was reported later by some of the dinner guests that they were orgies of luxurious exuberance, above all the great dinner of the fat satrap Atropates went down in history woven with legends. At this most lavish feast Alexander showed himself to be in the wildest high spirits, drinking an enormous amount, but also in another respect: every half an hour he withdrew with Bagoas or some other child in make-up into the back rooms. It was by chance on this evening, that the doctors began to take seriously Hephaestion's inexplicable illness. The fever did not get better, but, on the contrary, the patient was almost always to be found unconscious, with agonising fantasies.

The king was informed in the proper way about the general's condition, when he returned home towards morning from the satrap's amusing event. The heavily drunken man babbled and waved them aside. Glaucias, the conscientious and faithful doctor, withdrew in dismay from the reeling Alexander.

The next morning the king paid visits, first to a few of the Persian leaders, and then also to his suffering friend. As on this day the Dionysian celebrations began with great sacrificial ceremonies, he could not stay longer than a few minutes. Hephaestion did not recognise him. The gaze of the sick man, in which there seemed to be nothing left but great fear, did stray across him but without seeing him. Thus Alexander was glad to be able to go again; he promised the doctor Glaucias cursorily some reward for his devoted services and hurried to reach the festival procession, where the people demanded his presence.

He showed the people, who were cheering mechanically, his dead smile, and his grand gesture, which had become rigid. The women could detect that he had become fatter; but he had also become more dignified. His wider eyes below the high-arched brows lacked the lustre which had been capable of conquest. But still today they could exert mastery and enchant with a dead and mysterious forcefulness. They were set in deeper shadows, the women found, which shaded over from crimson into a blackish colour. Above all his mouth seemed to be distorted. How long ago was it when this mouth was childlike. Now it hung bluish and limp, and also looked greedy. Many found this mouth repulsive, but others certainly found it especially charming.

Countless women, who stood as a guard of honour, to see their foreign king pass by, discussed together all the details of his worn out face. One woman asked her neighbour: 'What will mother say, if he goes back to Macedonia? He left her a fresh radiant man, but he returns a tired and ruined one.' After that some of them laughed, but others kept silent.

In his carriage drawn by white beasts, Alexander, in his splendid tight-fitting costume and with the tiara above his brow, projected his dead smile constantly out over the crowd.

The sacrifices were followed by the great contests and theatre performances, and Alexander in his adornments was absent from none of them. His face, framed rigidly with precious stones, appeared again and again, majestic and fixed, above the people, whenever they had gathered together to shout and cheer. And next to him was the painted, shy grimace of the sweet hermaphrodite, who, on the streets, was already being called the 'queen'.

The rumour that Hephaestion was ill disappeared. Would the king have appeared otherwise? He would have been sitting at his bedside, if the friend was suffering, instead of appearing in the royal box with the hermaphrodite. Alexander distributed garlands of honour, bowed, smiled, and thanked people. In the evening, he boozed with the princes and generals, tarts, actors, up-and-coming merchants, in the villas of the rich or in his own palace.

It was the last day of the Dionysian festivities, during the contest between the adolescent boys, when the doctor Glaucias visited the king in the stadium. The doctor was seen to whisper to Alexander with a worried look, and the latter was seen to wave him aside irritatedly, his eyes directed with a dead desire at the wrestling lads. The grey-haired man withdrew shaking his head, only to reappear after an hour. He whispered in a more earnest way, which was seen by all the people. Finally the king got up.

He arrived too late. Hephaestion's gentle patient eyes had already closed. From the curtained room which the king entered, there withdrew shyly weeping women and troubled men. After such a long time Alexander found himself alone again with his Hephaestion.

Only Alexander revealed himself to be changed, for Hephaestion looked as he always did, and perhaps even more beautiful. His peaceful face seemed to shine in gleaming whiteness, and a comforting brightness emanated from his hands. Why had Alexander forgotten for so long how kind this friend was, how pleasant, how mild? Finally he dared to speak to him again.

He kneeled beside his bed; in a trembling voice he asked his beloved: 'That stupid business with Eumenes recently, you've forgotten it, haven't you? Haven't you?' He asked again as his friend did not answer.

Only when Hephaestion remained silent at the king's more and more urgent questions, did he begin finally to understand. There occurred an enormous silence. Desolation grew and swallowed every sound, every colour, devoured all sense of life, and even tears were not allowed to flow in it. The king sat in the middle of a solitude which enclosed him like a wall.

To break it apart he began to scream. He threw up his arms and screamed, screamed, screamed. A horde of courtesans came, military men, and doctors bent down busily. Ladies pressed little cloths to their faces. Having thrown himself over the corpse, the king roared, foaming at his wide open mouth. They wanted to hold him, but he struck about himself, and his eyes were bloody.

No mortal should be heard to scream out like that. In that scream there was no mourning, no sound of human pain; rather there was a loneliness, a despair, the like of which is never given to *us*, and which only the despairing gods know.

Over the dead face, which had become beautifully calm, of his peaceful lover, the tragic mask of his distorted face swayed, with its gaping mouth and eyes from which blood flowed instead of tears. One night passed, then the day, then one more night, and then another day. The miserable man did not sleep, ate nothing and drank nothing. He did not close his eyes, which had not seen anything for a long time already. His screaming became a whimper, his whimper a wheezing, but his disconsolate hands still moved with horrible stubbornness over the face, hair, hands and body of the dead man.

The words of consolation of his confidants, who dared to come near him, did not seem to be able to get through to him. People were already whispering to each other that he had lost his reason; nothing reached him any more, nothing concerned him any more. There was nothing left for him to do, but stare his fate, which had fulfilled itself, in the eyes.

After three days and three nights his strength weakened and finally he was found to be sleeping. So they lifted him carefully from the corpse, over which he still lay stretched out, and put him in his own bed. He slept for forty-eight hours.

When he awoke again, he bore a changed expression. He did not wail any more, but gave orders. It was as though he had taken his revenge on the whole of humanity for Hephaestion's death. His orders were curt, terrible and radical.

The most horrible thing was: Doctor Glaucias was to be nailed onto a cross. The king did not even allow the man who was pleading for mercy into his presence; his life, he explained briefly, was as good as over, as he had not been able to save that of the favourite of the gods. In all the temples the magi had to extinguish all the fires, which was no different than if the monarch himself had died. Hephaestion could only be talked of as though he were a demigod. The king let it be known that this was at the pain of death! Dancing and singing were forbidden for weeks in the whole world empire, from Macedonia to India. The walls of the surrounding fortresses were razed to the ground, the donkeys were shorn, the tails of the horses were docked.

The king had the exact keeping of all the decrees supervised with inexorable strictness: anyone who was found to be singing was tortured. Meanwhile he himself designed with his architects the funeral pyre which was to be erected for Hephaestion in Babylon. A hundred thousand talents were to be used for its decorations; and the same amount for funeral festivities, the contests and ceremonies. General Perdiccas was entrusted with leading the procession for the corpse.

With the greater part of the enemy Alexander took the route to Babylon across the mountains, where the Cossaeans lived. He had decided to chastise this mountain people, who it was true were refractory but also harmless, as an example. All men capable of bearing weapons were murdered, and the women, children, and old men sold into slavery.

4

Alexander became acquainted with a new feeling: fear.

Being used to experiencing every adventure to the outermost boundary of the possible, he gave himself over to this one as to intoxication. The world around him changed in an uncanny way. From every tree, every human face, from the whole horribly distorted landscape, the certainty of death grinned at him, the assurance, that everything had been in vain; his great experiment had failed.

Gloomy prophecies, which he would at other times have overlooked contemptuously or reinterpreted politically, confused and horrified him. The same Initiated One who had also known of Hephaestion's death in advance, now asserted that that of the king was near. He wrote about it to one of the officers, who had made enquiries: the liver of the sacrificed animal had lacked a lobe.

It was all horrible, but the most horrible thing was that he had to go to Babylon. Everywhere the clouds drifted along only in order to ridicule him, and everywhere water was his enemy, as were the rough earth, the moving foliage, and the whole of Nature, which had rebelled against him; but in Babylon all danger had become concentrated inescapably: here they were lurking in the grimaces of the bearded bulls with men's heads, in the reflective depths of the black walls and in the clever, mysterious eyes of the magi.

In addition there came the warning from the Chaldaeans before the entry. This was certainly politically suspect. The old men might well have an interest in postponing the arrival of the monarch, if not of preventing it; for how had they administered the reserves of money, which had been entrusted to them for the renovation of the Bel-Marduk Temple? Alexander tried to treat them in a cool and haughty way, when they came riding by on their white little asses with red-coloured ears and tails to let him know: it was not recommended that he enter Babylon, for the gods did not wish to see him. The king shrugged his shoulders, and he informed the old men: the entry had already been decided. Then they in their turn added: so would he *not* choose the eastern entrance at least, which was especially dangerous. He countered defiantly, that he would choose the entrance, which was in the most practical situation.

The answer sounded confident and impudent; but the heart of the one who had dictated it trembled with a fear, which it did not understand. The little old men rode away shaking their heads. Incidentally they were found murdered on the very same day, to the panic-stricken terror of the whole population. Alexander had the perpetrators of the bloody deed hotly pursued, but they had no success in throwing light on it.

Thus the reception being prepared for him was a cool one: they attributed the guilt to Alexander for the bloody deed, which must have harmed the standing of the whole city with the gods.

At the entrance to the palace, Roxane was waiting for him, sterner and tenser than ever, surrounded by her armoured ladies, and fantastically made-up in a way she had not been seen since the wedding: with her hair powdered a golden-green, a longish precious stone of a fierce violet colour on her forehead, and a close-fitting dress covered with silvery scales jangling with jewels, snake belts and hard and glinting decorations. She stretched her hand towards him; as he kissed her, she looked past him with icy coldness. He said shyly: 'I am glad to see you again.' She replied sharply: 'I too, my dear, am glad. How is Princess Statira?'

Her imprudence made him speechless. She used this silence to ask him with icy kindness: 'And how is your friend Hephaestion?' As he remained reproachfully silent, and did not know where he should look, for tears rose to his eyes, she remembered and said more explicitly, with a sparkle in her eyes: 'Oh of course, he died.'

Inside delegations were waiting, and during all of the following days deputations announced themselves, and people who were complaining about something or wanted to offer congratulations on something, who brought gifts or expected them. Envoys appeared from Hellenic lands and also from Macedonia. Some complained about Olympias, the others about Antipatros. They were constantly at loggerheads: it was hell at court. His mother, the Queen, interfered in each and every matter; she wanted nothing the way the Regent of the Empire wanted it. In the process she referred to the will of her son, from whom she pretended to have secret orders. Antipatros for his part, a pedantic and stubborn old man, claimed to be still receiving instructions on all matters from Philip.

Envoys came from the Etruscans, the Carthaginians, the Libyans, the Iberians, the European Cythians, the Celts, the Ethiopians and also from the Italian peoples. All brought the compliments of their lords, and many also gifts: golden wreaths, splendid clothes, tamed predatory animals, baskets full of delicious things. The people who brought them touched the floor in front of the throne of His Majesty with their brows and said, that he was the Greatest of all Mortals, the Son of the Deity, Ruler of the World. Under the baldachin he thanked them with a proud nod.

As long as the envoys were with him, he remained rigidly dignified. The broad painted face, in which the eyes seemed to be almost closed beneath the dark lids, appeared to be flabby and tired, but of an unassailable and tyrannical self-confidence.

In reality there was nothing else behind this mask than fear. Hardly had the envoys, delegations and petitioners left him alone, than he summoned the magi, to ask them about the results of the many sacrifices.

The future could be read from *everything*, if one only knew the right methods. Everything became meaningful, and from everything the secret intention of the deities could be guessed and established: from the flight of the birds, above all from storks; from the way the clouds drifted, the fluctuations of fog, the rays from diamonds, from insides of many flowers, and especially from dreams. The king made a note of the troubled visions of his nights with anxious care. If the dream had had something to do with Hephaestion, then he became happy; then things could turn out well.

Everything *had* to turn out well, for his plans were enormous. The whole world was not yet conquered by a long way. It must however be conquered completely, for the main thing was to know everything. Only he who has conquered everything, knows everything.

The most important plan was to sail round Arabia. The quarrelsome coastal peoples of the enormous peninsula had to be conquered, and the country integrated into the world empire.

In Arabia there were said to be, according to reports which had come to him, exquisite and rare spices. Myrrh and incense, spikenard and cinnamon. As far as gods were concerned, only two were worshipped there, Uranus and Dionysus, and the latter expressly because of his journey to India, which was remembered as being glorious. Alexander, who had gone further than Dionysus, declared concisely to some Arabian envoys: that he considered it suitable for him to be worshipped as the third Arabian deity.

He worked feverishly, had discussions with ship designers, military men and scholars. The commission for the fleet which was to be newly built was given to Phoenicia. Everyone, who could bring forward new information on the conditions and state of affairs in the country of Arabia, was received by Alexander, listened to and rewarded.

In the meantime the land army also had to be enlarged, for it was necessary to conduct war against various peoples, who were definitely too high-handed. In Italy there seemed to be opponents of the world monarchy: they would have to be subdued. Above all however Carthage, which was the only financial power of the inhabited world which was worth considering besides his own. As he had succeeded in taking Carthage's fat mother city Tyre, so the puffed-up daughter would also have to fall.

He sat amidst his colossal plans and calculations. At night he hardly slept, for he worked uninterruptedly, and in between he made sacrifices and received fortune-tellers. He did not dare to go out, for he was afraid of the sweetish stench of the alleys, which had already exhausted him the last time; but he was also afraid of being murdered.

Towards morning he had Bagoas give him the sleeping draught that only the cunning hermaphrodite could prepare. When the king was falling asleep Bagoas had to lie next to him, stroke him, calm him, caress him, and kiss him on the ear and brow. As he was falling asleep, Alexander thought, as the practised hands of this creature brought him relief:

So this is the last person who is left for me. The last one then.

After weeks of fanatical and embittered work he was overcome with unrest, which drove him away from his papers. Suddenly he could not bear the air of Babylon any more. 'It's completely poisonous,' he explained with sudden hysterical aversion.

As the fleet for the great Arabian enterprise was not yet ready, he decided to undertake a little expedition down the Euphrates to the Pallacopas Canal, which he had been told had to be reconstructed.

The stagnant water stank and was foul, and the officers who were accompanying him felt ill. Alexander also seemed to have a fever, but he insisted on travelling onto the lakes which were connected to the canal and led as far as Arabia. Here he suddenly had the idea of founding a city, the thirty-seventh Alexandria. He settled it with Greek soldiers. 'So I've also got to know this area,' he declared with agonising satisfaction, when they started the return journey. No other landscape had been so ugly. The water of the canal gleamed an oily-violet colour, and on its unsavoury smooth surface swam filth, dead animals, and all kinds of green-ish mud. And what a sulphurous dead sky hung over them. It was oppressively sultry, without sunlight. If only a storm would come! But the wind, which passed over them, was not refreshing, for it smelled bad and was hot.

It was also malicious, for Alexander, who was dreaming with a rigid overtired gaze, had his hat torn from his head, around which the diadem was laid. The hat sank down, and the diadem got caught in the branches of a clump of bushes, which hung over the water and was reflected.

To fetch it a zealous sailor tore the clothes from his body and leaped into the water, which did not look exactly enticing. He got hold of the gem, and in order not to lose it while swimming he laid it around his broad head. What he did meant the worst: the sign of royal majesty on the brow of a stranger and what was worse of an ordinary human being. He could not hear them shouting faintly on the ship. The poor fellow, who handed over the piece of jewellery grinning and with a clumsy bow, did not know what was happening to him, as they grabbed him from behind and bound him. The captain advised that he be killed. Alexander nodded. He looked away in disgust, when the execu-tioner's assistants seized him.

In Babylon festivities were awaiting him, which several great lords organised for Admiral Nearchus, whose departure for Arabia was imminent. Alexander had to take part, just out of politeness towards the admiral.

In the end he even enjoyed it.

From a smaller river fleet, which explored the mouth of the Euphrates, all kinds of amusing items of news had come in: they had discovered in the Persian Gulf, south of the mouth, two islands; both were small, thickly forested and inhabited by peaceful, brownish people, who served Artemis. One of them was called Icarus, and the other Tylus.

The news of this not exactly essential find seemed to infuriate the king oddly. 'So there are still islands, races, areas which I don't know,' he said in torment. Incidentally he had reports made to him on all details of the vegetation, water conditions and climate of both the islands.

At the banquets for guests, each of which superseded and was more abundant than the last, he was found to have an over-wrought cheerfulness, which sometimes, in a suddenly worrying way, went quiet. Just a few seconds ago he had laughed in a re-sounding way, and then suddenly he sat there sunk into himself, and his eyes seemed to be extinguished. During the last of these feasts which took place under the special patronage of Roxane, it proved to be necessary for Alexander to exchange at least a few official words with his wife.

'I hear that the Princess Statira is expecting a son from you,' said Roxane, who was serving him wine, with her horrible politeness.

Alexander, who did not know what to reply, took the goblet. While he was drinking, she observed him with a penetrating look.

During the day the king was very busy, as he had to view the newly enlisted troops. For hours he had the young men, who would fight and probably die for his fame, parade by him. '*For my predestined fame*,' he thought gloomily, while he was inspecting them.

They were strong young men of various races: Macedonians, Persians, Greeks, Egyptians, and also Indians; they had light and dark skins, smooth or frizzy hair, stocky or delicate legs; but all had the same shy and devout look for Alexander, in the humility of which there was also mixed horror. With this timorous and disinterested look one does not look at human beings, but idols, which are not alive, incapable of suffering or of joy, which are nothing but powerful.

On one of those mornings occurred something unsurpassably painful and awful, which more than all other bad omens put the king and his entourage into a state of fear bordering on panic.

In a pause between the reviews the king had gone with several officers to the pond in the park, to refresh themselves. He had left the royal cloak, the diadem and the decorated sword on the throne. When they came back, a stranger was sitting on his chair. They turned pale at this impudence, for he had also put on Alexander's cloak, and had his diadem on his head, and his sword in his lean fists.

They walked nearer and then they saw: he had goldish-brown absent-minded eyes, a wide oversensitive, and distorted mouth, which could do nothing but babble, and over the low angular brow hung tangled hair. It was Arrhidaeus, who it was believed had been lost.

In a voice which was hoarse Alexander bawled at him: 'What are you doing here?' The one on the throne scoffed, as though he had always been watching his brother, always seen him and wanted to ape him: 'I am the King of Asia.'

To the horrified officers he seemed really to be that; he was the distorted double of their king. They knocked him off the raised chair, but Alexander indicated by a wave that they should not beat him. He had become calm.

'It's the ghostly spirit that comes before the end,' he said quietly.

5

The river, the course of which they followed downstream, became more and more dangerous. Ten dusky rowers groaned away, but still they scarcely made any headway. Whirlpools and shallows, drifting wood, and also monsters caused them a lot of trouble. All kinds of swarming creatures rolled themselves up into ugly knots; Alexander stabbed at them from the prow of the ship with his lance. But next to them crocodiles were already raising their frightening heads.

It was the Euphrates which they were travelling up. They wanted to reach its source; but what were they seeking there? Alexander while he was fencing with the swarming creatures and evil spiked fish, thought about it, with his eyebrows drawn together in concentration.

With him in the boat were several friends, Hephaestion, Philotas, Clitus, and some boys; he recognised the blond youth. He missed the long-standing faithful men. Where, for example, was Parmenion?

Hardly had he thought about it – he was still brooding about the whereabouts of the old man – when before his very eyes Philotas dissolved into nothing with a sad little noise. He was gone, had vanished, complaining softly; immediately after him the blond youth faded away. Alexander could do nothing but just stare. Had the crocodiles and the scaly winged monsters which shook their swollen heads over the edge of the boat, swallowed them with their mysterious snapping?

Around them it became wilder and wilder, the rocky mountains made the river darker, and the current became stronger, and with it the groaning of the rowers. There had long ceased to be any trees and grass, and there was nothing but a fissured wasteland. Predatory birds circled in evil silence over the peaks, and in the abysses blackish little animals crept around, probably hyenas, as Alexander thought suspiciously.

Then it was the rowers, who disappeared with a more resentful than complaining grumble and groaning. Alexander, Hephaestion and Clitus jumped out onto the bank. They decided, without a word, that they would continue on foot.

While they cleared a way through thorn bushes and stone rubble, Alexander thought things over as hard as he could. He did not know what he was looking for. His face was bleeding, and the faces of both his last friends were also wounded. They did not complain and did not ask about the goal. Silent and bloody they followed their king.

It became more and more unbearable with the dragons; they had to hew their way right and left. There were some among them, which spewed fire, and others, whose breath had a poisonous stench. They howled from behind rocks, and sometimes you saw them fluttering in the air; many especially repulsive ones crept along the ground, where they left a slimy trail behind them.

The three silent heroes fought with sword and axe. If one of them was going to sink down, then the other held him, wordless, but comforting him and holding him firmly. – Alexander was thinking with extreme urgency: *Where am I taking them?*

They could still see between rocks the course of the Euphrates, which had become narrow. They noticed that they were almost at the source. To find this source seemed to them at first all that was important. Stooping down they looked for it. When they stood up they were standing before a high gleaming black wall which took up the whole width of the landscape and the end of which could not be seen.

Then Alexander knew what he had been seeking. He turned to make a solemn address.

He spoke as though to an army, with broad and emotionally masterful movements of his arms. Clitus and Hephaestion, with their bleeding faces lowered full of deep respect, listened to their commanding officer. He shouted 'Macedonians! Hellenes! It is an honour to you, my bands of men, that you have followed me this far. History will praise you, together with me! Even the fame of the great Cyrus will be as nothing next to ours. *No one* has come this far, none of all the kings of Asia or Europe.' He stretched himself in triumph, and there was a glow in his eyes. 'Do you know then, where we are? *We are at the gates of Paradise*. There remains only *one* battle which must be fought out, the final and last one, and then we have conquered *all*, then we will know *everything*. Hellenes! Macedonian men!' He stood with his arms stretched out against the impenetrable wall as though crucified, but rejoicing in it. 'The realm of happiness and ultimate bliss can only be realised on earth, when we have also conquered the hordes of heavenly armies, our most tenacious opponents, the angels. Only then, my friends, only *then*!' After a pause he added, and there came into his voice something like fear, exhaustion and lament: 'What have we achieved, if we have not established the realm of happiness and ultimate bliss on earth?'

This question, which contained the whole sorrow of his life, still rang in the ears of his friends; then he turned with his blazing sword towards the wall, which stared towards him mysteriously. He shouted, spurring them on; and Clitus and Hephaestion also rushed forward with their gleaming weapons.

Which enemy was it against this time? They could not see him, and he was probably for that very reason the most dangerous one. They shuddered, for an ice-cold wind blew at them. They felt themselves become rigid and they were already sinking down. Their swords, which had so often conquered, fell from their hands which had suddenly become weak. They were still mumbling; was it a farewell greeting to their king? Then their lips which looked white became silent.

When Alexander noticed that they were dead, he was frightened of his loneliness. For a moment it seemed to him that it would be unbearable. Behind the wall a metallic voice warned: 'For the battle with us you had to be completely alone, Alexander. Even the last ones had to leave you!' A double gate sprang open, and a brightness, which was blinding, poured towards the king, who was ready to fight. He rushed forward, his weapon stretched out again, so inexorably determined as never before to put everything at stake, absolutely everything.

He did not recognise the hordes of armies which came out of the open gate towards him. They seemed to be completely dissolved in light, and only he, and he alone, was in shadow. He felt a boundless fear before the wild brilliance, which moved valiantly towards him. But with incomparable defiance he hurried towards it – he, the isolated dark one, towards the vindictive mass of light – there he stood before the silvery armoured leader.

With a severe and delicate grace the head of this charming enemy rose above the glittering armour. He wore no helmet, but his hair hung free. Now Alexander noticed that he was also unarmed. He held only the palms of his hands defensively towards the attacking rebel. They were bare palms, very moving, the clear lines of which spoke an intelligent, insistently silent language.

Alexander was brandishing two arrows. The bright front of his opponents yielded before his lowered attack, as did the archangel with the defensive hands.

With a coarse roar Alexander stabbed both arrows into both of the hands held out by the beautiful figure.

The doctors could hardly hold him down, as he reared up so much. His fever rose, he screamed, was delirious and struck about him. The rumour that he had been poisoned spread around; many claimed it was by Roxane, who had poured him wine at the last banquet for guests.

The soldiers wanted to see him; they had to lie and console them. The army felt deceived; if he died, they regarded themselves as having been improperly cheated. Only on condition that he would live had they taken part in all this. What should they do in Babylon without him? They distrusted everyone, who offered themselves as prince to them, Perdiccas and Craterus for example. Mostly they still had sympathy for the poor Arrhidaeus, who had turned up again so inexplicably; he was all the same the half-brother of their king.

When Alexander was conscious, then they almost wished that he would have his feverish fantasies again; for it was a sad state of affairs. They should not talk to him about affairs of the empire; there was unrest in India; a new scandal in Athens, and administrative problems in Egypt, but he did not want to hear about anything. He waved it aside in disgust.

On the other hand he thought with a melancholy stubbornness about things, which everyone in his circle had forgotten. 'Do you remember?' he asked again and again. 'That time in Anchiale we found the saying on the statue of a king: "Anchiale and Tarsus were founded by Sardanapal in one day. But you, stranger, eat, drink and make love! Anything else that Man has is not worth talking about."' He turned away with closed eyes, when someone wanted to contradict him. 'Just let me sleep,' he said weakly. 'Liar – ' His entourage fell into a dismayed silence.

He thought much and with a shudder about the Babylonian fairy tale, which Clitus had told. 'It was generally a nasty fairy tale,' he asserted feverishly, 'but especially the end was so bad. They wanted us to believe that this Gilgamesh had a dialogue with his dead Enkidu. Gilgamesh, in his sinful curiosity, asked the spirit about the state of his fellow spirits, especially about the condition of those who have no carers – *but who has a carer?* – To this Enkidu replied with a hollow scornful voice: "He must eat the dregs left in the pot, and morsels thrown away in the street." You see, he does not say anything more. Dregs left in the pot – Oh, and who has a carer?' With such laments the king became delirious again. His gaze became confused and he slurred his speech.

With a slurred voice he spoke to Hephaestion: 'Hephaestion, tell me, Hephaestion, have I really been sent to deceive humanity and cause them pain? – And all of you? – Oh! – So what was the enormous effort for?' Having thrown himself back he wept, he spasmodically roared, and wailed, so that it became unbearable to listen to him. Friends and doctors left the bed on which he was suffering in cowardly flight.

Then finally the angel was allowed to enter.

He was still wearing the silver armour, but now it was decorated with flowers. In his bright hair he had blossoms, with a sweet scent. Both his hands, which Alexander's arrows had wounded, he had bound up, so that they appeared thick and clumsy. They were the only awkward and heavy things on his slim figure.

'I come as a messenger!' called the angel and stretched out his arm, as befits a messenger.

'So, are you Hermes?' asked the stubborn Alexander, although he knew that he was speaking nonsense.

'I do not know the name,' replied the angel brightly and in a very friendly way.

'Ammon?'

'You are being ridiculous, Alexander.'

As he raised his arm, his whole body jangled. The face, voice and hair seemed to be made of metal. Only his gaze and mouth were alive.

'Where are you to take me to?' groaned the king.

The angel stretched himself further. 'You'll burst apart,' shouted Alexander. 'Be careful, you'll burst apart with all the sparks!'

The angel made a cracking sound, roared and thundered. Alexander complained amid tears: 'I thought the last hour would be quiet and peaceful. It does become peaceful when you reach your goal. But you make such a noise that I'm going blind. – *Why does Clitus revenge himself in such an abominable way?*' he shouted suddenly, with his arms thrown up. 'Why, Clitus, do you go so far?' It was the first time that he dared to mention Clitus' name.

'You sacrificed another, not yourself,' said the angel reproachfully. 'You have essentially failed in your mission. So you should have realised that the hour of your death would be no festival of joy.'

'I'm afraid,' wailed the horribly doomed man. 'Already I can't see anything anymore, only circles and this frenzy – oh, how it's all spinning around in confusion – '

'The judgement does not come in a gentle way,' thundered the authorised representative, who was continuously changing, like a flame blown by the storm.

'All those I killed loved me,' the man on the bed defended himself.

And the angel, no longer wild but completely devout and composed and dignified: 'The next time you will have come so far, that you can die for those whom you love.'

The king went quiet. After a pause, which was a long one, he asked imploringly: 'Will I be allowed to establish the realm of bliss on earth?'

At this the angel wept. He let tears fall, which made his flowers wet and which also fell on his thickly bandaged hands. He leaned over the dying man, who believed he recognised him. He had already seen this face. Was it simply the blond youth? It was one of the countless such men who had died for him.

'Now you do not sparkle any more,' whispered Alexander and breathed more softly with gratitude. The angel, with the bright weeping face, said: 'Alexander, your young face is devastated. What ugly wrinkles. And your skin is completely slack.' Alexander, who was now also weeping, said: 'You are the first person, Angel, to weep over my slack skin – Am I nevertheless damned?' Instead of answering the envoy enquired: 'What was more difficult, victory or defeat?' 'I cannot distinguish the two of them any more,' Alexander reflected ruefully. 'For in the victories I could already sense defeat in advance.'

He remembered. Alexander, who had never yet related anything, started to tell his story. He lay his worn-out head in the open arms of the angel. The experienced being nodded. 'Just tell me,' he encouraged him gently.

So he started with the children's fairy tales of Olympias, which had prepared the mission. 'Without the mission everything would have been different,' he asserted, as though he wanted to excuse himself. The angel above him rocked his head understandingly, smiled and wept.

Only cursorily did Alexander mention Philip with his rough skills and his unpleasant death. But he described everything related to Clitus in great detail on the other hand; above all the night, on which the words 'You're disturbing me very much!' had been spoken. At this point he felt the tears of the angel flowing most plentifully. The flow became yet stronger, when Alexander came to the night with Hephaestion on the deck of the ship. 'No one will learn about that,' the dying man said proudly, with his face on the angel's breast. 'But even Hephaestion did not want me.' 'He did not dare to believe that you wanted him,' the angel corrected him, tenderly, but precisely. 'No one dared to believe it, no one,' complained the man confessing at his breast.

He continued to confess. About Roxane, who was not permitted to have a son by him, 'I could not grant her a wedding night,' he said disconsolately, but proudly. 'Neither to Clitus nor Hephaestion, and least of all to her. I killed the man I love, and my wife takes revenge for that.'

The angel, who understood him, stroked him more seriously and compassionately.

The whispered confession approached its end. Alexander's voice, which became weaker, confessed also the way he lost himself sinfully with the indecent Kandake, and later with Bagoas, the sweet hermaphrodite, and the faithless inexcusable estrangement from Hephaestion.

When he remained silent, the angel also did not say anything more. 'And finally I wounded your hands,' Alexander added after a long pause. He laid his mouth on the bandaged hands. 'Now you don't need to answer any more,' he still had breath enough to say. 'You spoke your judgement already before the confession. Oh, essentially, I failed – '

The knowledgeable angel had never heard these remorseful words from the mouth of any Greek. Thus he felt: this man is ready. And he promised him, more certainly than the first time: 'You will return, in a different manifestation.'

At this Alexander asked, as inquisitive as he had been as a boy by the well in the grove: 'To establish the empire, Angel? *To establish the empire?*'

But the contours of the angel with the wounded hands dissolved, and Alexander grasped at him in vain. The question, which he had put with the last feeling of passion in his life, remained unanswered in the air. And with it there remained the angel's promise, his blessing.

When the friends and servants returned, they found their king in a milder light. He lay there peacefully, calmed and pious. 'Carry me into the gardens,' he asked them. 'I want to see the soldiers once more.'

The soldiers wept, not so much because they noticed that he must die, but because they found him so moving and changed.

He lay covered up and weak in his chair, and he gave everyone a final smile. Some of them, who bowed to kiss his hand, he stroked gently over their brows and hair.

All passed by: the veterans, all those who had not been sent home, and also the young ones, whom he had only recently inspected. For all of them he had, beneath his tired lowered brow, a look that was growing blurred and distant, but was good. When he wanted to speak to them, his voice failed him. Smiling with difficulty he raised apologetically the hand which he had only ever raised to give orders.

Behind him the generals exchanged worried looks. The troops were still listening to hear if any words came. But Alexander's mouth was silent.

Notes

1. This refers to an actual well at an oasis in the Libyan Desert known to have been visited by Alexander and which was associated with a temple to the god Ammon. The water in the well was said to maintain a constant temperature, being cool by day and seeming warm by contrast at night. Its existence was recorded by the Greek historian Herodotus (485–425 BC).

2. Aristotle (384–322 BC), one of the most famous philosophers of the ancient world. He was a student of Plato, and is known to have been the tutor of Alexander the Great. He wrote on a large variety of topics, including metaphysics, physics, rhetoric, poetry, drama, government and biology.

3. Zeuxis (also spelt 'Xeuxis') was a famous painter, born c.464 BC in the Ionian Greek city of Ephesus.

4. The Sophists were a group of intellectuals in the fifth century BC, mainly in Athens, who used rhetoric to persuade others of their opinions and philosophical convictions. Plato and Aristotle regarded them as employing the ambiguities of language in order to deceive.

5. This is 'Geist' in the original German, and it is a rendering of what Aristotle calls later in the text 'nous'. For him 'nous' was the mind or intellect as opposed to sense perception.

6. 'Ideas' here refers to the concept in Plato's philosophy of external abstract forms of which individual existing things are imperfect realisations.

7. In ancient Greek philosophy the term 'eudemonic' (also spelt 'eudaemonic') was used to describe that which is conducive to happiness and wellbeing. What was considered good was also regarded as the most useful. For Aristotle this meant maintaining moderation in all things.

8. Hellas is the ancient Greek name for the country of Greece.

9. The young sister of Alexander should not be confused with Philip's niece and second wife of the same name, who is mentioned a few paragraphs later.

10. This was the formal title of the ruler of the Persian Empire, Darius Codomannus (see note 11).

11. Darius Codomannus (380–330 BC), or Darius III, was 'Great King' of Persia from 336–330 BC, and last of the Achaemenid dynasty.

12. A stade (stadion) was a variable Greek measurement of distance (about 600 feet).

13. Proskunesis (also spelt 'proskynesis') refers to the traditional Persian act of prostrating oneself before a person of higher rank. The ancient Greeks only performed this act to the gods and they regarded it as barbarian when performed before human beings.

14. The cynics were a school of ancient Greek philosophers, who held ease and pleasure in contempt.

15. The term 'gymnosophists' (meaning 'naked philosophers') was used by the Greeks to refer to certain Indian philosophers who practised extreme asceticism, regarding food and clothing as a hindrance to the purity of thought.
16. The term 'manas' and those terms used in subsequent paragraphs (prāna, kham, atman and Brahman) are Sanskrit concepts to be found in the Hindu scriptures.